MIDSUMMER MURDER

MIDSUMMER MURDER

CECIL M. WILLS

Galileo Publishers, Cambridge

Galileo Publishers
16 Woodlands Road, Great Shelford,
Cambridge
CB22 5LW UK
www.galileopublishing.co.uk

Distributed in the USA by SCB Distributors
15608 S. New Century Drive Gardena,
CA 90248-2129, USA

Australia: Peribo Pty Limited
58 Beaumont Road
Mount Kuring-Gai, NSW 2080
Australia

ISBN 978-1915530-32-5

First published 1956 by Hutchinson & Co
This new edition © 2024
All rights reserved.

Series consultant Richard Reynolds

Printed in the EU

FOR

DOUGLAS AND CYNTHIA

CHAPTER I

THE last stroke of midnight boomed from the cathedral spire, hung trembling in the air, then softly died into silence. A silence almost unbroken in the silver-flooded stillness of the moonlit Close. Almost, but not quite.

The good folk of Storminster (for surely those who dwell in the Cathedral Close must merit the term) keep early hours. Not a light gleamed in a window of the neat, Georgian houses; not a soul was awake to hear the stealthy tread of the figure that slipped from shadow to shadow, paused, glanced furtively around, then hastily slipped a note into the letter-box of one of the houses.

Rosalind Ashburn surveyed her husband from behind the cover of the *Storminster Clarion*. The survey was, of necessity, imperfect; for he was equally entrenched behind *The Times*. She glanced again at the slip of paper which lay on the table before her. It had been amongst the morning letters, but differed from its fellows in that the envelope bore only her name. No stamp; no address. Nor had the note a signature—unless a crude red-ink drawing of a pair of scales could be so described.

She was in two minds as to her course of action. Her first, and decent, impulse was to tear the thing up and burn the pieces; her second, and truly feminine, was to try the effect it might have upon her husband. "After all," urged her second self, "if it doesn't mean a thing—then there's no harm done. On the other hand, if you just destroy it and say nothing, then it will keep coming back to your mind. You won't have any peace; you know you won't!"

Second self won.

"Rodney," she said suddenly, trying to make her voice casual, "Who is Anita Pedler?"

Her husband gave a perceptible start and the knuckles of the hands holding the newspaper whitened. That, at least, was

1

what Rosalind thought she observed. A few moments later she questioned the evidence of her senses.

"Who?" asked Rodney, a piece of toast arrested on the way to his mouth.

"Anita Pedler."

"My dear, I haven't a clue. Probably some film star—or maybe a crooner. Why?"

"Oh nothing. Just a reference to her in this paper. I thought she might be someone one ought to know about."

Breakfast proceeded as usual and in due course Rodney Ashburn kissed his wife and left for the office where he carried out the duties of Diocesan Architect. But a trivial incident left his wife a prey to uneasiness. Just as he was about to step into the Close he turned back, slipped into the breakfast room and came out again carrying the *Clarion*.

"Thought I'd just take this along to glance at between whiles," he said airily. "Sometimes there's a call for the services of an architect in the advertisement columns. Never so busy that I can't take on a new job; and do we need the money!"

Maybe, she told herself as the front door slammed; but he'd never before shown any interest in the local paper.

Arrived at his office Ashburn dealt tersely with his secretary; also with the pile of correspondence she proffered. A method of procedure so unusual with him that when he had disappeared into his 'holy of holies' (his personal drawing office) where none dared disturb him, she gaped at the red-haired office boy in amazement.

"Well!" she said with a toss of the head, "whatever's come over him! Not so much as a good morning!"

"Had a row with his wife, like as not," retorted Albert with the worldlywise knowledge of sixteen. "Where there's trouble, look for the skirt. That's French," he declared with finality.

As for Rodney, once in the privacy of his office he

flung himself into a chair and began a painstaking and methodical scrutiny of the local paper. But beyond acquiring an undesired knowledge of heterogeneous local affairs his labours went unrewarded. Nowhere did the name of Anita Pedler appear.

He threw the paper aside and lapsed into moody and unhappy reflection. He had believed that the tragic affair had been forgotten. It was so long ago; and he had been so young—and inexperienced. The years rolled back and he was once again at Cambridge. Only son of a widowed mother he had been brought up under the tutelage of a retired clergyman and had led an unnaturally sheltered life. He had imbibed a generous share of such education as is necessary for the passing of examinations but had remained blissfully ignorant of all the things that matter most in life.

With what astonishment he had discovered worlds unknown. Free for the first time in his life, was it any wonder that he had kicked over the traces with zest and gusto? He thought not.

Anita. His first love! Of course there had been girls at 'parties', carefully chaperoned by eagle-eyed mothers, or seen only amidst a throng of their own kind. Certainly he had weaved impossible and romantic stories about some of them. Stories in which he played the part of the hero who rescues the fair lady from dire peril. That they remained quite unconscious of his (for the moment) undying adoration was a foregone conclusion; for he was shy both by nature and training. And so these idyllic episodes had never exceeded the realms of make-believe.

Thus Anita had found him an easy prey. But was that quite the right word to use? Might it not have been, as he firmly believed at the time, that she really did love him?

The meeting had been as romantic as even he could have wished.

It was a lovely morning in early summer and the urge to get out into the country was irresistible. There was a lecture; but on a subject in which he was well versed. It could be cut.

It was.

He wandered along the river with never a care in the world. Not that part of the river sacred to the colleges, where he could hope for no privacy; but the less urban reaches.

A girl came downstream, paddling a small canoe. As she drew level with him she gave him a summer morning smile. Before he could recover from his not unpleasurable surprise—for she was a very pretty girl—the canoe had shot past him. He turned to follow its course with his eye and the girl also turned to look back. Exactly what happened then he could never recall with any clarity, but there was the girl, struggling in the water and calling for help; while the canoe drifted away with the current.

When he brought her to the bank and helped her to climb ashore he noticed two things: that she wore a jumper and slacks; and that these were an excellent medium for advertising the fact that she possessed an aggressively attractive figure.

After that they were bound to meet. The meetings had the added charm of clandestinity.

Looking back on those events in the light of more mature understanding he felt he could fairly say that she had made the running. And colour was lent to this belief when he discovered that she was an expert swimmer.

Events took their new yet ever hackneyed course. To him—possibly to both of them—it seemed that there never had been such a romantic affair. The world was theirs and no one else mattered.

And then she was found drowned.

The inquest proclaimed it suicide; for the usual motive

was present. But even without this, her skill in the water almost precluded accident in the tranquil reach where she was found.

Since they had taken pains to avoid being seen together his name was never mentioned in connection with the tragedy; but his conscience insisted that he was in effect her murderer. He was too young, too inexperienced to ask himself why she had not confided in him; and his real affection for her, coupled with a moderate conceit, never caused him to doubt that he, and he alone, was to blame.

The incident had affected him deeply; the more so since he had no one in whom he could confide. In an endeavour to forget, and to stifle the prickings of an over-sensitive conscience, he threw himself into his work with an abandon which won him the praise of his tutor and an honours degree.

Gradually the matter had receded to the back of his mind. Never quite forgotten but, save for an occasional fit of remorseful depression, no longer in the forefront of his memory.

Since that time there had been other girls in his life; but his early experience had so reacted upon him that, with these, he had no cause to reproach himself—though the ladies may have thought otherwise. No doubt it was his lack of ardour—or his remarkable control of what ardour he may have felt—which brought to nought these early essays into the realms of love. But in any case, his work came first.

It was only after he had established himself, at a phenomenally youthful age, as Diocesan Architect to the See of Storminster, that he met Rosalind.

This, he realised, was the real thing at last. There could be no doubt about that. Nor had she any doubts. They married, obtained a house in the Close and were ideally happy. But it had been apparent to him from the first that his wife was of a highly romantic nature. Unlike the majority of modern girls she placed great store by such old-fashioned virtues as chastity and faithfulness; and he felt that she would never have understood that early affair. Besides, such an impression had it made on him, fostered by weeks of morbid brooding, that he had come to believe himself morally guilty of Anita's murder. An exaggeration, perhaps, but natural under the circumstances of his inexperience and early upbringing.

No, he. felt, the episode of Anita was one which he would never be able to confide to Rosalind.

And now, somehow, she had got hold of that name. What did it mean? Who had told her? And how much had she been told? More urgent was the question as to what he was to do next. Should he have it out with her as soon as he got home? Ask the direct question . . .? Or should he try to behave in a perfectly natural manner, and thus dispel any possible suspicions?

All day long he wrestled with the problem. At the thought of deception, the first in their married life, he recoiled. But he recoiled more at the thought of confession. In the end deception won. It was for the sake of her own peace of mind, he told himself with facile self persuasion.

He searched again through the pages of the *Clarion* and sighed with relief when he found an invitation to architects to submit plans for a memorial hall. Not the sort of thing to attract him in the ordinary way; but good enough for his purpose.

So it was with a cheerfulness almost unnoticeably forced that he greeted his wife that evening, flourishing the paper as he did so.

"Must be something in hunches," he declared buoyantly. "I somehow felt there might be a job in my line in this rag. A sudden feeling—just like that. And how right I was! We can do with a little more cash now that we've decided to get a car; and here is a job I can very easily tackle. Of course, I may not get it. It's open to competition; but I can at least have " a cut at it."

"How nice, darling," said his wife; but her tone lacked conviction. Moreover, he reflected gloomily, yet with a shamefaced feeling of relief, it was her evening for the W.I. When she returned it would be bedtime, and discussion could be avoided.

And so the first hint of restraint came between them. The initial success of the virus distilled by an unknown poison pen.

There were to be others.

CHAPTER II

How you have the patience to bother with those fiddling little things I never can imagine. They'd drive me mad!"

The bishop raised his round and smiling face, somewhat suffused by stooping, and chuckled.

"We must be thankful for small mercies. Suppose I'd been born a 'Roman'! Those soutanes must have many more buttons than a mere pair of gaiters. You know," he continued as he laid the button-hook on the dressing table and lit a cigarette, "I have at times thought of starting a fashion in zip fasteners. But I'm afraid there would be adverse comment from some of the dear old ladies. Might as well scrap breeches altogether and wear trousers—if the gaiters are to lose their buttons. Like taking the cords out of the episcopal hat."

"Or dispensing with the apron, I suppose," agreed his wife with a smile. "And, if the truth must be told, I think the clothes become you very well, my dear."

The bishop glanced at his well rounded stomach over which the apron spread smoothly. "Maybe you're right. At least it proclaims me a man of substance! You won't, of course," he continued as he put the final touches to his toilet, "forget the bazaar committee meeting at eleven?"

Mabel de Poynton made a grimace. "I'm not likely to do so. I've been groaning about it for the last three days. Dear me! It's a sad reflection on humanity that so many worthy people are so dreadfully dull and narrow-minded."

Mathew de Poynton, Bishop of Storminster, and his wife Mabel, née Plenderby-Scaithe, were a well-loved couple. His round, rosy and usually smiling face was just what a bishop should possess; while her bright eyes, twinkling forth from a mesh of delicately traced wrinkles reminded one irresistibly of currants in a bun—a very nice bun.

In the ordinary course of events it might have been thought that a bishop had duties more important and time-engaging than attendance upon a bazaar committee. But this was a special bazaar, in that it formed part of a vigorous drive for funds for the replacement of the organ. The object of the appeal had, in itself, roused instant criticism, not to say opposition in the diocese. Surely, argued the 'antis', an organ never needed replacing. At most a thorough overhaul should meet the case. Not so, argued the professedly musical. It had never been a good organ and it had been placed in a ridiculous position. Sell it, said they, to some other cathedral, or church, whose supporters did not know the difference between really good and rather bad music.

The campaign was given weight by the staunch partisanship of Nicholas Borroway; not only the local millionaire but a man of decided (and frequently pronounced) opinions. He it was who, when the bishop modestly declined the honour (and cost) of living in the historic bishop's palace, came to the rescue by buying it at a figure which endowed the new episcopal residence in perpetuity. Faculties, and worse, had been necessary; but Nicholas had not remained a millionaire by baulking at trifles. Remained, because he had certainly been born one. His was no meteoric rise to fame. His father, even his grandfather before him, had been powers in the world of steel and had made their mark up in the north. But they had always been too busy to acquire a family estate. Nicholas, now retired, saw fit to remedy the omission. And how more fittingly could this be done than by buying a palace—albeit an episcopal one?

So there he lived in state, and everyone was happy; from the local tradesmen, who thereout sucked no small advantage, to Storminster 'Society', who were offered verily palatial parties on a scale which no mere bishop could (or should) provide.

And it was in one of the lesser reception rooms of the palace, kindly loaned for the occasion (vide the *Clarion)* that the committee meeting took place.

In the chair was the bishop; on his right hand Mrs. Emily Prinnett who kept an antique shop, possessed a handsome but questionable son, and was reputed to be something of a social climber. She owed her seat beside the bishop to her office as secretary of the committee. She was secretary of many committees.

On the left of the chairman sat Nicholas Borroway himself, flanked by Mabel de Poynton. Facing her across the table was The Reverend Selwyn Sneddicombe, Vicar of the church of All Souls; bright as a bee and a tower of strength at bazaars and the like. Next to him sat Mrs. Battersby, a lady of financial importance though not to be included in the same class as Borroway. Mrs. Battersby was always on every committee, as were Miss Tatchet and Miss Pruin. It is probable that Mabel de Poynton had these ladies in mind when she bewailed the dullness of the worthy. Both spinsters were ladies of uncertain age; and both were narrow in their views; but these were the only points they had in common; for there was bitter rivalry between them.

Two men brought the total number to ten. These were John Archer (nicknamed Don Juan by some), who combined the roles of literary critic and social reporter for the *Clarion,* and who was acting as unofficial publicity agent—having been wheedled into the position by Mabel (who had a way with her)—and Sir Derrick Mathers, an impecunious baronet of ancient lineage and pugnacious temperament.

The bishop opened the proceedings with a short prayer and then called on Mrs. Prinnett to read the minutes of the last meeting.

She gave a little nervous cough, smoothed back a

straggling lock of greying hair and began to speak; but not to read the minutes.

"My lord, ladies and gentlemen," she announced in a thin voice, "I don't know if I am in order in bringing this to light, but having a high regard for my fellow-members I think it my duty to do so. I may say that I have been very upset. Never before has such a thing happened to me. Of course, one should ignore anonymous letters. And so I would, in the ordinary way. But where they refer to others. . . ." She broke off and glanced apologetically at the bishop and then at the rest of the committee.

"On the point of order, Mrs. Prinnett," said the bishop with a smile, "the matter does not appear to be on the agenda; but, since we all know, and appreciate, your never failing good offices in matters ecclesiastical, and since whatever it may be that you have to tell us is causing you some mental *dis*order, let the one cancel out the other. Pray proceed."

Mrs. Prinnett smiled gratefully. "This morning I received a letter. It did not come through the post—since it was un-stamped and un-postmarked; but it was in the letter-box with the rest of my correspondence. I will read it to you:

"'Why give your services to a corrupt committee? Do you know that one of the members has a large holding of shares in the company that is to receive the contract for the new organ?' That is all," continued Mrs. Prinnett. "There is no date, heading or signature—unless you can call a crude drawing of a pair of scales a signature. Let me say at once," she pursued hastily, "that of course I do not for one moment credit this abominable slander; but I felt it only fair to all present to let you know that there is in this town some evil-minded person who is working against us."

"One of those blighters who have been against the new

organ from the start," volunteered Sir Derrick Mathers in his booming voice. "Take no notice of it Mrs.—er,—Prinnett."

Nicholas Borroway gave a deep and comfortable chuckle. "I'm with you there, Derrick. Anonymous letters! Why, I've had hundreds in my time. Think nothing of 'em. And I don't mind betting I'm the one the writer's getting at. I did have some shares in the company—and not long ago. But I got rid of them. You may remember a line in the Press. I gave them to the Handel Strong Memorial Fund; thought them suitable for a fund raised to commemorate a great organist. . . . They weren't paying too well in any case," he added with a grin.

"As to that," announced the bishop, "it is possible that I myself might be the guilty party! I have little knowledge of financial matters; I leave them entirely to my broker—a cousin. It may well be that I hold some of these shares. Dear me! I must make inquiries. It's a terrible thought! The guardian of morals himself guilty of corrupt practice! *'Quis custodiet ipsos custodes?'*"

"No one, my dear bishop," purred Mrs. Battersby in her suety voice, "could for one moment speak of you in the same breath as corruption!"

"No breath of corruption, in fact!" said Selwyn Sneddicombe with a giggle, instantly repressed, and followed by a look of apology towards the chairman. "May we see the note?" he asked swiftly to cover his confusion.

The anonymous letter was passed from hand to hand. There was little to be learned from it. The paper was of the cheap type sold by the packet with envelopes to match, in every small stationer's shop. The envelope was square; the wording typed. The drawing of the scales executed, somewhat melodramatically, in red ink.

"Pity you've all fingered the darned thing," said Sir Derrick when the note came to him. "Might have been prints on it that would have helped the police. No good now, of course."

"I hardly think, Sir Derrick", put in his neighbour, Miss Pruin, "that this is a matter for the police. Vulgar publicity is surely the last thing we want for a committee of this standing."

"I entirely disagree," said Miss Tatchet snappily. "Persons who write these disgusting things deserve to be treated with the utmost severity of the law. But perhaps Miss Pruin has reasons for——"

"Mrs. Prinnett will now read the minutes," interposed the bishop hurriedly.

Thereafter the business became such as could interest only those concerned; except for a spirited encounter between Sir Derrick, who advocated a wines and tobacco stall, and Miss Pruin who, as a lifelong teetotaller and anti-smoker, viewed the suggestion with horror. The dispute was tactfully closed by John Archer's remark that he believed that a licence would be necessary, and he thought it extremely improbable that the magistrates would grant one.

"Got any ideas about the author of the letter?" asked Sir Derrick of Nicholas Borroway as they left the room at the close of the meeting.

Nicholas chuckled. "My dear fellow, if I worried about every anonymous letter that came to my notice I'd soon be in a mental home. Haven't the least idea; and couldn't care less. Why? Have you?"

"Well, between you and me, I wouldn't put it beyond either of those two old tabby cats Pruin and Tatchet."

"My good sir! I don't suppose either of them has ever touched a typewriter in their lives. Besides, that's a most libellous suggestion! Lucky you only said it to me."

CHAPTER III

NIGEL VILLIERS (formerly Tom Prinnett) was bored. A dull cathedral city after the vicissitudes and excitements of a touring company seemed to him the end of awfulness. But he had no choice. He was not a brilliant actor. It was chiefly on account of his looks that he had managed to get a part in a second-rate company touring the lesser towns. And then *Girls Galore* had flopped. Even the least sophisticated of the provincial towns had failed to show enthusiasm to the extent of filling the house. So the good old British impresarios Schmaltz, Labrinski and Aaron, through their manager, paid off the company at Brogden-in-Ash and left the members to find their own ways home.

Of course the towns had been frightful; still, there was always a bit of life in the company, and the weekend moves had prevented absolute stagnation. One or two passable girls in the show, too. Not quite his class, of course; but good enough to pass the time with.

At the thought Nigel fondled his small, dark moustache and smiled reminiscently. Well, there it was. With the show up the spout and not a bean in his pockets there was no other course but to come home to mother. She was always good for board and lodging, even if the trimmings were sometimes lacking. And, of course, he'd soon get another job. As soon as the unwonted heat wave was over the theatre trade would be looking up; and with his looks— not to mention his talent— they'd be crying out for him.

The entry of his mother broke in upon his reflections.

"Oh, hullo Tom. You ought to be out in this lovely weather; not sitting indoors. And you ought to be trying to get a job, you know. Funds are running low."

"My dear Emily" (he scorned to call her mother—so dating!), "what sort of a job d'you think I could pick up in a one-horse hole like this? It's not only the buildings that are suffering from senile decay. Why, there isn't even a 'rep' company. And I wish you wouldn't call me Tom. Why d'you think I bothered to take the name of Nigel Villiers if Tom Prinnett would have done as well? My dear! Just fancy: 'Leading man, Tom Prinnett'!"

"Well, dear, it doesn't seem right or natural to call you Nigel. You always were Tom, and I haven't seen enough of you since you started your stage career to get used to the change. And I don't like you calling me Emily. I may be old-fashioned; but I don't like it. As to a job, I quite realise that there aren't any openings in your profession in this town; but, after all, you had your full time at Cambridge. Surely that should have fitted you for a job in any walk of life?"

Nigel laughed discordantly. "My dear Emily—oh well; mother, if you will have it so—you certainly are old-fashioned! I admit I had a damned good time at Cambridge, and met some of the best people; but as for learning to earn my own living—you make me tired! Besides, the stage is my natural profession. Once an actor, always an actor. But never mind about me. How did you get on this morning?"

"It was much as usual. Of course the bishop was very gracious—he always is. No false pride about him. He doesn't mind the fact that I keep a shop."

"An antique shop," qualified Nigel. "There's a whale of a difference."

"Not in the minds of some. Oh, I'm good enough to be secretary of this and that committee, and do any odd jobs that are going; but that doesn't mean that I'm *persona grata*—as Miss Tatchet would say—with persons like Mrs. Battersby. I can just hear her saying to that nitwit of a husband of hers: 'Committees, yes; receptions, no! After all, we must draw the line somewhere. Don't forget she keeps a shop!'"

Nigel had not listened to the last part of his mother's diatribe. His thoughts were following a line suggested by the name of Battersby.

"That Battersby girl—Helen, isn't she—has turned into a nice piece of homework. Not exactly a 'Miss Storminster' perhaps. I'd reserve that for Rosalind Ashburn. Boy! has she a figure! but there's Ashburn to consider; and he looks as if he could be tough. But the Battersby childling has pots; at least, her mother has. And that, with my charm put to work, is much of a muchness."

His mother smiled fondly. "Tom—I mean Nigel— you really are a disgraceful boy! If I didn't know how your tongue runs away with you I'd be shocked. Talking of married women and available heiresses in the same breath! Oh! that reminds me. That's what that woman said to the bishop. You weren't up this morning when I left for the meeting, so I hadn't a chance to tell you. I had an anonymous letter this morning."

"You did!" There was incredulity in his tone. "Why, I thought you'd always led a most blameless life. At any rate you seem to be tied up with every religious and charitable show that's going in this burg. Tell me all; let me know the worst. Am I a foundling? Or merely illegitimate?"

"Don't be silly. It wasn't personal. It was sent to me as secretary of the Organ Fund Committee. It said that one of the members had a lot of shares in the company that's got the contract—that is, if ever we raise the necessary cash."

"Is that all? Well, why not? Any chap who had shares in a company would be a damned fool if he let the contract go to a rival firm."

"You don't understand, darling. You've never had to worry about business ethics. So you must take my word for it that it's a very serious matter—particularly in connection with church affairs."

"I will take your word for it. Did the unknown correspondent name the guilty party?"

"No. But Mr. Borroway confessed that he had had shares in the company in question. He said that he'd given them all away to a memorial fund. It was in the papers. No doubt that's how the writer got to know that he ever had them."

"But if he'd given them all away——?"

"He said he had; and the papers printed his statement. It may be true, of course. Then the bishop said that, for all he knew, he himself might have shares in the same company. He didn't know anything about money matters but his broker— some relation or other—might easily have got him some. But it's my opinion he only said that to relieve the tension and to avoid Mr. Borroway taking offence. We don't want to lose his patronage."

"I can understand that. Pity he hasn't got a presentable daughter."

"Even if he had a daughter it's probable that she wouldn't be what *you'd* call presentable. He's not terribly good-looking; nor, I'm told, was his wife."

"My dear Emily, any girl with a father as rich as old Borroway couldn't fail to be presentable. Well, *faute-de-mieux,* and on the principle that half a loaf's better than no bread, I'm off to wangle a chance to pick up our little Helen."

White Gables was a house which registered wealth rather than taste. It had been built in the most unfortunate Victorian period by a rich and retired builder who had been his own architect. As its name implied, it had gables; also pepper-box turrets. And on the top was a lead flat complete with teak rails and flagstaff. Its grounds were extensive and, in terms of gardeners, rated four. No other description is desirable.

The imposing, gilded, cast iron gates which gave entrance to the property stood at the foot of a long, serpentine drive, and were on that side of the house which faced away from the centre of the town. But there was a garden gate which gazed townwards; and here, parked against the kerb, stood a smart, scarlet coupé. It was this coupé which was engaging the attention of Nigel Villiers. It was obviously a young girl's car; and it was parked by the garden entrance to White Gables. Ergo, he reasoned, it was on the cards that Helen herself would shortly be coming to claim it.

He took a look around. It was a road lined with imposing properties. All the houses stood well back from the highway and on rising ground; for the road lay along the bottom of a small valley. Luck was with him—it usually was, he reflected smugly. Exactly opposite the garden entrance stood the gates of a house which was for sale. Shrubs bordered the drive; the gates stood open.

There was no one to observe him as he deftly unscrewed the valve cap of a rear wheel of the coupé and, depressing the valve stem, let the air escape from the tyre. Then he took refuge behind a bush in the accommodating drive; a post from which he could watch the car.

Presently the garden gate opened and a pretty girl, wearing a yellow jumper, green slacks and a cherry coloured beret, stepped across the pavement towards the car. Nigel left his station and walked openly down the drive, arriving at the car just as the girl pressed the self-starter button.

"I say!" he said, raising his felt hat with a slightly theatrical gesture (one he had learned in *Girls Galore*), "d'you know you've got a puncture?"

"Oh hell!" said the girl. "That would happen just when I'm in a hurry. I suppose I'll have to go back and get Hoskins."

"If the worthy Hoskins is your chauffeur," said Nigel with a carefully cultivated 'charm smile', "perhaps I can sub for him? I'm quite good at changing wheels."

The girl regarded him with interest. There was no doubt about his good looks, and his manners were charming. After all, why not let him help? Obviously he wanted to make himself useful. Helen was well accustomed to young men who wanted to make themselves useful.

"O.K.," she assented gracefully. "Jolly decent of you. The spare's in the boot at the back. I'll unlock it." She got out of the car then paused suddenly. "I say, didn't I see you coming down the drive of The Maples?"

"If that" (he pointed) "is The Maples, you did indeed. I saw it was for sale so I went to have a look. Who knows?— one day I may be in a position to buy a house for myself. But why the interest?"

Helen eyed him narrowly. "Oh, nothing; but it was pretty quick of you to spot my flat tyre in the few seconds you took to walk down the last bend of the drive."

Nigel laughed. "Say! You're quite a detective. But it wasn't all that smart of me. I noticed the tyre before I entered The Maples."

When the wheel had been changed Nigel brushed the dust from his hands and smiled. "You wouldn't be going down into the town, I suppose?" he asked.

"I am, as a matter of fact. Want a lift?"

Helen drove with temperament and Nigel was thankful that he had no nerves.

"D'you live in Storminster?" she asked. "I don't remember seeing you about."

"Not really. I'm on the stage. But at the moment I'm staying in the town—at that antique shop in the High Street. Maybe you know it?"

"Mrs. Prinnett's? Oh yes. Mother often goes there. . . . She rather fancies herself as a judge of antiques," she added with a little laugh. "Is that where you want to be dropped?"

"I'm in no hurry. What about a spot of tea at Meakin's? Oh, I forgot; you're in a hurry."

"It's too early for tea, anyway," retorted Helen. Then a look of mischief crept into her blue eyes. Her mother would have several fits if she saw her daughter having tea with a young man whom she had just picked up—or had he done the picking up? Well, why not? Her mother was safely at home. And he *was* good-looking. Moreover he'd be a nice change from the young presentables of the town; she knew them all, only too well.

"Look," she went on, "my appointment will only last half an hour. I'll meet you at Meakin's at four o'clock, O.K.?"

"More than O.K. But if we're going to have tea together we'd better know each other's names. I'm Nigel Villiers, very much at your service."

"And I'm Helen Battersby. All right. We'll be meeting."

And meet they did; in a secluded alcove of Meakin's rightly renowned café, where the cakes had to be eaten to be believed. Nigel had taken care to arrive in good time; hence the alcove.

"Look!" he said, leaning over the table when they had given their order, "I've a terrible confession to make. You probably won't speak to me again when I've told you the worst!"

Helen gave him a quizzical smile; but her eyes became wary. "Oh, I can guess. Although you pretended not to know me, you knew all along that I was the only child of the Battersbys. Well, at least you're honest enough to say so."

"But I didn't! Twice. I mean, I didn't say so and I didn't know you from Adam. Well—I mean to say! You don't look much like Adam, particularly in that jumper thing; so that's rather an exaggeration. But it's intended to convey the idea that I didn't know who you were. All right. So you're the daughter of the Battersbys. Who are the Battersbys? Am I supposed to tremble with awe, or commiserate with you?"

Helen gave him an incredulous look and then burst into a laugh. "Oh, of course! I was forgetting you're not a native. My dear, every young man I come across knows that my parents are much better off than they've any right to be in these days. The more they try to conceal it—the young men, of course!—the more they give themselves away. But, if you didn't know, then what have you got to confess?"

"I think I'd better tell you a little story first. Quite short. An enterprising but, at the moment, out-of-work actor (or 'resting', as we prefer to call it!) has returned, like the prodigal son, to his family for sustenance. His family being represented by Emily Prinnett, who is his mother. Difference in names not due to second marriage, but to snob-value from a stage point of view. Handsome actor, wandering at a loose end in the saintly but rather too respectable town of Storminster, sees a lovely girl tripping along the Cornwalk. He is alone; so cannot ask: 'Who is that lovely?' In default, he follows her, at a discreet distance, and harbours her at a substantial house labelled White Gables. Fortunately for him she wasn't using her car that day. Quite impossible to get to know her socially—since the White Gables district is ultra-exclusive. Not likely to have social connections in the antique or theatrical worlds." Nigel bowed sardonically.

"Very well. So enterprising young actor—have I said he's very good-looking?—haunts the vicinity of the said house and has the luck to find very feminine car parked at garden gate. Couldn't be better. Well screened from the house. Whereupon, being quite devoid of those uncomfortable things known as scruples—or, maybe, even without morals—he removes valve cap and deflates tyre. Result: boy meets girl. Hackneyed; I admit. But our mutual attractiveness gives the old situation a new slant.

Or wouldn't you say so? Well, anyway, there it is. I've come clean. Do I get the sack?"

"You can hardly be sacked from a job you never had. But, seeing that tea is ordered—and potato cakes, of all things!— I'm jolly well not going to waste them. So I suppose we'll have to go along on a basis of friendly neutrality."

"Rosalind," said Rodney Ashburn, with the courage of desperation, "we've got to come to grips. What's on your mind?"

Rosalind busied herself with her cooking of the evening meal and kept her face averted.

"I'm sure I don't know what you mean. Nothing's on my mind except to wonder whether I put salt in the potato water."

"Damn salt; and damn the potato water!"

"Certainly, if it gives you any pleasure."

"Oh, look here; it's no use pretending that all is well between us. Sudden death is better than suspense. You're worrying about Anita Pedler—aren't you?"

Rosalind turned and faced him squarely.

"All right, Rodney. I confess. Decent of you to be the first to mention it. I've been afraid to; and that was rotten of me. I had an anonymous letter. Of course I ought to have burned the beastly thing and thought no more about it. That's what decent people do—in books, at any rate. But I just couldn't. At least, I did burn it; but it keeps coming back: 'Ask your husband about Anita Pedler. A life for a life' and then a silly drawing of a pair of old-fashioned scales. But now you've brought up her name yourself I feel much better already. I'm sure it's all rot. Some former flame of yours trying to make me jealous!" She gave a watery little smile.

But Rodney failed to return it. Instead he looked preternaturally grave. "I'm terribly sorry, darling; but it's not as easy as that. As for former flames. . . I can at least swear that there " haven't been any—since Anita. But I'm afraid you're going to be terribly hurt. I've often longed to tell you; but I—well, I suppose I've been a moral coward. But I told myself that it couldn't do any good. It was past and done with and it would only upset you. And, believe me, Rosalind, I care quite a lot about upsetting you."

Rosalind left the potatoes to look after themselves and sat on the edge of the kitchen table, patting its formica surface in invitation to her husband. But he preferred to remain on his feet and paced up and down the diminutive kitchen while he told her the whole story of Anita Pedler. When he had finished he stood gazing unromantically into the sink, not daring to look into her eyes. He could hardly believe his ears when he heard her joyous laugh.

"Oh, my dear! And is that the guilty secret you've been hiding from me for our two whole years of married life! You poor darling! Knowing you, I can guess how you've suffered; both from remorse and because of deceiving me. Oh, why didn't you tell me right at the beginning?"

"I was afraid. You see. . . I wanted you terribly. And I felt sure that—with your innocent sort of outlook—you'd give me my marching orders. I simply didn't dare."

Rosalind laughed again. "My dear babe! No grown girl of today is half as innocent as you think—or as you are yourself! I can just see that poor, silly little thing. I don't doubt for a moment that you were only one of several. And, believe me or believe me not, in nine cases out of ten it's the girl who makes the running. You've been reading too many Sunday papers! 'Betrayed girl takes own life. Guilty man severely censured by coroner.' And then columns of sickening twaddle with bits out of the letters the poor things wrote to each other. Ugh! Well, I'm jolly glad that's all washed up. There have been times when I thought you had something on your mind. You poor, silly dear. But I wish now I'd kept that letter. The police could probably have done something about it. Oh Lord! Look at those potatoes; what a mess on the stove—and I scrubbed it all clean only yesterday!"

Rodney laughed with relief. "Never mind; I'll do it again— as a tribute to a pearl among wives."

So was the first dose of poison neutralised. But what of the others?

CHAPTER IV

HELL what a crowd. Can't think why Jane Battersby has to ask every Tom, Dick and Harry every time she has one of her what she calls 'functions'. Matter of quantity, not quality I should say, when I take a look around." Sir Derrick Mathers perked his moustache and scowled at his companion of the moment.

The Rev. Selwyn Sneddicombe gave him a glance from his bright eyes and adopted a look of intense seriousness.

"Well, Sir Derrick, if that's the way you feel I rather wonder why you make one of such a gathering."

Sir Derrick smote his thigh—thereby spilling part of his third cocktail. "Damme, *touché!* That's one on me, padre. By Gad it is! Why *does* one come to these blasted 'do's?"

"Well, if I am to indulge in a little plain speaking, I'd say that you have one of your reasons in your hand— or, at least, a part of one of them. For myself, I like the Battersbys; and. . . Miss Battersby."

"Oho! Blows the wind in that direction? Nice enough young filly, I suppose. But, my dear chap, Christian charity and all—I suppose it's your duty to shoot a line like that; but you can't really *like* the Battersbys. Why, he's just a nincompoop, and she's a domineering old go-getter if ever there was one."

The padre regarded him with disfavour. "If that were the way I felt about them, I shouldn't be here," he said flatly. "But, on an occasion like this"—and he glanced meaningly at Sir Derrick's glass—"I don't take you too seriously."

Sir Derrick shot his adversary a look from beneath his shaggy eyebrows and seemed about to make an angry retort; but, if such had been his intention, he thought better of it.

"You remember that anonymous letter at the committee meeting?" he asked instead. "Well, would you believe it? The fellow's had the damned impertinence to send me one!"

"Indeed!" said Selwyn with lively interest. "And what, if one may ask, was the purport?"

"Eh? Purport? Oh. . . ah, yes. Purport. Of course. You mean what's it all about? Well. . . hardly fit for a parson's ears, I suppose; but there it is. The writer claimed to know some blighter who says he's my son! And that if I don't mind my p's and q's he'll be calling on me! Ever heard such damned impertinence?"

Selwyn raised his eyebrows. "But I don't quite see the point. I thought you were a bachelor."

Sir Derrick gave a hoarse laugh. "So I am. But what the hell difference does that make?"

"Have you still got the note?"

"'Course not. I burned the darned thing as soon as I'd read it. Only thing to do with muck of that sort. If I could lay my hands on the blighter who wrote it I'd horse-whip him within an inch of his miserable life. Why d'you ask?"

Selwyn looked diffident. "Well, I've got the one sent to Mrs. Prinnett. I. . . I thought I'd try a spot of detection. And the more examples I can collect, the more chance I'll have of tracing the author."

"Oh, you thought that, did you? 'Pon my soul you're a queer little chap for a padre. All long faces and artificial accents in my young days. Well *tempora mutantur;* and I won't say the change isn't for the better." He raised his glass. "Good luck to you! That's all I say. If I get any more notes I'll keep 'em for you." He sauntered off towards the bar and Selwyn breathed a sigh of relief. It was all very well to be all things to all men; but sometimes the duty exceeded his histrionic ability.

"Oh, hullo Selwyn," said a young and pleasant voice

behind him, and he turned with alacrity to greet Helen Battersby.

"D'you know Nigel Villiers, the actor?" she continued with a wave of the hand towards her companion.

Selwyn regarded the good-looking young man and a smile twisted the corners of his mouth.

"Well, not under that name. I used to know a young chap called Tom Prinnett who looked remarkably like him."

Nigel grinned. "Good for you, padre. Some memory! Hell, it must be years since you used to lecture me for misbehaviour at choir practice. But that's all passed and done with. I'm a reformed character now. As Helen says, I'm on the boards."

"I'm not all that ancient!" protested Selwyn. "It couldn't be more than a few years ago—six, at most. That's when I first became a curate at All Souls."

"And now, so Helen tells me, you're vicar. So we've both done pretty well for ourselves. And both in the same line, when it comes down to brass tacks."

Helen was claimed by another guest and the two were left together in a corner of the room.

"Hardly the same line," corrected Selwyn.

"Of course it is. Don't tell me you believe in all the old twaddle you have to preach about. Why, man, all parsons are actors—have to be, if they're to get by with it. Take a look round you and see what a hell of a mess this blasted world's in. Hydrogen bombs! There's brotherly love for you. Not to mention plagues and pestilence; floods, fire and famine. Don't tell me there's a God who cares a darn about any blooming one of us."

Selwyn smiled. "Hardly the time and place for a theological discussion. But we'll talk of this again. You wouldn't adopt that attitude if you didn't want to be convinced against your reason. 'Methinks you do protest too much!'"

"Who was that young man, Helen?" asked her mother sharply when the last guest (Sir Derrick) had reluctantly departed.

"Which young man? There were quite a lot."

"Don't be perverse. You know quite well which one I mean. The only young man in the room not known to me personally—or to your father. How did he get here?"

"You must mean Nigel Villiers. He got here because I invited him. After all, the party was supposed to be for me. You said so, anyway; so I suppose I can ask a friend."

"Friend indeed!" ('is a friend in need!' piped Mr. Battersby ineffectually, with a smirk). "I've never seen him before."

"I only met him yesterday; so that's not surprising. He picked me up, as a matter of fact."

"Helen! I hope you're not serious. If that's the way they taught you to speak at your Swiss finishing school I am sorry we sent you there."

"Sorry, Mother. No, of course I was only joking. As a matter of fact I had a puncture and he helped me to change a wheel. He was awfully nice about it. I could hardly do less than ask him to have a drink—and the party seemed the right place to do it."

"Does he live in Storminster? Who are his people? Is he respectable? What does he do?"

Helen gave a forced laugh. "My dear Mother, what a lot of questions. Which shall I answer first? He does live here—for the present. He seems respectable—he's certainly good- looking; and that's just as important. As for who his people are, he's only got one. His mother's Mrs. Prinnett."

Mrs. Battersby glared. "Helen! Fancy bringing her son to my house! I should have thought you'd have more sense— even with your ridiculous socialistic ideas."

"But I thought you liked and admired Mrs. Prinnett," said Helen with wide-eyed innocence. "I'm sure I've often heard you say how worthy and hard-working she is."

"In her place she's extremely efficient and hard-working. On a committee she is admirable. In her shop, no doubt, she is equally at home. But in my house—as a guest!"

"Oh Mother! You really are too out-of-date for belief. All that rot has gone to blazes nowadays. My best friend in Switzerland was the daughter of a fishmonger. You're literally antique!"

Harold Battersby coughed nervously. "Helen, my dear, I don't think you ought to speak like that to your mother. You——"

"I'll take care of this, Harold," interrupted Mrs. Battersby curtly. "I find a change in you, Helen; and not for the better. Goodness knows what parents pay good money for, if their children are to be taught to lose their respect for them. But I make allowances for your being excited by the party. When you are calmer, you will regain your senses. As for that young man, I forbid you to see him again."

Helen was saved an overt act of insubordination by the entry of Craven, the family butler. In his hand he held a silver salver on which reposed a white, square envelope.

"Excuse me, madam, I found this in the hall after I had ushered out the guests. I thought it might be important."

Mrs. Battersby took the envelope, which bore nothing but her name, and tore it open. The next moment she gave a cry of outraged anger.

"Who left it, Craven?"

"That I couldn't say, madam. I did not notice it until I had handed out the last of the hats and coats. It may have been concealed by the hats."

"Very well, Craven. That will do."

"What is it, my dear?" asked Battersby when the door had closed behind the butler.

For answer his wife handed him the missive in silence.

It read: "Does your husband know that your father was a village postman?" For signature there was a crude drawing of a pair of scales.

Battersby read it out slowly, a wondering note in his voice. "Why, Jane my dear, this is stupid! Who on earth wrote it? You told me your father was mayor of his town."

"And so he was. Mayor of Turton; and highly respected. It's a pity he died before we met. You would have looked up to him." There was an almost defiant pride in the statement.

"Then. . . this postman business is all rot?"

"Of course it is. Do I look like the daughter of a postman?"

Helen laughed aloud. "Oh mummy, you are priceless! D'you really suppose postmen's daughters look any different from anyone else? And why shouldn't you have one for a father? I don't believe in all this rot about ancient lineage. There was a girl in Switzerland who's father was a French marquis—and she was an awful little squirt; an absolute outsider. Everyone hated her. Personally I like postmen. They do a jolly good job, and often under beastly conditions. Isn't it better to have a postman father than to trace back to some disreputable type who got a title for providing the king of his day with mistresses?"

"Helen! I am shocked. I won't have you speaking like that. I can't think where you get your ideas. The aristocracy are the backbone of the country!"

"Sir Derrick, for instance. Then the country's got curvature of the spine. What *was* grandfather, anyway?"

"He was. . . in commerce, I believe. But I was educated away from home; and my parents didn't believe in young girls knowing anything of business affairs."

Helen, who sensed a certain embarrassment in her mother's reply, hastened to change the subject.

"Mother, do let me have that note—for Selwyn. I over-heard him saying that there had been others, and that he was going to try his hand at detection—running the writer to earth. Though, if the others are no worse than this one, I shouldn't think it worth his while."

"Certainly not!" said her mother, snatching the note from her husband and tearing it into small pieces. "The very idea of this going the rounds! I'd be the laughing stock of Storminster. I forbid you to mention the subject to anyone. Your father should never have read it aloud!" and she flashed an indignant glance in his direction.

"What? Oh, sorry, my dear. I didn't think. But since it isn't true, you know, I don't see that any harm's done. What?"

"What was it like? Did you say I had a headache?"

"I did. The Lord forgive me. But she knew all right. She said: 'Ah yes. Headaches come on so quickly—don't they? And vanish just as quickly. Give the poor dear my love.' So there you have it—for what it's worth: the Battersby's love."

Rosalind made a little grimace. "Oh well, it can't be helped. I don't care if she does know it was just an excuse. I simply can't stand that woman. She's a snob of the first water, and patronising with it. Just because she's on the permanent cathedral restoration committee and you're 'only the architect' she seems to think that makes her an officer and you an 'other rank'. As for me—well, I'm even less than that. Only the wife of an 'other rank'; not even in the army!"

"Sort of a rank outsider, eh?" teased Rodney.

"That is not worthy of you. I wonder who her forbears

were, anyway." She laughed. "But there! Don't mind me. A sauce curdled on me—hence the spleen. Well, what was the party like?"

Rodney flung himself into a chair and grunted: "Lousy! Far too many people, all talking too much; and far too few drinks. But worst of all, what there were had been watered. All the same that didn't stop old Derrick from having his share. Perhaps that's what loosened his tongue. I heard him telling Selwyn that he—Derrick—had had an anonymous letter; scales and all. So we're not the only favoured ones."

"Really? What was his about?"

"Well, he said that the writer claimed to know a chap who said he was Derrick's son—and Derrick a bachelor! Selwyn was on it like a smell dog on a scent—the note, I mean; not the bit of scandal. He said he was going to try his hand at a spot of detection and asked Derrick if he still had the note; but of course the fellow had burned it. I had a mind to tell the little parson that we'd had one; but I didn't. He's making a collection of them, you see."

Rosalind smiled. "I like little Selwyn. He's always so bright and cheerful; and so much in earnest in an inoffensive way. He never makes you feel you're beyond the pale, even if he's trying to rescue your immortal soul. Anyone else of interest?"

"The usual crowd. Oh, there was one newcomer. Good-looking chap in his twenties, I'd say. I had an odd word with him. He appears to be an actor named Nigel Villiers. I should imagine he has a pretty good conceit of himself. He and Helen were getting along fine.

"Poor Helen! She deserves a break. If only that mother of hers wouldn't throw her at the head of every eligible man in sight, she might get hold of some really nice young fellow. She's pretty enough; and I think she's a lot wider awake than ever mother realises." He lit a cigarette. "You know, Rosalind, I don't like this letter business. It was bad enough when you got one—though you were a darling about it. But if the thing's becoming general—Derrick said that the Organ Committee had had one—there's no knowing where it will stop. I'm fond of Storminster, and a thing like that can upset the whole tenor of life in any community. Everyone suspecting his neighbour of being the author— quite apart from the harm done by the raking up of old scandals and the rattling of skeletons in cupboards. No. I don't like it."

Rosalind nodded thoughtfully. "You're quite right. But I don't see that we can do much about it. Anyway, if Selwyn is on the warpath something good may come of that. He's persistent; and he's got a way with him that opens all hearts."

"True enough. But d'you think a poison pen addict has a heart?"

Late that same night the Rev. Selwyn Sneddicombe, on returning to his vicarage, where an aged housekeeper, Mrs. Teeming, and a young country girl 'did for him', found on the floor inside the front door (he did not run to a letterbox) a plain, square envelope. It bore as superscription 'Reverend Sneddicombe, Private.'

His heart gave an extra beat when, on tearing it open, his eye lighted on a crudely drawn pair of scales. An addition to his collection, was his first thought. Then he read the message above the drawing: 'Lay off and keep your nose out of what doesn't concern you. If not—take the consequences.'

The light of battle shone in the bright brown eyes of Reverend Sneddicombe as he placed the letter carefully inside his note-case and went upstairs to bed.

CHAPTER V

(From the *Storminster Clarion*).

GAS FATALITY IN STORMINSTER

WELL-KNOWN CATHEDRAL WORKER DEAD

E ARLY this morning Mr. Munro Briggs of 18, The Precincts, was returning to his home after a dance at The Priory, the well-known country property of Sir Edmund and Lady Crombie, when he detected the smell of gas. This he traced to the neighbouring house, that of Miss Arabella Pruin, a much esteemed and old-established resident of our city; and an indefatigable worker in all matters pertaining to the cathedral.

Having ascertained that the gas was coming from the front door of No. 17. Mr Briggs rang the bell and hammered on the knocker. There was no reply. Becoming alarmed he broke a window and forced an entry.

In the kitchen he discovered the body of Miss Pruin, her head in an oven and the gas turned fully on. With commendable promptitude Mr. Briggs turned off the gas, carried the inanimate form to another room and rang the police. Then he returned to the kitchen and opened all the windows.

Inspector Holmslade—who, our readers will remember, conducted so skilfully the inquiry into the recent theft of rare orchids from The Priory—accompanied by the police surgeon, Dr. Forsythe, arrived at the house within ten minutes; but life was already extinct.

An appreciation of the work of Miss Pruin will be found in another column.

A few days later the bishop sent for Selwyn Sneddicombe

and spoke to him gravely and suitably about the untimely death of Arabella Pruin.

"A very shocking thing, poor soul," he said. "I sent for you, Sneddicombe, because she resided in your parish and, I believe, attended All Souls—when not worshipping in the cathedral. Apparently she left a note addressed to the coroner stating that she was taking her own life because she was suffering from malignant cancer. But the pathetic part of the whole unfortunate tragedy is that her medical attendant tells me that this was entirely imaginary. She was, for her age, remarkably fit.

"But what I want you to do is this: official matters connected with the fabric of the cathedral are, I need hardly tell you, the affair of the dean. But, like our Organ Fund, there also exists a Cathedral Maintenance Fund. Both entirely voluntary and, for that reason, organised and staffed by lay helpers who work quite independently of officialdom.

"For some recondite reason I have been nominated Chairman of both the committees concerned with these matters." A twinkle appeared in his eyes. "One would have thought that the dean, being responsible for the fabric of the cathedral, might well have been asked to take this post. But. . . worthy as, beyond doubt, is he, he seems to have the knack of. . . how shall I phrase it. . .?"

Sneddicombe smiled. "Might one say, my lord, that he is more given to ecclesiastical matters than to the study of female temperament? The ladies, I regret to say, seem to hold him in a veneration—perhaps awe—which inhibits their free expression. They find that they cannot work on committees where he presides."

"Yes," agreed the bishop, returning the smile, "I think one might venture so far—though I am not sure that I appreciate the implication in my case! Now to business. Miss Pruin was, as I don't doubt you know, honorary treasurer of the Maintenance Fund. In this work she was assisted by Mrs. Prinnett. An admirable woman, Mrs. Prinnett. An indefatigable worker and always ready to undertake anything that comes to hand. But I gather that Miss Pruin was not endowed with what we may call a financial mind. Rumour has it that she offered herself for the post because she heard that Miss Tatchet had been suggested. 'Nil nisi. . .' of course; but the rumour does not seem to be out of drawing. Now, perhaps, Miss Tatchet will succeed to the post; but that is a matter for the committee.

"What I want you to do is to assist Mrs. Prinnett in preparing the accounts of the Maintenance Fund for handing over to whomsoever may be chosen to fill the post of honorary treasurer. You have a good head for figures, as I have had occasion to remark, and you have your full share of tact. I could, of course, ask some accountant to look into the affair but. . ." The bishop's manner became increasingly grave. "You will remember the anonymous note that Mrs. Prinnett received on behalf of the Organ Fund? Very well. I, myself, have recently received a note suggesting that all is not well with the Maintenance Fund. One's natural instinct is to destroy such poisonous communications and try to forget them. The first I did; but, having regard to poor Miss Pruin's death—added to the fact that she was not suffering from cancer. . . ."

"I think I follow you, my lord. Of course, if there were anything irregular one would naturally want to prevent it from becoming public knowledge—if such a course were ethical."

"Exactly. Hence my choice of you. I know that you get on well with Mrs. Prinnett and, since Miss Pruin was one of your parishioners, it will arouse no remark if you are known to be associated with the former lady in settling up the ecclesiastical affairs of the latter."

It was all very strange, reflected Selwyn as he trod the

sun-warmed pavements on leaving the bishop. Surely the dean should be the one to deal with these matters? In any event, the final report—as far as the handing over of any cash balance and accounts was concerned—would have to be made to him. It was not properly the affair of the bishop. But there it was. Since lay workers were bound by no episcopal protocol they could, he supposed, choose their own method of working. Refused this—well, there just wouldn't be any lay helpers. What a pity that the dean—invaluable in his own, official line—should be so completely devoid of tact, and so impatient of the frailties and whimsicalities of the feminine sex. His too agile mind was ever ready to prompt a witty and scathing comment on any suggestion with which he did not agree. The plain fact was that no woman would serve under him. And that was that.

Selwyn's walk brought him to the antique shop of Mrs. Prinnett. It was an Elizabethan cottage, rich in old beams and lattice windows; and it snuggled in a backwater off the High Street within a stone's throw of the cathedral and The Close.

Behind the diamond panes appeared the usual assortment of objects of vertu or otherwise. Over the window, in gilt, neo-gothic characters, appeared the legend: 'Treasure Corner'; and in small white letters above the door: 'Mrs. Prinnett. Antiquarian."

The bell jangled loudly as he made his entrance and Mrs. Prinnett appeared from a door at the back with the promptitude of a jack-in-the-box.

"Oh, it's you, Mr. Sneddicombe. What a pleasure to see you. It's not often that you pay me a visit."

Selwyn smiled. "The stipend of a parson hardly justifies him in visiting such an emporium of treasures," he replied lightly. "Dear me, that's a nice Queen Anne desk you have there."

Mrs. Prinnett patted the surface of the desk with loving appreciation. "Yes, it is rather a beauty. And ridiculously cheap. Only two fifty! I bought it at a bargain price in a sale, and I never seek to make an undue profit."

"Small profits and quick returns?" suggested Selwyn. "Well, I hope some connoisseur with that amount of money to spend may soon relieve you of your treasure. But can I have a word with you in private?"

Mrs. Prinnett was flurried. "Of course, vicar. Of course! Oh dear, have I been guilty of some indiscretion?" She led the way to her back room, a combination of parlour and kitchen where a kettle was boiling merrily on a gas cooker.

"I was just about to make myself a cup of tea. Perhaps you will join me?—that is, unless our roles are to be confessor and penitent!" She finished with a nervous laugh.

"Far from it, my dear Mrs. Prinnett. I am here as your assistant. In the matter of Miss Pruin, you understand."

Mrs. Prinnett's face fell as she poured hot water into the teapot and swirled it round.

"Indeed! What a tragic affair. Whoever would have thought it of her. I should have said that she was the very last person to take her own life. But there! One never really knows one's neighbours. And cancer! Yes, one can excuse a great deal with the threat of that ghastly disease before one."

"Yes indeed. But Miss Pruin was not suffering from cancer. She was remarkably fit for her age."

Mrs. Prinnett put down the teapot and stared at her visitor's face. "Not suffering from cancer?" she repeated incredulously. "Then why. . .? Oh! the poor, poor soul. You mean she was mistaken? That she thought she had it but was really all right?"

"It would appear so. Yes, a very sad affair. But I had better tell you why I have come."

And while Mrs. Prinnett infused the tea he explained

his mission.

"That is most kind of his lordship," said Mrs. Prinnett emphatically. (She was a little prone to the use of titles where opportunity offered.) "And of you too, of course. I should indeed welcome some help in settling the maintenance accounts. To tell you the truth, Mr. Sneddicombe—one lump or two?—dear Miss Pruin had not a very good head for figures. I often wondered why she took on the job of treasurer. To speak quite plainly, she hadn't an idea of how accounts should be kept. That is why I helped her; though officially I had no right to do so. Secretary of the fund I am; but not treasurer. However, I was, of course, only too pleased to—cream?—do all I could to assist."

Tea being duly imbibed Mrs. Prinnett went upstairs for a hat and her bag while Selwyn amused himself in examining the stock. Then they set out together for the house of the late Arabella Pruin. It appeared that Mrs. Burdock, who was the late spinster's daily help, had a key to the house and would, if she were following her usual routine, be engaged in her domestic duties at the moment. This proved to be the case.

On explaining their business they received an almost enthusiastic welcome from the voluble lady, immediately tempered with suitable lamentations. It was plain that working alone in the house of tragedy had got on Mrs. Burdock's nerves and she was glad of company. At the same time her sense of fitness imposed a mournful countenance and the declamation of an elegy.

"Such a shock it was, as you can believe me, Mrs. Prinnett, ma'am. I says to Albert 'Whoever would ha' thought it! Fancy,' I says. 'But for that Mr. Whatsisname coming 'ome late that night I might 'ave bin the one to find 'er,' I says. I never shouldn't have recovered from that. My 'eart, you know. But there, we never knows when our call is to come. Mind you, it wasn't everyone as appreciated the poor lady. Reserved, she was. Didn't find it easy to mix with folks, if you know what I mean. No, it wasn't everyone as got on with 'er. But I always managed well enough. Temper she did 'ave—at times. But I always says: 'oo 'asn't? It would be a poor sort of world if all was alike and lying down like lambs under provocation."

"Provocation?" queried Selwyn, refraining from the obvious comment that with a world peopled by lambs there would be none to occasion provocation.

"Well, sir, that Miss Tatchett. Mind you, I'm not sayin' a word against the good lady. I knows me place. And no doubt she's a very respeckable lady. But she and Miss Pruin never did hit it off together, as you might say. Argue! Why, there's been times when I've 'eard 'em in me kitchen and been of a mind to come in—casual like—to stop 'em. For it never did my lady no good. Always on edge she were, after them rowdybouts."

"Did Miss Pruin ever complain to you about her health, Mrs. Burdock?" asked Selwyn.

"That she never did. No sir. She enjoyed the best of 'ealth. Barring what it might be a bit of an 'eadache—megrims, she called 'em—as you or me might get any time, she never 'ad nothin' wrong with 'er. Not in all the ten years I've bin with 'er."

"So she was perfectly normal when you last saw her?"

"Well, sir; yes. But when you say normal, it did seem to me as she were very worrited about somethin' the very last day of 'er life—as it came out to be; though little we thought it, I'll be bound. Short with me, she was. But I never took no notice—but for to make 'er a extra cup o' tea."

"Perhaps she had something in the post that upset her?" suggested Selwyn.

Mrs. Burdock shook her head. "That she never. Post

comes after I arrive of a mornin'. Took it in meself. There wasn't but two of them circular things and a postcard. Not a great lot of letters did Miss Pruin 'ave—barrin', of course, times when she'd sent out appeals. Treasurer of somethin' she was. To do with the cathedral, I believe; but I never knew rightly what. Mrs. Prinnett 'ere, she'd be able to tell you better 'n me— isn't that so, ma'am? For 'twas Mrs. Prinnett who 'elped the dear lady. No 'ead for figures, Miss Prain 'adn't. Nor for money neither. I 'ad to do the shoppin' for 'er. Bless 'er, she never knew the price of a bunch of greens like. But there, sir and ma'am, you'll 'ave come on business. You won't want to stop talkin' to me. I've left all 'er papers as they was—but for top dustin' and puttin' 'back. I'll be makin' you a cup o' tea while you get to work." And Mrs. Burdock, now somewhat breathless, betook herself to her kitchen—only to return a moment later with an envelope containing several keys.

"You'll no doubt be wantin' these," she explained. "The perlice 'ad a lend o' them the day as it 'appened; but I wouldn't let 'em out of my sight. I felt responsible like. You see, Miss Pruin 'adn't no lawyer or the like. Didn't believe in lettin' other people into 'er affairs, she used to say; though goodness knows as she 'adn't the 'ead to look after them 'erself. So I'm glad you've come along."

Left to themselves at last they got busy. Mrs. Prinnett, who seemed to know where things were kept, produced the account and receipt books and handed them to Selwyn.

"Perhaps you'd be kind enough to check these," she said. "And I'll give you the pass book as well. It should be in Miss Pruin's writing desk." She tried one or two keys and eventually opened the desk. From this she took a receipt book and a black japanned cash-box. "I'll just check through the petty cash balance," she suggested, seating herself at the desk. "There shouldn't be much, as we used to pay any money there was into the bank at the end of each week."

Selwyn settled to the task of checking entries in the cash book against the receipt counterfoils when he was suddenly interrupted by a low cry from Mrs. Prinnett.

"Good gracious! Look at this!" She turned in her chair and held a white, square envelope at arm's length. "D'you know, that's the dead spit of the anonymous letter I had about the organ committee. Addressed in the same way, too; 'Miss Pruin. Private and Personal' in type; no stamp or postmark." She laid the letter on the table in front of Selwyn and he picked it up with some curiosity, turning it over in his hands.

"It's been opened," he reported. "Well . . . under the circumstances I think we are justified in seeing what it contains." He drew forth a single sheet and read aloud the few typed lines which it contained: 'What did you do with Miss Carson's hundred pounds? My eye is on you. Watch the newspapers. Be sure your sin will find you out!' Beneath was the usual signature of a pair of scales, roughly drawn in red ink.

"What did I say!" said Mrs. Prinnett in triumph. "I just knew it was one of those vile things!" Then the gist of the contents began to dawn on her. "My goodness!" she gasped. "What d'you think it means? It can't mean that Miss Pruin. . . took money that wasn't hers!"

"Precisely what it does mean," retorted Selwyn with set lips. "But whether there's any truth in the accusation is an entirely different matter. Was Miss Pruin treasurer of any other societies or committees?"

Mrs. Prinnett shook her head. "Not as far as I know. I should think it extremely unlikely. If she had been I'm sure she would have asked me to help her."

"Then the assumption is that this thing"—he flung the letter on the table with a gesture of disgust—"refers to a subscription towards the Maintenance Fund." He glanced rapidly down the last few pages of the account book and " shook his head. "There's no entry for anyone named Carson," he reported slowly. "I'd better look through the receipt book."

Several minutes passed while Mrs. Prinnett waited with barely concealed anxiety, watching her companion as he went carefully through the counterfoils of the book. He looked up at length, his finger marking a place.

"Come and look at this," he invited in a strained voice.

Mrs. Prinnett leaned over his shoulder. There could be no doubt. One counterfoil had been neatly cut from the book. Only the fact that the pages were numbered drew attention to the absence of one of them. Selwyn sat back and passed his hand across his forehead.

"I don't like this, Mrs. Prinnett. There may be a perfectly simple explanation, of course; a receipt blotted, or a mistake made. But then one would expect to find the counterfoil still in place and marked 'cancelled' or some such thing. Do you know this Miss Carson?"

Mrs. Prinnett pursed her lips doubtfully. At length she declared: "There is a Miss Carson who lives at Wythet Oak— about five miles out of town on the Boxted Road. It's a large place and she's reputed to be very rich; but. . ."

"You don't think she can be the one?"

"Well, no. She has the reputation of being eccentric; almost a miser, you might say. I shouldn't have thought it likely that she'd give a hundred pounds to anything."

Selwyn picked up the telephone directory and turned its pages.

"Here we are," he said, "Carson, Miss Beatrice; Wythet Oak, Fernhampton. Telephone number Boxted 1987. I'll give her a ring." He suited the action to the words and in a few moments was speaking to Miss Carson herself.

"This is the Reverend Selwyn Sneddicombe. . . No. Sneddicombe. . . . I daresay; it's not a common name. I am ringing up on behalf of the Cathedral Maintenance Fund committee. I believe you were good enough to subscribe a hundred pounds to—— Anonymous? But of course. No, no. I assure you. I merely wanted to be certain that you had been sent a receipt. We must keep the books in order, you see. No, not for publication, I promise you. You did? I see. I wonder if it would be troubling you too much to ask you to give me the number of the receipt? Yes. . . Yes. . . that is why I am settling up the accounts on her behalf. Yes, it was most tragic. So unexpected. Yes, I'll hold the line. Thank you so much."

Selwyn turned from the instrument and reported jerkily, the receiver held to his ear: "She did send a hundred; and got a receipt. But the gift was anonymous; seemed curious that anyone knew of it besides Miss Pruin."

Mrs. Prinnett nodded knowingly. "What did I tell you? I said she was eccentric—and a bit of a miser. Didn't want her name to appear in case others wrote for subscriptions."

"Maybe. I've asked her to get the number of—. . . Yes, I'm still here, Miss Carson. Yes, I have a pencil." He wrote down a number on a sheet of paper while a spluttering voice could be heard at the other end of the wire. "Thank you; thank you very much. That is most kind of you. I'm much obliged. No, no word of your gift shall go beyond the officials of the fund. Goodbye."

He replaced the receiver and turned gloomily to Mrs. Prinnett.

"It's the same number as the missing counterfoil. Oh dear! It does begin to look as if something were not quite right. But Miss Pruin! Of all respectable old souls! I should never have dreamed——"

"Still waters run deep, they say," said Mrs. Prinnett profoundly. "But I agree. I should never have thought it; and I've worked with her. What do we do now?"

"I'm afraid we must make inquiries at Miss Pruin's own

bank. Do you know where she had an account?"

"I don't. But I expect we'll find a paying-in book in her desk. We can't leave matters as they are, I'm afraid. Better that we should find out the truth than that some hide-bound lawyer should do so. Someone will have to clear up her affairs."

Together they searched through the drawers of the desk. They soon found a passbook in Miss Pruin's name and an entry showing a credit of one hundred pounds laconically labelled 'Carson' and dated a week earlier.

"Poor old soul," said Selwyn compassionately. "Sudden temptation, I suppose. Being an anonymous gift it must have seemed too easy. But. . . I thought Miss Pruin was comfortably off?"

Mrs. Prinnett shook her head. "Oh no. A man wouldn't notice, of course; but any woman with an eye could see that her clothes were out of date and even repaired in places. Look round this room. You won't see much evidence of luxury here. No, I imagine she had just enough to scrape along on. Look at these!" she continued, dipping into the open drawer and pulling out a sheaf of unpaid bills. "Here's one for the rates. 'Final Demand' printed on it in red." She piled up the bills on the table and then, at the bottom of the drawer, came upon a long envelope inscribed with admirable brevity: "My Will."

CHAPTER VI

"WHAT ought we to do?" asked Mrs. Prinnett, balancing the heavily sealed envelope in her hands and gazing anxiously at Selwyn.

"Open it. There's no name of an executor or lawyer on the envelope; so we can't deliver it to the proper authority. No doubt the Will itself will appoint some executor. But we can't tell who it may be until we open it, can we! So we must do just that; and, if an executor is mentioned, seal it up again at once without reading the rest. Then we can deliver it to the person so named."

"You do it," urged Mrs. Prinnett, passing over the envelope as though it were burning her. "I'm terrified of legal things."

Selwyn slit the seals with his pocket knife and drew out the single sheet which the envelope contained.

"One of those things you can buy at any stationer's," he remarked as he smoothed it out before him. "My goodness! Listen to this: 'I appoint the Rev. Selwyn Sneddicombe, Vicar of All Souls, to be my executor.' What d'you think of that? How extraordinary. I knew the good lady, of course but not all that well."

"You were her parish priest. I suppose that's why. She'd no close friends, poor soul. Well, that makes things much easier. Now you can read the Will with a good conscience and we shall know what to do."

Selwyn nodded and read for a few moments in silence.

"According to this," he said at length, "she had precious little to leave. This house and its contents. That's all. No mention of a mortgage. And that's funny, you know. You'd think she could have raised money on the house, rather than. . . well, do what she did do."

"Probably had a horror of mortgages. Lots of people have—even those with a business sense; and poor Miss

Pruin hadn't that. Poor soul! She must have been desperate to take a chance like that. But—I hadn't thought of it before—how on earth did the person who wrote that anonymous letter know about the hundred pounds? How could he—or she, for that matter?"

"Ah! there you have me. How do people like that garner their evil knowledge? But it was the threat of exposure, without a doubt, that caused the poor thing to take her own life. Writers of letters like that"—he flipped the anonymous letter as it lay before him—"have a lot to answer for. I wouldn't care to be one of them on the Day of Judgment."

"Indeed no! Well, I suppose we'll have to tell the police; and then the whole scandal is bound to come out. And after the poor creature took her own life to avoid the disgrace. What a shame!"

Selwyn frowned in thought, his head between his hands, and for a while there was no sound but the ticking of a clock. The peace was shattered by the entrance of Mrs. Burdock, bearing a tray on which a teapot steamed and thin bread and butter lay tastefully displayed on a green, china plate shaped like a vine leaf.

The break gave him a chance to collect his thoughts and come to one of the sudden decisions which characterised him.

"Look, Mrs. Prinnett," he said as he drank what was his third cup of tea that morning, "what I'm going to suggest may be unorthodox—even unethical; but I cannot see that the ends of justice will be better served by bringing to light this sad affair. The inquest has been held and a verdict of suicide while the balance of the mind was disturbed has been given. If we hand this letter to the police then scandal will be added to scandal; and the verdict would be the same even if they were able to reopen the inquest; which I doubt. Let us spare the poor lady's memory as much as we can. As to the hundred pounds, I myself will pay that into the fund—anonymously. So no one will be the loser. What d'you say?" His bright, brown eyes sought those of Mrs. Prinnett with an appeal it was hard to resist.

"Very well. You know much more about these matters than I do. Certainly we don't want any scandal that can be avoided—both for the sake of Miss Pruin and the cathedral. But the hundred pounds!—isn't that an awful lot for you to pay out of your own pocket?"

Selwyn made a rueful grimace. "Well, I can't truthfully say that I shan't miss it. But never mind. 'Lay not up. . .' you know."

"Well, I call it very fine of you. And no one will even know how generous you have been. But I suppose that's what you want. I'm afraid I'm not that altruistic myself. By the way, how does Miss Pruin leave what money she had? Perhaps you could pay yourself back out of that?"

"I wouldn't if I could. But I can't. It's quite plain. All her possessions are to be sold and the money so raised is to be given to St. Ethelreda's Home. You know, that home for faded ladies on the outskirts of the town. Poor Miss Pruin! She herself might have been happier as an inmate. But," he added with a roguish twinkle, "what would Miss Tatchet have thought—and said! Dear me; I'm afraid the best of us are apt to suit our actions to conform to the opinions of others."

When they left the house Selwyn had the anonymous letter and its envelope tucked into his wallet. He now had three specimens on which to work—though he had no clear idea how to set about his self-imposed task of detection. Nor was he quite easy in his conscience. Was it not his obvious duty to give the letters to the police—who were trained in these matters? But this would mean reflections on at least two cathedral workers; one of whom had already atoned for her crime. And the Church of today had too many enemies as it was. Anyway, he decided with an aggressive thrust of his chin, he'd made his decision; and that was the way it was going to be.

But now *The Clarion* again took a hand. In a two column spread on its front page it shrieked:

POISON PEN AT WORK IN STORMINSTER! LEADING CITIZENS ATTACKED

The poisoner, the blackmailer and the anonymous letter writer may surely be classed amongst the lowest and most despicable criminal types. Such a person is at work in our city. Although we cannot at the moment give details or names, it has come to our knowledge that several people of unimpeachable respectability and position have been attacked by the cowardly writer of anonymous letters. Some of these have even been of a threatening nature. All of them have attempted to sow discord and mistrust; be it in family or civic life.

HELP IN THE CRIME HUNT!

What can be done about this pest? We appeal to all our readers to help in unmasking the criminal. The police are powerless to act unless we assist them. They must have evidence. And it is a deplorable feature in a case of this sort that no one cares to go to the police and make known to them what has been alleged in an anonymous letter. For usually there is at least a substratum of truth in the accusations.

But we must all sink our private feelings for the good of the community. Remember that your confidence will be respected, and that in the event of a prosecution it is the usual procedure to keep the names of witnesses out of the proceedings and so, of course, out of the Press.

CRIMINAL IS NIGHT BIRD

A peculiar feature of these anonymous letters is that they are all delivered by hand; and at night. So, if you are out late, take particular notice of any other late wayfarers and observe their movements.

There followed further diatribes against the poison pen wielder and the blackmailer, with instances, dug from the record, of previous incidents in the history of Storminster. But Selwyn Sneddicombe skipped these. What he had read was sufficient for his needs; he had been struck by an idea.

He strongly suspected that John Archer had inspired the article. And this belief was strengthened when he recalled that Archer had been present at the committee meeting when Mrs. Prinnett had read aloud the letter she had received. But how had he come to learn of the other letters? Could he know about the one which Miss Pruin had received? The one which, undoubtedly, had caused her death? There was only one way to find out.

John Archer held a peculiar position on the staff of *The Clarion*. There were those who thought that *The Clarion* itself was a peculiar paper. Belonging to that rare-becoming group of locally-owned journals, under no obligation to bow the knee to the great News Barons, its methods were not in keeping with the majority of its more powerful contemporaries. It was owned by a retired publisher who had settled in Storminster some years before the events which are now being chronicled. He had wanted something to occupy both his time and interest. *The Clarion* came into the market on the death of its proprietor, and the ex-publisher bought it. From a weekly organ he converted it into a daily—though local news had to be padded generously with items supplied by the national agencies. And amongst his staff he had placed his nephew, John Archer; thereby killing two birds in the traditional manner: he earned the gratitude of his widowed sister, and obtained the services of one whom, he fondly believed, he could control; one who would toe the line unquestioningly. It had not worked out quite like that. John, who had had some experience of newspaper work in a small town, held his own views as to what he liked and what he didn't like. Combining the functions of critic (which in a town containing but two theatres and one music hall, were not onerous) and society reporter, he allowed himself more licence than would in general have been granted to him. His, indeed, was the poison pen article; and if not on strictly journalistic lines it at least reflected his personality. And the editor, perhaps with thoughts of uncle, had passed it with but the slightest use of the red or blue pencil.

The critic-journalist was in his diminutive office, shared with his part-time typist secretary, when Selwyn called.

"Come in, padre, and welcome," he said with a smile. "What can I do for you? Another appeal?"

Selwyn shook his head and glanced at Miss Moorloft, who sat expectantly before her typewriter; fingers poised over the keys and a shorthand pad at her side.

"Time for your elevenses, Mabel," said Archer, interpreting aright the glance of his caller.

"It's this article," explained Selwyn, when they were alone. He spread out the morning's *Clarion* and pointed to the poison pen effusion. "I suppose you wrote this?"

"Honesty compels where modesty might forbid. Yes; all my own work."

"I thought so. Now, what I want to ask you is: how do you know that people have been receiving these letters?"

"My dear padre, there's no mystery. As you may know, I am supposed to be a social reporter. That means that I go to most parties—and the cups of tea I have to drink would ruin any constitution less robust than mine! I met Derrick Mathers at one of them the other day, and he was full of a letter he had which threatened a filial visit from one of his offspring. Others have confided in me. Furthermore, a little bird whispered to me that poor Miss Pruin was so honoured, shortly before her lamented death."

"Her housekeeper, of course? Listening at the door no doubt."

"A rhetorical question, I take it. As you know, no newspaper ever divulges the source of its information. Wouldn't get any if we did."

Selwyn smiled. "Maybe something in that. Anyway, your little bird told you the truth for once. And it's about that very matter that I have come to see you." He proceeded to explain how he had come upon the note and ended by producing it.

"I suppose I ought to have gone to the police; but I didn't want to create more scandal. So I thought I'd work on it myself. I'd already decided to do that with the first one—the one we both heard at the committee, for I kept that note. Then I had one myself. Telling me to lay off! So now I've got three to work upon. Then I read your article and thought that two heads were better than one; and that, as you seemed interested, we might put those heads together."

John Archer nodded slowly. "Might be something in the idea. As for the police; I don't know, but I very much doubt whether they could take action in either of the cases we are discussing. There's no definite libel of any one person; nor are there any specific threats—or blackmailing demands. I don't see what they could do. All right. I'll have a stab at it. Let's have a decko at Miss Pruin's note."

He read it through slowly and gave an exclamation.

"By jove! Unless I'm greatly mistaken this was typed on

a machine of mine!"

"You. . . you don't mean that Miss Moorloft——"

Archer laughed joyously. "Good Lord no! Why, my dear padre, she's the very epitome of respectability. I almost wish she were capable of such criminal activities. She would, at least, be interesting."

"I'm much relieved. I have the same opinion of her— that is, of course, the first part of your opinion. She sings in my choir, you know. Well then, what do you mean?"

"I mean that I firmly believe that this note was typed on a machine that I used to own. It began to get a bit wonky, so I sold it. Let's have a look at the other notes. I only glanced at that one at the committee. Never thought of examining the type faces."

Selwyn hunted in his over-stuffed wallet and produced them.

"Yes, there's no doubt. I'd know that 'w' with a chip out of the left leg; also the 'i' which is slightly out of alignment—yes, and that drunken 'r'. But I can make quite sure. I've got some old typescript at home that I did on the machine—articles that were never published. Let me borrow these specimens and I'll make certain."

"You can have them, of course. But I don't see that it helps us much if you sold the machine—unless you sold it privately."

"Well, I didn't. I sold it to a secondhand dealer in such wares. Now I wonder. . . . I might be able to trace it. But it's some time ago. Anyway, I'll do my best. But look! A word of warning. If I get on the trail, by means of the typewriter, I reserve the right to keep the matter to myself until such time as I've rounded up enough evidence to incriminate or clear the person who bought it—if it is possible to find that out from the dealer. You see, it may have passed from hand to hand a number of times. It may even be in some small office where half a dozen chaps could get at it if they chose their time. Besides," he added with a grin, "I'm first and foremost a newspaper man—though there may be many who'd declare otherwise—and as such I reserve all scoops for my own paper. 'Watch the Press!' indeed. Darned cheek!"

Selwyn returned the grin. "That's quite O.K. as far as I'm concerned. I'm not taking on this job because I like it, or because I fancy myself as a budding Sherlock Holmes. It's simply that I realise what harm can be done by such letters and I want to find out who's responsible and get them stopped. If you can do that for me, so much the better. I'll even be generous! Anything I may discover I'll share with you at once!"

"Ah! Returning good for evil, eh? Well, after all, that's your trade."

Nigel and Helen met frequently, either for elevenses or afternoon tea. The risk of being seen by her mother added, for Helen, a spice of excitement to these adventures. Nigel, on the other hand, confident of his power to charm, would have welcomed discovery. It might bring matters to a head.

They quarrelled almost as frequently as they met, but that, Helen told herself, was a refreshing change from the behaviour of the young men of her acquaintance (the young men approved by mother) who agreed with everything she said and whose every action shrieked the word 'heiress!.' For it just doesn't do to offend heiresses—not, that is, if you want to marry them for their money.

They were quarrelling now. "Don't be silly, Nigel," said Helen brusquely. "One would think I was asking you to sign your death warrant!"

"Well, I'm likely to die—of boredom—if I do as you ask. Tea with Miss Tatchet! Tea, to begin with, which I abominate above all other meals—except, of course," he added hastily, "when it's tea with you. And Miss Tatchet of all unbelievably frightful people. My dear, what have I in common with Miss Tatchet?"

"Or I, for that matter?" countered Helen tartly. "D'you think I want to go any more than you do? It's simply that mother can't—or won't—go; and I've been detailed to represent her. I'm simply not going alone; and you promised yesterday that you'd come with me. Besides, if you're half as good an actor as you make out, then you can be all things to all men—or women. Here's an excellent chance for you to put on an act. I don't believe you can do it. That's why you're making all this fuss."

Nigel bowed to the inevitable. Quite apart from the estimated cash value of an alliance with Helen he was beginning to find himself mildly interested in her. At least it was better to run around in her company than to go alone or with some pick-up, as long as lack of funds condemned him to this dull, cathedral city.

"All right," he said with an ill grace. "Little Nigel will play juvenile lead opposite you at the old snoot's tea party. Think I can't act, do you? Well, you just wait and see!"

Helen smiled the secret smile of the moral victor as she led the way from the museum where they had met. But Nigel paused as another, and appalling thought struck him.

"Good Lord! I shall probably be the only man there!"

"Nonsense. Selwyn's always there. He'll keep you company."

"I said 'man'."

"How perfectly foul you can be, Nigel. Selwyn's a man if anyone is."

"A *clergy-man*; not quite the same thing. Hell's boots! These church types give me the willies. I've no use for churches."

"How they must miss you. All the same, it might do you a spot of good if you went to one—just now and again. You might learn something."

"Not for me; thanks a lot. I had enough of that when I was mug enough to be in the choir. And I wouldn't have been, but for the odd bob or two they paid me. Frustrated spinsters and tame old tabbies. They're the sort that make up congregations. That is, of course, as long as the parson's reasonably good-looking. Getting as near to a 'near' man as they can—poor pathetic old hags. Religion's the dope handed out to the less fortunate in life in order to keep them down and under. A mere sedative pill coated with alleluias, to prevent mass risings. Oh! but I'm forgetting the younger members. Also prescribed for the sentimental fools of both sexes. Soporific and soothing."

"D'you know, Nigel, at times I think you're a perfect swine. A stinker, in fact. And yet you think yourself so clever."

"Item by item. Like all women you ask about, or pronounce upon two different subjects in the same sentence. Item one: I *am* a realist—what you call a stinker, no doubt. Item two: I don't *think* I'm clever; I *know* I am. And what's more, my beloved shrew, you just adore me the way I am."

Helen pursed her lips and frowned. "I'm not so sure," she said slowly. "I rather think I hate you and all you stand for."

"Bad grammar and bad psychology, my pet. If you really want to change a man you must never—but never!—tell him directly to his face the things you don't like about him. If you do he'll only dig in his toes and become more so. All must be done by subtle innuendo. . . . Oh well, to hell with all that. If we've *got* to go to old mother Tatchet's, let's get cracking."

CHAPTER VII

Miss TATCHET, well boned, frizzled and rouged, stood (according to Storminster Society protocol) just five paces from the folding doors of her 'withdrawing' room. Here she received her guests with a handshake nicely graded according to their social standing. There was the frigid or non-committal shake, for those whom policy, rather than regard, had caused to be invited. This started with her right hand at shoulder level and consisted of the merest touching of fingertips followed by a slight oscillation of the wrist and a quick renunciation of the temporary prey as though, tasting something unsavoury, she promptly eschewed it. This was calculated to keep such persons in their places. It usually did so.

Then there was the friendly shake. This followed the conventional pattern so closely that it needs no elaboration.

Lastly came the over-familiar greeting in which the hand of the visitor was firmly grasped in both those of the hostess and given a series of short but vigorous shakes. This was reserved for those from whom much was expected: potential donors to the charity of the moment, or those from whom invitations to this or that were solicited; and, naturally, those who bore titles or the golden chains of worldly prosperity.

"My dear!" she said in her high, reedy voice as Helen made her appearance. "But how nice. I hope your dear mother is not indisposed?" and Miss Tatchet offered the friendly shake.

"Afraid she is, Miss Tatchet. So I've come along to do duty —that is, I'm here in her place. And I've brought Nigel Villiers, the celebrated actor, to keep me company." She waved a hand at the reluctant Nigel.

Miss Tatchet adjusted her pince-nez and surveyed the

young man with cool insolence, from polished shoes to Bryl-creemed hair. "Indeed! Not, I imagine, Shakespearean?" And Miss Tatchet bestowed upon him a sample of the frigid shake. "How do you do?" she murmured without interest.

"That remains to be seen," said the irrepressible Nigel, as he cast a dubious eye upon the meagre and strictly teetotal refreshment displayed on occasional tables.

Miss Tatchet was disconcerted. Used to lip service and ready acquiescence (she was reputed to be very rich), she had no appropriate rejoinder for the retort discourteous. But she quickly recovered her poise and addressed herself exclusively to Helen.

"I've no doubt you'll find plenty of people you know. Your dear mother would have, at any rate. Excuse me, my dear," and she turned with obvious relief to new arrivals.

"What an old bitch," said Nigel, grinning sardonically. "Typical church worker, I feel sure."

"S-sh!" rebuked Helen. "You can't talk like that here. Don't forget you're amongst the cream of Storminster Society. Please try to behave as such—even if it comes a bit hard."

Nigel made a comical grimace. "You've said it!—I say! There's that little tame cat parson of yours that you got so het up about just now. Let's go and worry the life out of him."

Selwyn Sneddicombe was standing in a corner of the room in the attitude of a stag at bay; but there was but a single hound to represent the pack—and she of the female gender. This took the form of an over-substantial woman who pressed urgently upon him. When he espied Helen and her escort coming towards him his face lightened.

"Oh, hullo Helen," he cried with alacrity, dodging beneath a waving arm of his adversary, "where's your mother? I wanted to see her about——"

"Indisposed," said Helen crisply. "But," she added with a smile, "don't let that distress you unduly. It's something that comes on 'all of a sudden' when she's due to attend a show of this sort. I used to suffer from the same thing on Monday mornings—when it was time to go to school. You know Nigel?" and she pushed forward her companion.

Selwyn gave a cautious glance over his shoulder, observed that his late sparring partner had retired (presumably in a dudgeon) and extended his hand.

"Oh yes, indeed, Helen. We're quite old friends," and he gave his ready and attractive smile. "As I told you, I remember Nigel when he was quite a young boy."

At that moment Helen was co-opted by a bulky lady in black satin and bugles and the two men found themselves at a forced tête-à-tête.

"Rotten job, yours must be," began Nigel patronisingly. "Having to turn up at these *Walpurgis Nachts* of the tabbies of Storminster."

Selwyn eyed him carefully. "Oh, I don't know," he replied; "All is grist that comes to my mill. But, if I may say so, I should have thought that you were somewhat of a fish out of water."

"The flies go where the honey is," retorted Nigel sardonically. "Tell me, does anything ever happen in this deadly town?"

"Don't you read the papers?"

"You mean Miss Pruin killing herself? Not surprised. Better than dying of boredom, anyway." He gave a harsh laugh. "Don't see why she had to use an oven, though. I should have thought there was enough gas in the air!" and he waved a scornful hand to indicate the hum of conversation.

"I don't know that I like your attitude," said Selwyn quietly. "Miss Pruin was a friend of mine."

"Really? Then your faith doesn't seem to have done her a power of good—or perhaps she was eager to get to a better world?"

Helen's return saved Selwyn the necessity of replying.

"What are you two talking about?" she asked brightly. "You look as though you were discussing a funeral—or the state of the stock market!"

"As a matter of fact," supplied Nigel, "we were just discussing the only bit of news that has hit this town in the last century: the death of Miss Pruin."

Helen's expressive face took on a look of compassion. "Poor old darling. Hounded to death by some filthy person with more ink than decency. If I could lay my hands on that poison-pen monger I'd——"

Selwyn registered shocked surprise. "My dear Helen! What are you suggesting?"

Helen gave a little laugh. "Oh, it's no secret. Everyone knows she got one of those filthy letters. And she's not the only one. Would you believe it?—and her blue eyes opened wide—"even mummy had one the other day. Digging into her sticky past. The only trouble is, of course, that she hasn't got one. Oh Lord!" she added with a little grimace, "I quite forgot. I wasn't supposed to breathe a word." She smiled at Selwyn. "As a matter of fact I asked her if I could have the beastly thing to give to you. I knew you were collecting them. But she shied at the idea and said I wasn't to mention a word to a soul. And now I've gone and told the pair of you. Forget I said it, see?"

Both men gave smiling nods and Helen, to change the subject, said hastily: "I've been telling Nigel that a spot of church wouldn't do him any harm worth mentioning. I strongly suspect he's an atheist."

"Agnostic would be the better word," amended Nigel. "I don't see how you parsons can reconcile all the blah you talk about a 'loving God' when there are things like floods, bush fires and earthquakes cropping up everywhere; not to mention diseases and people born crippled or moronic. And what about dire poverty alongside people who stink of money?"

Selwyn's eyes twinkled. "I rather suspect that's a freely adapted passage from one of your plays. But even if I thought you were serious this is hardly the time and place for a conversion talk."

"Oh?" sneered Nigel, "I thought it was your job to preach the Gospel in season and out of season; at all times and in all places. Isn't that what you're paid for?"

"Shut up! Nigel," said Helen indignantly. "You're being a perfect swine. Sorry," she said, turning back to Selwyn and presenting a very firm little back to Nigel, "He's such a ham actor that he can't get a decent job anywhere and is peeved in consequence; so he vents his spite on anything too decent for his comprehension."

Far from being abashed Nigel burst into a roar of laughter.

"So our little Helen has steel beneath the velvet glove. Whoever would have thought it? Well, well! I can see I'm not wanted. Always one to take a hint, is Nigel Villiers." And he left them with a mocking smile.

"I'm sorry about that," said Helen simply.

It was Selwyn's turn to smile. "Don't worry, my dear. We parsons are used to that sort of thing. It's what we're paid for—as your friend justly remarked. He's evidently one of those unhappy people who can't get to grips with themselves and are therefore at loggerheads with the rest of the world. But tell me, did your mother really receive one of these anonymous letters?"

Helen nodded. "She did; but, as I said, I was forbidden to mention it. It accused her of being a blacksmith's daughter or something! As if anybody nowadays cared a hoot—except mummy herself. You know what the darling is!"

"Can you tell me when she received it—and how?" Selwyn's tone was both serious and eager, and Helen looked faintly surprised.

"You sound quite excited about it!"

"I am. Look, Helen, I didn't want to say so before Tom Prinnett—Nigel Villiers, if you prefer it—but Miss Pruin did get one of those letters; and there's little doubt that she killed herself because of it. This thing is becoming a menace that threatens to destroy the social life of Storminster and I'm out to stop it if I can. When anonymous letters start going the rounds it's not long before everyone suspects everyone else— then goodbye to any chance of a decent life. As you said just now. I'm collecting these letters; but not like a chap collects stamps or autographs. I'm going to do all I can to find out the guilty party and put an end to it. It's not that I fancy myself as a detective," he added rather shyly; "but just that I happened to be present when the first one was publicly discussed; and I managed to get hold of it. I thought it might be possible to trace the writer by one means or another. Then I found that other people had had them, though they had destroyed the things at once. Then a funny thing happened. I showed one to John Archer and he said that it had been typed on a machine that he once owned——"

"I say! How exciting," broke in Helen. "It sounds just like a thriller!"

Selwyn nodded agreement. "Yes, doesn't it? But, unfortunately, it's real life; and deadly serious. So can you help me—about the one your mother had?"

"Of course. Craven—our butler, you know—found it in the hall after mother's last party. He said he didn't notice it until the last of the guests had gone and it might have been concealed under the hats. . . . I say! What a funny coincidence. There is John Archer, talking to Miss

Tatchet. I suppose he's just arrived. They're looking our way. Probably discussing us!"

Selwyn glanced towards the pair and nodded. "Oh yes. He's usually at all these affairs. Part of his job as a reporter, I suppose. . . . So it was found in the hall after the party. Then it was probably, though not necessarily, brought by one of the guests. Not necessarily, because I suppose that on an occasion like that the front door would be left open or ajar; and Craven would usher guests upstairs. A determined person could have hidden in the garden in view of the door and watched for a suitable opportunity to slip in and place the letter. But the probability is that it was one of the guests. Can you get me a list of them?"

Helen's eyes widened. "My dear Selwyn! You can't suspect one of them. They were the usual crowd; people we've known for years, mostly; and all personal friends. You couldn't possibly suspect any of them."

Again Selwyn smiled. "You're very loyal to your friends, aren't you?"

"Of course," replied Helen simply. "What else are friends for?"

"Helen!" The high-pitched voice of Miss Tatchet broke in on their conversation and the lady in person confronted them. "I should like a word with you—in private."

Selwyn smiled a farewell and drifted away.

"Yes, Miss Tatchet?" said Helen in surprise.

"I am extremely annoyed with you, Helen. I have just discovered that that young man you brought with you and introduced under some silly, false name is really none other than Mrs. Prinnett's son!"

Helen nodded. "Quite true. What about it? And it's not a false name. It's his name on the stage; and it's usual for actors to be known by their stage names."

Miss Tatchet waved this aside. "You must have known

perfectly well that I would not have received Mrs. Prinnett's son had I known who he was. I am very displeased."

A slow flush mounted to Helen's cheeks. "But why on earth not? I thought you and Mrs. Prinnett were great friends. You're both on all sorts of committees."

"I have nothing whatever against Mrs. Prinnett, my dear. She is a most worthy person and an admirable worker. An excellent woman to have—on committees."

"I see. Worthy enough to be patronised on committees but not in your own home."

"You speak like a child. You are quite old enough to realise the importance of what few social distinctions are left. I should never dream of asking Mrs. Prinnett to one of my 'at homes'. Nor, I am quite certain, would your dear mother."

Helen felt a twinge of discomfort as she recollected her mother's views on the same subject, and the thought made her defiant.

"And I should jolly well hope she wouldn't come if you did! You don't imagine I'd have come if mother hadn't wanted to get out of it? They're crashingly boring—oh! I say!" she added contritely, "that was beastly rude of me. I'm terribly sorry, Miss Tatchet. I never ought to have said that."

Miss Tatchet pursed her thin lips and drew a deep breath.

"No apology can atone for such rudeness; such unjustified and wanton rudeness, Helen. One does not expect the young people of today to have any manners; and in your case, after what I have observed of the laxity with which your mother treats you, I suppose it is not surprising. Nevertheless——"

"And now you're insulting my mother. All right, Miss Tatchet. I'm going home. And. . . I'm sorry I said I was sorry!"

"Why all the hurry?" demanded Nigel as Helen shook

the dust from her feet on Miss Tatchet's doorstep. "First you positively force me to come to the beastly tea party and then you whisk me away just when I'd found someone with a glimmering of common sense to talk to. That chap Archer——"

"Sorry, Nigel," said Helen with a little laugh, as they fell into step on the pavement. "But Miss Tatchet's just what you called her. She was frightfully rude to me. But," she hastened to add with an impish grin, "she wasn't the only one to be rude!"

"Rude to you?" echoed Nigel frowning. "Old bitch she may be; but I should have thought she'd be meticulous about her duties as a hostess—boring though she and all her works undoubtedly are. Let's think this one out. She certainly wouldn't be rude to you without cause. At least, what she considered just cause. Could it be that she resented the presence of little Nigel as much as he resented being there?"

"Don't be silly! Why should she?"

"That's no answer. So I'm right. Own up!"

"I. . . I think you're being very silly," faltered Helen.

"You said that before; but it doesn't alter facts. So I was the bone of contention. Didn't like an actor in her house, I suppose." He gave a laugh. "My dear! How sweet of you to try to spare my feelings. But even I realise that there are still a few antediluvians who regard the stage as a sink of iniquity. What a laugh!" And he proceeded to illustrate it.

Secretly relieved, Helen let him continue in his ignorance.

In the room which they had just left, Miss Tatchet was greeting a late arrival.

"How good of you to come, Mrs. de Poynton. And the dear bishop? Too busy, I suppose, to attend social gaieties?"

Mabel de Poynton grimaced inwardly at her hostess's estimation of her party but smiled outwardly.

"We're all rather busy just now, Miss Tatchet. What with the

Organ Fund and other things. That is why I'm a little late. And that reminds me, is Mrs. Prinnett here? I wanted to see her about the Book Guild."

"Oh no, Mrs. de Poynton. She. . . well," there was an artificial laugh, "she's not on my 'at home' list. A very worthy woman, of course, but. . ."

"Yes indeed. I frequently have her to our house. I don't know what the committees would do without her. What a sad thing about poor Miss Pruin. So unexpected."

Miss Tatchet's mouth became a grim line and her eyes hardened. "Of course, one is not supposed to speak ill of the dead; but I have always abhorred hypocrisy, and I do not see that death can alter the life character of a person. I cannot pretend that Miss Pruin came high in my estimation. She was, I fear, a very unbalanced woman; and extremely bigoted. It was quite impossible to reason with her. I never felt, indeed, that she was a true Christian. And how right I have proved to be! Her taking her own life against all Christian tenets has put her quite beyond the pale; a blasphemous and unforgivable crime."

"Let us hope," said Mabel de Poynton gently, "that she is now facing a more merciful Judge." And she passed on leaving Miss Tatchet tight of lip and high of colour.

In a corner of the room Rosalind Ashburn, wife of the Diocesan Architect, and Selwyn Sneddicombe were talking together when Mrs. de Poynton came up to them.

"Ah, Rosalind, my dear. I haven't seen you for quite a while. And how is Rodney? Not working too hard, I hope? And Mr. Sneddicombe! How is the inquiry proceeding? With good results?"

"I'm afraid there's nothing very definite as yet, Mrs. de Poynton. But I am no longer alone in the search. John Archer is my partner. That is to say," he added with a smile, "I tell him all I discover—little enough to date!—and he tells me what suits him."

Mabel's dark little eyes twinkled. "A malady common to the gentlemen of the Press—though by no means confined to them. But, seriously, I am very worried about the affair." She turned to Rosalind. "We are speaking of these horrible anonymous letters which have broken out like a plague in Storminster. I trust that neither you nor Rodney have received any?"

Rosalind turned scarlet. "I think people ought to go to the police," she said a little shakily.

"Ah! my dear, a counsel of perfection. I only wish that they would. But the trouble is that there's usually a certain amount of truth in the contents of these letters; a certain unpleasantness. I suppose that most of us have some little things we would rather not have known. Not necessarily shameful, of course; still—something we do not wish to become public knowledge."

Selwyn took up the argument. "And the police cannot act unless someone lodges a complaint, and produces some sort of evidence. It's a difficult position. I have managed to obtain one or two specimens of these notes, and hope to get others; but there is little to go upon. However, John Archer thinks he has a clue from the typewriting."

Mabel de Poynton nodded and then smiled. "I see. Well, if the bishop or I receive such a letter you shall certainly add it to your collection."

Selwyn smiled in return. "I'm afraid there can be little hope of that! One can hardly imagine either of you keeping a skeleton incarcerated in the episcopal cupboard."

As soon as the bishop's wife had left them Selwyn turned to Rosalind and asked quietly: "What did *your* letter say?"

She flashed him a startled glance. "What do you mean? What makes you think that I've had one?"

"Your face gave you away, my dear, when 'Mrs. Bishop'

asked you; and I noticed how swift you were to switch the conversation."

Rosalind nodded dejectedly. "Rodney always says I give everything away by my expression. Yes, I did have one. It turned out all right in the end; but it could have caused a frightful lot of harm. And, as Mrs. de Poynton says, it wasn't the sort of thing one could possibly tell the police. I'm afraid that's why I said that to her. I didn't want to tell an actual lie—I always get caught out if I do, anyway!— and I thought if I said that about going to the police she'd assume I couldn't have had a letter. D'you think," she asked anxiously, "she guessed?"

"I think she's a very shrewd—and very lovable—woman; and that whatever she may have thought, your secret is safe with her."

CHAPTER VIII

EMILY PRINNETT poured the coffee and handed a cup to her son. Her face wore a troubled expression.

"You know, Tom—oh, all right, if you must have it, Nigel—it's not doing you any good hanging around here. If you don't fancy getting a job in the town—and I admit that it might be hard to find anything suitable—why don't you go up to London and worry the agents? They aren't likely to give you anything when you're just sitting down here and not caring a bit."

Nigel smiled with moderately affectionate superiority.

"Don't you worry, Emily. I know darned well what I'm doing. I'm never going back to that one-horse touring business. To speak quite frankly, I'm too good for it. Oh no; I have other plans. I've just about got the little Battersby filly on the curb. Why, she actually had a row on my account with that old hag Tatchet! It seems the old faggot resented my presence in her house—doesn't approve of actors, presumably—and Helen gave her hell and walked out on her. Oh yes, she's in the bag all right. Ma's a bit of a trial, I admit. She'll take a bit of persuading; but I flatter myself that when I take the trouble to turn on the charm she'll come to hand all right. With the money they'll have to fork out when I marry Helen I mean to launch into Actor-Management. That's the way to get on—and to make money, if you know your job and have plenty of capital."

Mrs. Prinnett shook her head. "You're not the sort for an easy life. You're just like your father in some ways. He would never work unless he was made to. If you could sit back and feel that you didn't have to earn your living I know what would happen: you'd get careless and things would begin to slide. You know, Tom—yes, I'm not going on with this silly Nigel business when I'm talking to you seriously—you've got a lot of conceit in you. You rely too much on the 'charm' you've just mentioned. If you were free to choose what you would and would not do, then goodbye to any real, steady work. And another thing: you'd never manage to run a company. You'd want all the limelight for yourself, and if you didn't get all the applause you'd get sulky; and then you wouldn't be able to act."

Nigel raised his eyebrows quizzically. "Well! I never thought you had so much perception. Talk about a prophet having no honour in his own country! And, to be as candid as my dear mama has been, I'm ready to admit that I don't intend to do a stroke more work than I'm compelled to do. On the other hand, I consider myself a born actor. I don't need to grind at it like some of these second raters, it's simply that I've never had a chance to show what I can do. Fiddling little touring companies! What a man needs, to get on in the world today—whatever his profession—is influence. And the best influence you can have is money; lots of it. Helen's not a bad little piece, anyway. I could be quite happy with her—for a time. After that—well! In the Profession there should be ample opportunity for extra-marital amusement."

"It's a good thing I don't take you seriously when you talk like that," said his mother severely.

"Perhaps that's just your mistake!" retorted her son.

On the outskirts of Storminster lies a golf course which is highly esteemed by devotees of the Royal and Ancient. Not only is it an excellent course from the point of view of the game, but it is charmingly picturesque.

It lies in a winding valley down which meanders a sparkling stream. High on the slopes on either side are stately beech woods while, jutting from these slopes, are close-cropped spurs which offer ideal situations for natural hazards, bunkers and greens.

Yet, as there is a fly in every ointment, so is there a major drawback inseparable from the course. A part of it lies over property owned by Harold Battersby; which is equivalent to saying 'controlled by Mrs. Battersby'. There came a time when the lease of this portion of the land required renewing and, to the dismay of the members, Mrs. Battersby suddenly developed a conscience which informed her that to play golf on the Sabbath was a desecration. She refused to renew the lease unless Sunday golf was banned.

Since most of the golfers were hard-working men whose days of leisure were confined to Saturdays (half-day only, for many) and Sundays, there was genuine cause for alarm. For a while it looked as though the club would have to close down. Then Rodney Ashburn came to the rescue. Himself an ardent golfer, he brought forward a scheme whereby the course could be so diverted that the Battersby land could be disregarded. To do this entailed renting more land from the other owner, Nicholas Borroway, the local millionaire, and considerable expense in the new layout. But this, it was generally conceded, was preferable to the extinction of the club.

In the event, such heroic measures proved unnecessary.

For when it came to the ears of Mrs. Battersby that she was likely to lose the rent for her portion of the land, and gain great unpopularity into the bargain, her conscience suffered a sudden change of front and she withdrew her objections to Sunday play. But she did not forget that Rodney Ashburn had been the man who had successfully challenged her dictatorship.

It was upon this course that John Archer and Sir Derrick Mathers were now playing a round.

The sun was shining, the stream sparkling and life looked good. That is, if one banished from the mind the thought of anonymous letters and their writer. But

thoughts on this subject—which he had made his own—
were never far from Archer's mind. He did not, it must be
admitted, worry unduly about the distress caused by such
missives. If people had uneasy consciences, he reasoned,
then they deserved what they got. Anyway, he flattered
himself, no one had anything on him. He was too careful
for that. Such little indiscretions as made life desirable
were conducted with the greatest secrecy; and the wives
were, surely, the very last persons to talk. But he took
his self-appointed role of amateur detective seriously. He
felt the problem to be a direct challenge to his wits and
ingenuity, and he was determined to get to the bottom
of it. Little Sneddicombe was all right, of course; a good
little chap who did no one any harm; but it was a laugh to
think of him as a sleuth. On the other hand, people had a
way of confiding in parsons, and it was quite possible that
the chap might pick up something worth while. In which
case, of course, it would come to the notice of his partner,
John Archer. Finally, if and when it came to a showdown,
the Press was at his disposal; and he would see to it that
his light hid beneath no bushel. Modesty was not unduly
present in his makeup.

Since his discussion with Sneddicombe he had made
some progress, as presently appeared. Sir Derrick and
he were walking towards the third tee when Archer
remarked, apparently casually: "About time these
anonymous letters stopped, don't you think? Have you
any ideas on the subject?"

Sir Derrick twirled his ample moustache and scowled.

"Lot of kid's play. Parcel of women scared to death at the
thought of the resurrection of their pasts. Damn me if any
blasted letter would scare me!"

Archer smiled. "Position's a bit different. You're
unmarried, and therefore your own master. You don't have
to worry about what a husband or wife would have to say

on the subject. Besides—if I may say so—your disregard of other people's opinions of you is notorious."

Sir Derrick gave a hearty laugh. "And I should think so!

What the hell do I care what a parcel of old women—male or female—think about me? Still, mustn't be egotistical. I can see that it's a bit awkward for some folks if their sticky pasts come to light. And I've a bit of a notion who's at the bottom of it all."

Archer became alert. "You have?"

His companion nodded portentously. "Simple matter of logic, my dear chap. Who's the bloke every woman in trouble confides in?"

Archer considered the point and hazarded: "The doctor, I suppose."

Sir Derrick made a gesture of impatience. "Not talking about physical ailments. Mental, my boy; mental. Seared consciences and the like. Why, the parson, of course—or priest, if they're Romans. Now look at that chap Sneddicombe.

High church if you like!—personally I don't. Why, damme, I've heard that he runs confessions in his church! Well, there you are. Gets to know vital secrets and then cashes in on them. Logic, my dear fellow. Logic!"

Archer burst into a roar of laughter. "You can't be serious! Why, Selwyn's the mildest and kindest little man I know. He'd never hurt a fly. Besides——"

"Still waters run deep. All that holy-holy business! Excellent camouflage."

"Beside, as I was saying, you talk of 'cashing in'. I've yet to learn that the writer of these notes has made a penny out of his knowledge, or even tried to do so."

"Biding his time. The bigger the scare the more the victims will be willing to pay."

"And have you any evidence for such an appalling

accusation—with regard to Selwyn?"

"Well, I ask you! Who else would be in a position to know the ins and outs of people's lives?"

"A pretty weak defence in a Court of Law—if you were summoned for criminal libel," Archer remarked drily. "And I seem to remember that, after the organ committee meeting, you were just as free in accusing either Miss Pruin or Miss Tatchet—or both. What of that?"

Sir Derrick looked a little abashed. "Well, maybe I was a bit hasty when I said that. Taken by surprise and hadn't had time to reduce the thing to logic. And I never could stand those desiccated old hags. All the same, I still wouldn't put it past either of 'em to do a thing like that—perhaps in partnership with the little parson. Oh! . . . dear me. Yes, of course. I forgot about Miss Pruin. God rest her soul."

"Well, I think I *have* got some evidence," said Archer surprisingly. "I've had the opportunity of seeing one or two of these notes, and I've remarked that they are all from the same typewriter."

It was Sir Derrick's turn to laugh. "My dear chap! You're joking. All typewriters must write alike. Stands to reason. Make for make, that is. They're machine made, aren't they? Of course, one realises there's different sorts and sizes of type. But given the same 'face'—I believe it's called—why then, of course they must all be alike."

"Oh no they're not. Not even machines made by the same firm. In fact I'll go so far as to say that it's far easier, and much less liable to error, to identify typewriting than it is handwriting. But what interests me is that I've traced the typing of these anonymous notes to a machine that once belonged to me."

They had reached the third tee during the discussion but neither had made any attempt to continue the game; nor were there any following players. Sir Derrick shot a glance at his adversary and raised his eyebrows.

"Is this meant to be a sort of confession?" he asked grimly. "Are you trying to tell me that you wrote 'em yourself? Or," he added as a second thought struck him and cleared the frown from his face, "d'you mean that someone in your office got hold of your machine and did the job on it?"

"I sold the machine some time before this business started. And when I said I had some evidence I was referring to the fact that I've traced the purchaser."

"You have, have you? And who might he be?"

"You, Sir Derrick."

The Reverend Selwyn Sneddicombe carried on a moderately peaceful existence in a little house in a corner of The Close. It was tucked away at the end farthest from the arched entrance and was, by contrast with its neighbours, a modest abode and well suited to its occupier.

Though Selwyn was by no means an Anglo-Catholic it was true that he favoured the High Church. He liked dim lights, altar candles, images; and veered so far towards Rome that he even had a predilection for incense in his church. But this, alas, was forbidden to him. Shortly after his induction he had made an attempt to introduce it—with disastrous results.

The elder of the feminine members of his congregation descended upon him *en masse* and threatened to change their purveyor of religion unless the obnoxious practice ceased at once. Much as they would have dealt with any other supplier of everyday necessities or luxuries. But confession he did have. He was not at all sure that his bishop approved; but there was a stubborn streak in Selwyn's, otherwise mild, nature which was perhaps toughened by his defeat over the matter of incense; and confession he would—and did—have. And it is strange to relate that many of the old ladies who had turned up their noses at (or protected them from) incense, were frequent attenders at this surely Romish practice.

A gentle man of kindly heart it always seemed to him that his job was to minister to the sick in mind or heart in the best way possible. He was not a firm adherent of protocol.

Following upon this principle he set aside an hour each morning when parishioners might come and visit him in his little house and there pour out their woes, ask his advice or seek religious counsel. These hours were, of course, quite separate from those of confessional.

On this particular morning his callers had been few; their woes of little import. He was feeling that all was for the best in the best of all possible worlds. Looking through his latticed window at the sunlit strip of garden he smiled with deep satisfaction. Life, he reflected, had been very good to him. He had a job which he loved and which, in spite of his innate modesty, he felt that he performed moderately well; sufficient stipend for his simple needs and a roof over his head. Not the vicarage roof, admittedly. Like his spiritual chief he had disposed of his vicarage—temporarily at least—and had been fortunate in being allowed to come to rest in the favoured and eagerly sought Cathedral Close. *Tempora mutantur*; and the Close was no longer exclusive to the cathedral. If there were one thing lacking in his life he gave no outward sign of it. Perhaps he had his secret dreams.

Suddenly he sat up, staring through the window in incredulous surprise as a trim figure opened the little gate and came hesitantly up the path. Then a smile of sheer delight broke over his face; but it had been replaced by one of conventional welcome by the time he opened the door to his visitor.

"Well! Helen. I little expected to find *you* a caller during my 'trouble hour'—but perhaps it's just by chance that you have come at this time. Come in, my dear."

He led the way, not to the room usually reserved for

those in search of guidance, but to his study; a cosy and cheerfully furnished room on the other side of the house which, at the moment, was lit by a flood of sunshine.

Helen sat on the edge of a chair and seemed ill at ease.

"No," she began in a strained voice, "it's not by chance that I've come now. I want advice ... and help. It's a beastly thing to have to talk about; and I nearly didn't come at all. Look, you'd better read the thing for yourself." With a gesture of distaste she handed him a paper which she had held crumpled in her hand.

Selwyn spread it out before him and his expression hardened as he read:

"You silly girl! Do you really believe that Nigel Villiers—as he calls himself—really cares for you? Don't you see that he's only after your money? He knew all about you before he picked you up. And don't think you're the only girl he's after!"

The missive concluded with the, to Selwyn, now familiar scales.

He looked up from the paper and forced a smile.

"Surely you don't take any notice of what some spiteful person writes in an anonymous note? Why, it's like all the others—just spite and, I should imagine, jealousy."

"Just like all the others," agreed Helen tonelessly. "They all have some truth in them—so I've heard. Oh, Selwyn, I've been such a fool! I really knew all the time that Nigel was much more interested in the money he thought I might one day have than he was in me. He gave himself away in heaps of little things he said. And it isn't as if I really cared for him. That's what makes me feel so cheap. It seemed ... well, rather fun at the beginning; to have a good-looking young man running after me. And one so different from any others I knew. You see, the men here— well, they're not exactly exciting, are they? And they always treat me as if they couldn't forget that my parents are horribly rich. So I thought I'd see for once what it was like to have someone really in love with me—even if I half suspected that it was pretence."

"In that case," said Selwyn quietly, "I don't see that any great harm is done by this thing," and he pointed to the note which he had thrown on the table.

"Oh, but there is!" persisted Helen. "Can't you see what it feels like to know that someone is laughing at you, and probably talking about you, behind your back?—and you've no idea who it is? Why, any one of the people I meet may be the one who writes these beastly things. Besides, what am I to do about Nigel? I can't just cut him dead. After all, we've been about a lot together. And I'm supposed to meet him this afternoon for tea. What on earth can I do?"

"You could just show him the note," suggested Selwyn weakly, not knowing what other advice to offer.

"Oh, that's silly! Of course he'd deny it. Besides, I couldn't do a thing like that; accuse him to his face of running after me for my money."

Selwyn reflected deeply, but hopelessly.

"Have you told your mother about this letter?" was all he found to say.

"Good heavens no! Why, she'd have a fit. I did take him to one of her 'at homes'—and you should have heard the rowing I got afterwards!"

"Well," said Selwyn, and for some reason he blushed, "isn't there . . . I mean, doesn't someone . . . care for you in the way this chap pretended to? Someone you like yourself?"

Helen avoided his eyes. "Well, if there is someone— someone I like, that is—he doesn't even know it. Why?"

"Oh, well, I just thought that if there were someone like that, you could just tell him about Nigel and leave him to deal with the fellow. But I see, when I put it into words, how silly I am. If there had been someone like that you'd never have gone round with Nigel."

Helen smiled faintly. "Dear me. You don't know much about girls, do you? That might have been the main reason why I did. But I ought not to have bothered you with this.

I realise now that it's hardly in your line, and that you can't possibly advise me. But . . . well, I haven't any really close friends and . . . somehow you seemed the obvious person to come to. You've always been so nice to me and we've known each other for a long time now." She rose to go; but Selwyn put a restraining hand on her shoulder.

"No, don't go. I . . . I can't tell you how much I appreciate your coming to me. Let's think this out. There must be a way if only we could find it together."

CHAPTER IX

T HE voice came tinnily over the car radio: "Calling car three; calling car three. Over."

Sergeant Trent picked up the transmitter and replied, while his driver automatically reduced speed.

"Two men and a woman reported quarrelling in summer house of Tolbay Park," the voice continued in a professional monotone. "Shot said to have been fired. No further details. Investigate."

Sergeant Trent acknowledged the call and gave curt instructions to his driver. Behind them two constables sat up and took notice.

"Shot fired!" repeated Tom Barnett with relish. "Don't get much of that sort of thing in Storminster."

His companion, Jim Merrowby, smiled tolerantly, though the smile was wasted in the darkness.

"Now don't you go getting all hotted up," he said as one instructing a child. "When you've been in the force as long as I have you'll get to know that things don't often turn out the way you think. Like as not there's nothing to it. Some hysterical female gone off the deep end. Heard a couple of chaps and a girl arguing the toss and imagined a shot. Sense of drama—that's what she's got!" and Merrowby finished with a chuckle.

"Who said the report came from a woman?" asked Sergeant Trent quizzically.

"Well," reflected Constable Merrowby judicially, "if it wasn't a female, then it might have been a kid. A man would have done something about it—had a try at breaking it up; instead of just reporting it to the police."

"I'm not so sure of that," retorted Trent. "A lot of chaps would feel like keeping out of a scrap of that sort— particularly if there were firearms about. Besides, we don't know that whoever reported the affair didn't do something about it, beyond just reporting."

" 'No further details,' " quoted Merrowby. "It's my guess that it was just a telephone report; otherwise they'd have found out a bit more at the station before calling us."

"Maybe you're right. Anyway, here we are."

The car pulled into the kerb and the occupants hurriedly disembarked.

Tolbay Park lay in the centre of Storminster and was both its pride and its pain in the neck. The pride stemmed from the extent of the grounds and the orderly beds well filled with all the most ordinary and unpleasing bedding-out plants. In addition there was an artificial lake at the heart of the park, containing an island on which was built a rustic summerhouse.

The pain in the neck came from the fact that the surrounding railings had been removed during World War II and, owing to the need for economy, had never been replaced. The younger members of the city council accepted the position with equanimity; but the elders pursed their lips and shook their heads. All well-conducted parks, they affirmed, should be closed at latest at ten o'clock at night. But how could they close a park that had no railings? Not even so much as a chestnut paling surround?

So the good citizens of Storminster shook their heads; and the not so good continued to enjoy the amenities of the park at all hours of the day and several of the night.

It had been argued that at least the summer house could, and should, be locked at dusk; and for a while this practice had been in force. But the cost to the city of constant replacement of broken locks had worn down the edge of the zeal which had inspired the elders, and they had followed the line of least resistance.

Sergeant Trent marshalled his men, including the driver, and gave short instructions.

"You, Merrowby, will double across to the south entrance in case anyone tries to leave by Portman Road. Question anyone who attempts to do so and, if necessary, detain them for questioning at the station. The rest of us will advance on the lake in extended order. No talking."

In flagrant defiance of the 'Please do not walk on the grass' notices the three men hurried across the sunbaked turf, keeping touch with each other by the fitful light of the waning moon.

Had Sergeant Trent been asked why he had deployed his men and what he hoped to gain by it, he would have been at a loss for an answer. Maybe memories of his wartime army service, before he entered the police force, suggested to him that it was always a good thing to do when advancing upon the enemy. Or maybe he had an idea that the men—if indeed there had been any quarrelling men—might try to escape from the field of battle across the grass rather than by the main path which ran from north to south across the park, skirting the lake and linking Houlton Road on the north with Portman Road on the south. On the other hand, they might leave the park by one or other of the sidewalks; but these wandered aimlessly and served no roads; moreover the eastern and western borders were hemmed in by private houses and their gardens; and what could one do with an army of but four bodies?

The three policemen met no one, and when they reached the edge of the lake they drew together by common consent.

Here the main path resolved itself into two minor paths which embraced the waters and reunited on the southern side. Trent and Tom Barnett took one path; the driver the other. They met at the bridge which connected the island with the mainland at a point where the two paths again converged. They had encountered no one and heard nothing.

The summer house was set amidst shrubs in the centre of the island and was only to be approached by the bridge which spanned the water; here no wider than a modest canal. After a whispered consultation Sergeant Trent stepped on to the bridge on reconnaissance bent, his subordinates remaining behind.

The moon chose this moment to take refuge behind a cloud and what little light there had been was no more. As he was about to grope his way off the bridge at the island end, someone cannoned into him violently, gave a grunt of startled surprise, sprayed him with the light from an electric torch, then turned tail and bounded back on to the island.

When Trent recovered from his surprise he remembered that he too had a torch. By its beam he could see a man, carrying what appeared to be a scarlet raincoat (which was odd; for he was also wearing one of a more sober hue), a few yards ahead on the path which led to the summer house. As soon as the light from Trent's torch fell upon the other he started to run, then left the path and plunged into the bushes. A moment later there was a loud splash.

Since there was no longer any need for caution the sergeant shouted to his colleagues, explaining that their quarry was in the water and telling them to run round the lake on opposite sides and prepare to receive boarders. He himself attempted to follow the man; but by the time he had negotiated the bushes and arrived at the water's edge his torch showed the escapee wading clumsily towards the distant shore and already several yards away.

Trent knew the lake. Had he not dragged it on sundry occasions—usually with disappointing results? Nowhere was it more than four feet deep. The man was in no danger of drowning. So the sergeant, seeing no point in immersing himself in the still waters, contented himself with spotlighting the wader, knowing that when he landed he would be met by a reception committee.

The chase was over in a few minutes. While the two constables were returning with their captive, Trent made his way to the summer house. He now felt that there might be something in the 'information received'. Why, otherwise, should a man jump into the lake because he had bumped into a stranger?

Then the moon came forth once more. Lying in the doorway of the summer house, face to the ground and arms flung wide before him, was a second man. Trent's hurried examination showed him, firstly, that he knew the man; secondly that he was dead. A small hole in the forehead suggested the manner of his death.

Trent stepped carefully over the body and flashed his torch round the single room which formed the summer house. There was no other person in the room, but the light of his torch was reflected by a bright object which lay in one corner. It proved to be a chromium plated compact. Trent left it where it lay.

By this time his companions had reached the door of the summer house, their prisoner between them.

"Coo!" said Tom Barnett in awestruck wonder. "That bloke's dead or I'm a dutchman."

"You're no dutchman," said Trent, stepping over the body and joining the others. He flashed his torch over the prisoner, though the moonlight made this hardly necessary.

"Why!" he exclaimed in astonishment, "it's Mr. Ashburn! Whatever were you doing here, sir?" Then, as the full significance of the situation dawned upon him, he adopted his most official manner.

"There's no need to make a statement, unless you wish to do so. But if you do it will be taken down and may be used in evidence in the event of police court proceedings. Now sir," he continued in a less formal tone, "you'll agree that we've no option but to ask you to come to the station. This man," he spotlit the corpse for a brief moment, "is dead. Shot through the head. And we find you running away from the scene of the crime."

Rodney Ashburn, pathetic in his dripping clothes, shrugged his shoulders. "Quite right, sergeant. Of course you've no option. But I'll reserve my statement until we get to the station. You won't believe me, of course, but I know nothing whatever about this. I don't even know who the dead man is."

Trent was about to enlighten him when he thought better of it. Though no detective, for the police car was a routine patrol one, he knew enough about sudden arrests to reserve his belief of any statements made under the stress of the moment.

Ashburn might or might not have killed the other man; and he might or might not know who he was. Personally, thought Trent, it looked darned like a clear case of murder, with the culprit caught on the spot. If so, then Ashburn must certainty know that the dead man was John Archer; for one doesn't murder an unknown man. On the other hand it was possible that Ashburn had fired in self-defence. Trent thrust the problem aside. It wasn't for him to puzzle it out; the C.I.D. would do that.

"All right," he said briskly, "we'd better get along." He blew his whistle and a few moments later Merrowby joined them. He reported that he had seen no one.

"Very well," ordered the sergeant. "You'd better stay here until relieved." Then, with Ashburn between him and Barnett, and the police driver bringing up the rear, they returned to the car.

The station sergeant thought the matter of sufficient importance to warrant the calling in of the superintendent, who lived on the premises. Superintendent Fuller looked, and to some extent behaved, like an army sergeant major.

Short cropped grey hair grew thickly on his narrow skull; his eyes were brown and extremely alert, while above a firm, narrow-lipped mouth, there flourished a luxuriant wax-pointed moustache which varied in colour between light brown and grey.

He listened in silence to Trent's statement, while the station sergeant took it down. When Archer's name was mentioned, Ashburn gave what, to the superintendent, seemed an exaggerated start.

"You say Mr. Ashburn was carrying a scarlet raincoat," he commented when the other had finished. "Where is it?"

Trent looked surprised. "Well, there now, sir! I never gave it another thought." He regarded Ashburn thoughtfully, trying to re-visualise the scene of the arrest. "He certainly didn't have it with him when Barnett and Salter brought him along to the summer house. What about it, Barnett?" and he turned with relief to the young constable.

Barnett shook his head. "He wasn't carrying any raincoat when he came up out of the water," he declared emphatically.

"That's so, Salter, isn't it?"

Salter, the driver of the car, nodded affirmation. "Only the one he's wearing," he supplemented.

The superintendent nodded and made a note. "This compact you mention. Did you handle it at all?"

"No sir." The answer came promptly and with a touch of pride. "I thought there might be prints on it; so I left it for the C.I.D. men."

"Quite right." He turned to Ashburn. "Well, Mr. Ashburn, I'm sorry to see you here under such circumstances. Would you care to make a statement? There's no need to do so; but if you do. . . ." The usual caution followed.

Ashburn smiled wanly. "Oh yes, I'll tell you what little I know about it."

He had been silent on the drive to the police station.

Had he, wondered Trent, been employing the time in concocting his story?

"I was working at home on some plans this evening— my wife being out at the weekly meeting of the Women's Institute. I got into rather a jam. Things wouldn't go right. When that happens I find that a walk clears my mind. So I went out for a walk, with no particular object in mind and not taking much notice of where I was going. A clock chimed the quarter before ten and that brought me out of my reverie, as you might call it. I found that I was at the south entrance to Tolbay Park; at least, at the point where Portman Road finishes; for, of course, there aren't any proper entrances now. I didn't expect my wife to get home until about half-past ten and decided that I had plenty of time to go through the park and home via Houlton Road. I was about half-way towards the lake when I heard a shot which seemed to come from the direction of the summer house on the island. I started to run, thinking something might be wrong. The moon was out and when I got to the door of the summer house I could see someone lying across the threshold. I stooped over him and saw that there was blood on the ground underneath his head. I felt his pulse and slipped a hand under him to feel for his heart. There was no movement. Apart from that I didn't touch or disturb him. Well, in view of the shot I had heard, it was pretty obvious that he'd been killed by a bullet. Might have been suicide . . . or murder. In either case I knew I ought not to move the corpse, or touch it more than was necessary to know that he was beyond help. So I flashed my torch over the body and took a look round the room beyond. But there was nothing and nobody there. Of course," he added with a slight smile, "I know now that there was a compact; but I didn't see it. I suppose it just didn't happen to reflect the rays of my torch. Besides, you'll realise, I was leaning over the body and so didn't get a very clear view. Well, I thought a bit and wondered what I ought to do. Of course the police should be informed at once and, I supposed, a doctor—though the poor chap was past medical aid. On the other hand, oughtn't someone to stay with the body until the police arrived? If I waited, someone might come along and I could tell them to get the police." Ashburn broke off and gave a keen glance at the superintendent; as though trying to assess the effect of his narrative; but Fuller remained impassive.

"Well," continued Ashburn after a pause, "it suddenly struck me that I was in a very awkward position. Here was I, alone with a corpse in the middle of a deserted park—at least, I hadn't seen anyone on my way across. There was only my word for it that I heard the shot that killed him before I was anywhere near the summer house. Then there was another thing: it looked to me as if he had been killed by a small calibre weapon. It's funny, you know, how minds work! I immediately thought that I had a——"

"One moment," broke in Fuller. "I've already cautioned you, sir, but I think I must again point out that you are not obliged to say anything ——"

"Yes, yes; I know all that," Rodney interrupted in turn.

"But I'm not giving anything away. You know darned well that I've got a Colt .32—since you yourself renewed my fire-arms certificate last year. I keep the pistol in a drawer of the desk in my study at home—where the police would find it at once if they had reason to make a search. Mind you, at that time I had no idea that I was going to be arrested on the spot; and I had it in mind to get rid of the weapon as soon as I could. Though I suppose that wouldn't have done much good—in view of the certificate. But I didn't get as far as thinking all that out.

"I suppose it was silly of me, but I panicked. My one idea was to get away from the place. I started to leave and had just got to the bridge when I crashed into someone. It was quite dark, for the moon had gone behind a cloud; but I was still carrying my torch and I flashed it on almost automatically. Imagine my feelings when I saw a police uniform! I simply turned and ran. Stupid, no doubt; but I didn't have time to think. I plunged into some bushes but it was no use trying to hide, for the fellow was too close, and had his torch shining on me. So I just jumped into the lake. I was obsessed with the need to get away. I expect you can understand that.

But I didn't have any luck. The chap behind me kept his light on me all the time and when I got to the opposite bank there were a couple of policemen to meet me. That's all there is to it."

Superintendent Fuller bent over the report dictated by Trent.

"You say that the clock struck quarter to ten as you entered the park?"

"That's so."

"And how long after that would it be when you heard the shot?"

Ashburn frowned. "Difficult to say. I wasn't taking particular notice of the time—and," he added with a nervous laugh—"I wasn't expecting to hear a shot. But I suppose I was about half-way to the lake, and that's a four or five minute walk."

Fuller nodded. "I see; about nine forty seven. And you, Sergeant Trent, received the wireless call at ten eight. Pretty quick work." He turned to the station sergeant. "Give me the incoming report sheet."

The station sergeant fumbled in his desk and produced a book.

"The first report of the affair came in at ten five, sir," he announced. "Sergeant Hudson was on duty at the time. Here's what he wrote." He handed the book to Fuller.

The entry ran: June 15. 10.5 p.m. Police call received through Central Exchange. A woman's voice stated that she had just come through Tolbay Park. As she passed the summer house on the island she heard the sound of men's voices quarrelling, and the shriek of a woman. Being alone, and frightened, she had hurried on and then, just as she got to the park boundary, she heard a shot. Fortunately there was a telephone kiosk opposite and she had at once rung the police.

A note followed the entry to explain that the woman's account had been given in an excited and disjointed manner and in an uneducated voice. The gist of it had been entered above. At the conclusion of the statement the woman had abruptly rung off. The call had been verified as coming from the kiosk in question.

"H'm," said Fuller, "another of these anonymous witnesses. Afraid of the publicity and, maybe, reprisals. Can't say I blame 'em—though it makes it darned hard for us." He made a note on a sheet of paper which he took from the sergeant's desk.

"Now sir," he turned to Ashburn, "would you care to add to your statement by explaining why you were carrying the woman's raincoat—and what you did with it?"

Ashburn gave a forced laugh. "So it has become a woman's raincoat now! I thought the sergeant said simply a scarlet raincoat."

"He did," agreed Fuller. "But men don't wear scarlet raincoats—at least I've never met one who did."

"Well, you needn't worry about that. The simple truth is that there never was any such garment—male or female, scarlet or otherwise. The only explanation I can think of is that he saw me flourish a large red handkerchief which I was carrying. I was sweating a bit, what with the hot night and being chased by the police; not to mention the discovery of a murdered man."

"I see. May I have a look at the handkerchief?"

"I'm afraid not. I must have dropped it when I jumped

into the water. I felt for it just now when I heard I was supposed to be carrying a scarlet raincoat. Mind you, I'm not blaming Sergeant Trent. His torch wasn't too bright, and the moon kept going in and out. . . ."

"Here's the torch, sir," said Trent drily, switching on a very powerful beam as he turned to the superintendent.

"Well, it didn't seem bright to me," maintained Ashburn; but his confusion was manifest and beads of sweat showed on his forehead.

Superintendent Fuller, with grave courtesy, announced that Ashburn would be detained for the night, for further questioning; and when the now silent man had been safely lodged, issued orders for the C.I.D. squad to proceed at once to the spot.

"I don't like the time element," he confided to Trent. "The woman reported at ten five—as I have noted here—and said that she heard the shot as she left the park. She at once telephoned from the kiosk—half-a-minute's walk at most. So the shot was fired at about ten three or ten four. Yet Ashburn claims that he heard it about nine forty-seven. Allowing for inaccuracy on both sides, eight minutes is too great a discrepancy. We know the time the woman telephoned; and Ashburn claims to have known the time by hearing the clock chime the three-quarters; so unintentional misstatement would seem to be ruled out. You could walk right across the park in eight minutes."

"You mean that Ashburn deliberately made it earlier—so that he wouldn't have had time to get to the summer house, sir?"

"I mean that that is a possible theory; no more than that."

"But in that case, why should he say that bit about hearing the clock? He could have been as vague about that as he was about his walk."

"Because he had already heard your report, and knew

that the murder—if it is murder—had been reported at ten five. So it was necessary for him to have a reason for knowing that it was only two minutes or so after quarter to ten that he heard the shot. The average man, on hearing an unexpected shot at night, doesn't pull out his watch and note the time. If Ashburn had claimed to have done that, we might well have been a bit suspicious. But to hear the chimes and remember where he was at the time, and then to remember where he was when he claimed to have heard the shot—well, that's quite plausible. That's why I said an unintentional misstatement seemed unlikely. I imagine that he at the park entrance at quarter to ten. Maybe he hoped that someone had seen him and will come forward to testify. So, if we believe his story of the shot being fired a couple of minutes after—then he's in the clear!"

"Well, I must get out to the park and see what those detectives are doing. We'll have to find the weapon—probably thrown into the lake—and the raincoat. By the way, you're quite sure there *was* a scarlet raincoat?"

Trent grinned. "Well sir, I couldn't swear to the actual garment; but it was certainly the size of a raincoat. If it was a handkerchief, then it's the largest one in existence. And that bit about dropping it! What a crazy thing to say. He must know that we'll look for it—and fail to find it."

"Yes. But he didn't stop to think. Said the first thing that came into his mind. He was badly rattled by that time. And what about that compact? Funny he should take the raincoat and leave the compact."

"Take the raincoat, sir?"

"Obviously. A man doesn't walk about at night by himself carrying a woman's raincoat. There must have been a woman there—remember the telephone report of the scream. I suppose she scrammed when the men began to quarrel and rushed off, leaving her coat and the compact behind. Ashburn took the coat with him because it would have been a clue to the woman. Maybe he didn't see the compact, as he said. Looks like another blasted triangle! And John Archer had the name of being a bit of a gay dog, you know. Looks as if both men had turned up for a rendezvous with the same woman—error on her part, no doubt—and had shot it out. But there! The best policemen don't indulge in theories without any evidence to support them. I'm off to get what evidence there may be."

"Just one moment, sir," said Trent hastily. "Ashburn said he'd no idea who the man was. He said that in the park; immediately after we'd told him he must come along to the station. Then, in his statement to you, sir, he said he didn't touch the body except to feel the pulse and heart." Trent paused expectantly.

"Quite right," agreed Fuller. "So what?"

"Well sir, if he didn't turn the chap over, or at least have a look at his face—how did he know he'd been shot by a small calibre weapon? And if he did have a look at the face, then he must have seen that the man was Archer."

"Trent, my lad, you've got something there!" said Fuller with appreciation.

"And now I must be on my way. I shall also have to see Mrs. Ashburn. I'm not looking forward to that, I can tell you."

CHAPTER X

IT was late that night when Rosalind Ashburn, advised by the police of her husband's detention, visited Rodney in his cell. Since he had not yet been charged with any offence the superintendent stretched a point and allowed her to see him alone.

He greeted her with marked restraint and to her anxious query: Darling, what is this all about?" said evenly:

"The police think I shot John Archer."

"But that's ridiculous!" exclaimed Rosalind. "Why on earth should you want to do that?"

"Your guess is as good as mine." said Rodney, accompanying the words with a cold stare.

"Darling! Rosalind appeared to be utterly amazed "what is all this? I don't understand you one little bit. What's happened?

"I suppose the police have already given you their version?"

"Well, they haven't. All they said was that John Archer had met with an accident and that you were detained for questioning. I asked if I could come and see you and they said 'yes'—so here I am. But I don't understand it at all. Is John really dead? And, if so, why do they suspect you? I just can't think straight."

"Look, Rosalind, I know everything. There's no need to put on an act. I know where you were tonight."

"Well, of course you do. I was at the W.I. meeting—as I am on this night every week. Besides, you saw me start off for it. What *are* you trying to suggest?"

"I'm speaking of where you went afterwards. When you left the meeting."

Rosalind's eyes widened. "After the meeting?" she echoed uncertainly. "Why, I just walked home. What do you mean?"

"By way of Tolbay Park," supplemented Rodney tersely.

"I certainly didn't! Why on earth should I go that way? Quite apart from the fact that it's much longer, I'd never cross the park alone at night."

"Perhaps not—alone. But what if you weren't alone? What if John Archer were with you? That would be different, wouldn't it!"

"Rodney! What on earth are you trying to say? You're just talking in riddles. Everything you've said since I came has been unlike you. I haven't an idea what you mean. I suppose you've had a pretty bad shock—being arrested or whatever it is; but this won't get you anywhere. Just pull yourself together, dear, and tell me exactly what's happened since I last saw you." Rosalind's words were firm but her manner of uttering them was tremulous. She was on the verge of tears.

Rodney shook his head wearily.

"It's no good, Rosalind, I tell you. I know everything. I know you were in the summer house in Tolbay Park with John tonight. I suppose there was a quarrel—and you shot him. But you needn't be afraid. I shan't give you away."

Rosalind gave a gasp of dismay. "Rodney, are you mad? Are you all right? You . . . you haven't been . . . drinking, have you?"

"No such luck," said Rodney bitterly. "It's no good, I tell you. You left your raincoat there—the scarlet one with the tear in the pocket. You also left your compact."

Rosalind's manner changed. "Look, Rodney," she said coldly, "as far as I can make out, you're accusing me of having an affair with John, and then of murdering him. As to the raincoat, I wasn't even wearing it tonight." She stopped and gave a little start. "In fact I'm sure it wasn't in my cupboard. I must have left it somewhere; I'm always losing things, as you jolly well know. Let's see . . . I can't remember when I last wore it. Not in the last few days, anyway, because it's been fine all the time."

"All right, Rosalind. You'd better stick to that story; it's as good as any. But it's a pity you can't remember when you lost it. Of course," he added, coldly reflective, "I could swear that you told me about it when you came home. But what about the compact? Probably covered with your fingerprints."

By way of answer Rosalind opened her bag, shuffled the contents and produced a silver and enamel compact which she displayed in triumph.

"There! Mine's here all right. See for yourself."

Rodney barely glanced at it. "Oh yes; I daresay. That's the one I gave you. But perhaps John gave you another? Most women have several. But you needn't distress yourself. The police aren't likely to suspect you, or take your fingerprints—while they've got me. And I shan't give you away."

"Rodney! You don't really think I had anything to do with this awful affair?" Rosalind's manner was anxiously pleading.

Under the stress of the moment her momentary resentment was forgotten.

"Oh, of course not. Not if you deny it. One should never doubt a lady's word. It wouldn't be chivalrous." The words fell with icy sarcasm. "But unfortunately I had previous warning of your proposed meeting. That's why I was there."

Rosalind had a flash of intuition.

"Rodney! *You've* had one of those abominable letters! But surely you weren't silly enough to believe it?"

"The *one you* had spoke the truth. Remember?"

An angry flush appeared on Rosalind's cheek; but she forced herself to answer quietly.

"Look, dear, we're getting nowhere. Suppose you tell me all about it; then we can think what ought to be done."

Rodney smiled sarcastically. "We can think up a good yarn for the police, you mean. Maybe you're right—if we can make the grade. I've no particular wish to hang by the neck until I'm dead. But it'll have to be a damned good yarn to get me out of this jam . . . without," he added slowly, "producing the guilty party."

Ignoring this Rosalind took his hand. "Come on now," she said with a pathetic attempt at gaiety, "tell mother everything!"

"Very well; since you've asked for it." He withdrew his hand. "A note was left at my office this afternoon. It was addressed to me and marked 'Urgent and Personal'. Naturally no one saw the person who left it. It was just found on the floor inside the front door. It said; 'Do you know what your wife does after her W.I. meetings? And why she gets home so long after they are over? Go to the summer house in Tolbay Park at ten o'clock tonight and stop being a blind fool.' It had a pair of scales at the end, drawn in red ink.

"Well, I tore it up at once and burned the bits in an ash tray. And I tried to think no more about it. But I couldn't get it out of my mind. It kept coming between me and my work. Then I thought of the note you got—and the fact that malicious as it was in intention, it was true. True in suggesting that there had been something between me and . . . that girl. Then I told myself I ought to be hanged for thinking that sort of thing about you. Yes, I told myself that! So I didn't say anything to you when I came home. But it seemed to me that you'd taken special trouble over yourself—considering that you were only going to a women's meeting. Make-up; clothes and the rest. And your manner seemed excited. That may have been just my imagination; because I was, perhaps, looking for it.

"That's what I told myself after you'd gone. But at half-past nine I set out for Tolbay Park. I told myself I was being a damned fool; but I knew that if I didn't go I'd never have another moment's peace.

"As I got near the summer house I heard a shot. I ran like hell—imagining awful things. When I got there I found—a dead man face down in the doorway. I turned him over to feel his heart and I saw it was John Archer. There was a bullet hole in his forehead. You may or may not know what sort of a reputation he has—or had—with married women. I flashed my torch—you see I'd gone prepared for the worst—and saw a red raincoat on the floor which looked like yours. Yes, there was the tear in the pocket. I turned Archer back so that he lay as I had found him. Later on I told the police I hadn't moved him and didn't know who he was. Then I picked up the raincoat. It's a pity I didn't see the compact. The police found that later. My one thought was to protect you. I suppose I was too stunned to feel what I ought to have felt about you— what I feel now. I bundled the coat under my arm and started to get away. On the bridge I ran smack into a policeman. Then I lost my head. I ran back and dived into some bushes, but the chap was hard on my heels, so I made for the lake. But even then I thought of the raincoat. Of course I'd no idea they'd already seen it over my arm when I was running away. So I stuffed it into the middle of a thick bush and jumped into the lake. There was no other way of escape from that blasted island. Anyway, I thought, even if they catch me they won't get the raincoat. Why should they trouble to search the grounds when they'd all the evidence they could want, with the body in the doorway and me running like hell?"

Rodney paused and smiled bitterly. "I might have known that those damned police have eyes like hawks. They'd spotted the raincoat all right. And they'll find it. But that needn't worry you. If I confess to killing Archer they'll not worry overmuch about unimportant details. I'll think up something to serve as a motive. I'll say that we met by appointment over a business affair and had a row—although that sounds damned weak. I could even say he attacked me first and that I shot him in self defence."

"What about the revolver—or whatever it was? Did you hide that too?" asked Rosalind, white and strained.

"The revolver? What d'you—Oh, I see! Very well. I suppose it's a good thing for me to get in as much practice as I can. Yes, we'll have to think about that. I suppose I threw it into the lake or is that too obvious? But I wish I knew whether it was a revolver or an automatic. I suppose you wouldn't care to . . .? Oh well, it doesn't really matter I'd better say nothing until they find it—if they do. And now perhaps you'd better go. I'll need a bit of rest if I'm to be charged and then hauled before the magistrates in the morning."

In the meantime the C.I.D. men were busy on the site of the crime. Photographs were taken, measurements checked and chalk marks made to pinpoint the finding place of the compact; the outline of the body; and so forth. The police surgeon made his examination and the body was dispatched by ambulance to the city mortuary. There were no footprints in the immediate vicinity of the summer house, for the path was of asphalt. They did, however, find well-marked prints amongst the bushes. These, no doubt, would prove to be those of Ashburn and Trent. In a bush close to these tracks was found the scarlet raincoat—with the supplier's name in evidence—'Stainforth'.

Superintendent Fuller sighed deeply. "No trace of the weapon, eh? That means dragging the lake once more. But we'll leave that until daylight." He arranged for a police guard to be maintained until the dragging party should take over and then dismissed his men. He himself, with inward qualms, went to see Rosalind Ashburn.

. . . . .

Next morning Superintendent Fuller sat at his desk reading the reports of his C.I.D., for Fuller combined the two roles of superintendent of the comparatively new Criminal Investigation Department and that of superintendent of the uniformed branch.

His interview with Rosalind had been peculiarly painful although, as he reflected, she had been astonishingly brave.

True, he had made no direct accusation against her husband; but the inference was there for any intelligent woman to see. He had, perforce, and with her permission, searched her husband's desk. The automatic was not there. He had hardly expected that it would be. He regarded Rodney's voluntary reference to the weapon merely as an attempt to disarm suspicion. The certificate, as the man himself had pointed out, made it certain that the police would, in due course, realise that he had such a weapon. Therefore it was a reasonable thing to be the first to mention it and where it was kept; since it would be only a matter of time before its absence would be discovered. He had not, however, told Rosalind for what he was searching.

And now the lake had been dragged and a Colt .32 had been discovered. It lay before him. There were two unfired cartridges in the magazine. Despite the weapon's immersion there were fingerprints on the barrel, though there were none on such portions of the pistol as would be held in the hand when firing. "Used a glove," mused Fuller.

The doctor's report had just come in and Fuller gathered that death had occurred through penetration of the brain by a bullet which had lodged in the back of the skull. The bullet was of .32 calibre and had been handed over to a professor at the Storminster Technical College who, when occasion arose, acted as police ballistics expert.

Fuller again regarded the pistol thoughtfully. There could

be little doubt that this was the weapon which had fired the fatal shot; but it must be sent to Professor Holt for confirmation by means of the comparison microscope. The fingerprints had already been photographed. He spoke through the 'intercom' telephone and a sergeant was dispatched to the Technical College, bearing the weapon.

The compact had also been tested by the fingerprint department but, most remarkably, yielded no prints.

Detective-sergeant Drover came in at this juncture, carrying the scarlet raincoat.

"I've checked up with Stainforth's, sir," he said; "but we don't get much help there. All they can tell me is that it is one of a batch of reach-me-downs that they had about three years ago. It was the only one of this colour, but the assistant who dealt with the sale of the coats at the time has since left the firm—no record of her address. As you know, sir, Stainforth's are a cash concern—no accounts. So there's no chance of tracing the purchaser. Between you and me, sir," Sergeant Drover assumed a crafty expression which went well with his foxy face and sparse red hair, "I'd say it belonged to Ashburn's girlfriend—left behind in a panic when he and Archer got fighting and the girl skipped."

Fuller raised his eyebrows. "Girlfriend? Why not his wife?"

Drover shook his head and smiled meaningly. "Chaps don't go to Tolbay Park at ten at night to meet their wives!"

"Well, you should know," assented Fuller drily; for Drover was married; the superintendent was not.

"What I reckon happened," continued the sergeant, much encouraged at this apparent acceptance of his deductions, "is this: Ashburn and Archer were running the same girl—unknown to each other, of course. Either the girl made a mistake and dated them both up for the same time and place, or she did it on purpose—hoping to see a little fun. Some girls are like that, you know. Gives 'em a sense of importance to see two chaps quarrelling over them——"

"Then why the shriek? And why did she run off when they started to fight?"

Drover shrugged the question away. "Didn't bargain for the pulling of a gun, probably."

"Well," declared Fuller, "I'll admit I put forward something of the sort last night when I first heard Mr. Ashburn's statement; but I've had time to think since then. You know Mr. Ashburn, I suppose? At any rate you know of him and his reputation?"

Drover nodded. "Oh yes, most respectable; has to be, of course—seeing he's Diocesan Architect. Can't imagine the bishop having a chap around who was known to be leading a loose life—like Archer, for instance! But that doesn't mean a thing. Believe me," again the sergeant assumed the crafty expression, "it's often those very chaps who play merry hell behind the scenes. Still waters run deep, you know."

"Yes. I seem to have heard that expression somewhere," said Fuller solemnly. "All the same, I've met Mr. Ashburn a good many times; and I don't think he's that sort. He's happily married to a very charming girl—so what the hell?"

"That's what you think, sir," retorted Drover. "But there's many a couple heading for divorce who've got the reputation of being Darbies and Joans in the making—if not of qualifying for the Dunmow Flitch! People don't wash their dirty linen in public; not in cathedral towns."

"How true. And I seem to have heard that, too; at least, the first part. Now if you were talking about John Archer— well, I'd be more likely to agree with you. I liked John. A very decent fellow he was; but he certainly had a weakness for the ladies. Being a bachelor I suppose he thought he could please himself. The only trouble was that the ladies themselves weren't always single."

Drover let out a long whistle. "So that's it! You think Archer was after Mrs. Ashburn and Mr. A. didn't like it. He got wind of their meeting in the summer house and went there to catch them. In that case he went there meaning murder. You don't walk about the town carrying an automatic for fun."

"You go too fast, Drover. I said nothing of the sort. Still, it's a possibility; and it's our job to consider every possibility. I shouldn't have thought it, myself; not of Mrs. Ashburn. But you never can tell. Women are kittle cattle."

"Now that's funny too," declared Drover with a grin. "I seem to have heard both those sayings before."

Fuller's eyes twinkled; but he made no comment.

"All right. Now here's a line you can take. Go around Mrs. Ashburn's friends and try to find out if she had a scarlet raincoat; and if so, if she's still got it. Be discreet. We don't want to start a major scandal for nothing. Also you can make inquiries about John Archer. Find out who were his current girlfriends. If we could lay our hands on the girl who was in the summer house I guess we could soon call the case closed.

She may not have been there when the shot was fired; but she must have been there almost up to that moment— because of the scream. And another thing: we'll get the local radio station to put in a bit before the news tonight asking the woman who telephoned us to come forward. The Chief Constable will have to arrange that. The odds are that she won't; as I said last night to Trent, she's either afraid of publicity or reprisals. Come to that she may not want anyone to know that she was in the park herself at that hour. Maybe she's married."

"By gosh!" exclaimed Drover, "I've got a brain wave.

Suppose it was the girl herself—the one who screamed! What price that?"

Fuller considered the suggestion. "Could be," he agreed after a while. "But in that case why did she tell us of the scream? Why let us know there was a woman there at all? I can see that she might have got really frightened when the two chaps started to scrap, and have run away; and she might telephone us hoping that we'd get there before any harm was done. But why say there was a woman in the case? Quite unnecessary. Besides, she said she'd heard the shot—so she'd be too late to do any good. Still, for all she knew it might not have been fatal. Well, we'll certainly bear your theory in mind. Yes, it could be. And in that case—goodbye to her coming forward as a witness."

"Yes, you're right there. If she'd been the sort that likes publicity, and letting people know she had two boyfriends who thought her worth fighting over, then she'd have given her name and address over the phone; or, if she was too excited to think of that, she'd have come to the station when she'd had time to think about it. Very good, sir; I'll get on with those inquiries. I'd better report to Inspector Holmslade and tell him what I'm doing, I suppose?"

"In due course. He's away for a couple of days, giving evidence at the assizes, as you probably know. But keep a copy of all your written reports and let him have them when he returns. Now, about this automatic. Prints on the barrel; none on the stock. And it's all metal, so there should be. What d'you make of that?"

Drover shrugged. "Chap wore gloves, I suppose. Nothing in that."

"Then why prints on the barrel?"

"Put them on when he was loading the thing at home, no doubt. These murderers always slip up on some silly point like that. Thought of gloves for firing; but didn't think of them when loading up at home."

"Maybe; but I shouldn't have thought so. Another thing: you noticed that the number had been filed off the pistol. What can we do about that?"

"Send it up to the Yard lab, sir. They've got ways of getting over that. Funny thing, I was reading about it not long ago. Seems that when a number is stamped into metal it does something more than just show the figures up. Hardens the metal underneath or something of the sort. By using reflected light, and mirrors and things, they can still read the number in spite of it having been filed off. I think that's how it goes; but I don't rightly know the details."

Fuller nodded. "Yes, I've heard something of the sort. All right; we'll do just that. And get our 'Dabs' to check up the prints with those Ashburn gave us last night."

CHAPTER XI

ONCE again Selwyn Sneddicombe had an unexpected visitor during his 'trouble hour'.

"My dear Rosalind!" he exclaimed as he rose to greet her, offering both hands. "It's not often that I have the pleasure of seeing you here. And how's Rodney?"

Rosalind sank into a chair. Her face was colourless but for two little patches of pink where a hasty make-up had attempted to disguise her pallor.

"Mr. Sneddicombe, I'm terribly worried. Of course you've seen in the paper about John Archer's death? And I expect you read that a man has been detained for questioning by the police? Well, that man is Rodney! And it's just as good as saying he's suspected of shooting Mr. Archer."

"My dear! What a terrible thing. Of course there's some stupid mistake. Don't worry; it'll all come right. No one who knows Rodney could dream for a moment that he'd hurt anyone."

"I'm not so sure. That's the awful part. Look, Mr. Sneddicombe, can I speak to you in absolute confidence? The police will be coming to question me again, I've no doubt; and I *must* know what to tell them. Can you treat this as a sort of confession? I know it's cheek my coming to you when I'm not even in your parish; but you have always been a friend of Rodney's and there's no one else I can trust in a matter of this sort. You see, I've heard how much you've done for other people in trouble and that you see anyone at your morning hour; so I just came."

"My dear Rosalind, of course I will treat anything you tell me as confidential; and if I can help you in any way, I shall be only too happy to do so."

Rosalind gave a wan little smile. "Thank you. And I shan't

be putting you in an awkward position by anything I say. For, you see, it's only my own opinion. I've no evidence of any sort; and I've no personal confession to make." She broke off to collect her thoughts and Selwyn took the opportunity of offering her a cigarette. She smiled gratefully as he supplied a light.

"As soon as the police came to see me last night," she continued, "and told me that Rodney was at the police station, and why—though they just said 'for questioning'— I asked if I could go to see him. Of course I thought, like you did, that it was just a horrible mistake. But before we left the house they asked if they might search Rodney's desk. Naturally I agreed; for I didn't imagine for a moment there was anything to conceal. But while they were doing it I remembered that he kept his revolver, or whatever you call the thing, in that desk. And it wasn't there! And then, the moment I saw him, my heart went absolutely cold. He gave me such a look— almost as if I were a complete stranger. And his manner was quite unlike him. We've always been so close, you know. There was a time when there might have been trouble—through one of those beastly poison letters that have been going about. But that was all cleared up and we were all the closer because of it. But now he's behaving as if I'd done something awful." She stopped and her eyes filled with tears. Selwyn looked troubled. Tears in a woman were a manifestation to which he had never become accustomed.

"Now don't upset yourself," he said gently. "Tell me just what is in your mind. What awful thing can he think you've done?"

Rosalind dabbed at her eyes with a little handkerchief and forced a smile.

"Yes, I'd better tell you straight out. He thinks—or else

he pretends to think—that I was having an affair with John Archer; that we met in the summer house at Tolbay Park and had a quarrel, and that I shot him. There! Now I've said it."

Selwyn was taken aback. He had been far from expecting this. In spite of the gravity of the situation his sense of humour invaded his mind for a space. What does one say to a person who tells you that she is accused of infidelity and murder? Does one say: 'Are the accusations true?' or 'Dear me! How provoking!' But he said neither of these things. Rosalind's tense little face, anxiously watching him, restored him to the normal.

"In that case he must think he has reason to believe such terrible things. Can you tell me what reason he has?"

"He hasn't any. At least . . . well, he did have one of those horrible letters. It said that I was meeting someone in the summer house at ten o'clock last night, and he'd better go there and see for himself. But he's not telling the police that—naturally; it would supply a motive."

"But you weren't there, of course," said Selwyn, more as a statement than a question.

"Of course I wasn't. But he was. D'you see what that means? He told me that at first he tore the thing up and tried to think no more about it; but it kept coming back to him. You see, I did go out last night—to a W.I. meeting. And it was while I was out that he started to have doubts. Well, he did go in the end. He says that just before he got to the summer house he heard a shot; and then he found John Archer lying dead in the doorway." She paused, as if in doubt as to how to continue.

"And so he might well have done," encouraged Selwyn.

"Yes. But. . . . Well, you'd better know. As I said just now, he made out that he believed I had been meeting John, and that I had shot him. He said he knew I'd been there because he found my raincoat inside the summer house. The police also found a compact; but I've got mine; the only one I use."

"And what about the raincoat? Was it really yours?"

"I suppose so. Rodney said he saw a tear in the pocket which has been there for weeks. He said he hid the coat in some bushes. If that's true the police have probably found it by now. But, as I told him, I lost it some time ago. I don't remember when. But I certainly haven't been in or even near the park for weeks. If the coat really was there, then I didn't leave it."

"You seem to think it might not have been there at all," prompted Selwyn.

"I don't know what to think. Perhaps he took it there himself. But no, that's silly! How could he have got hold of it—unless someone returned it while I was out. I don't remember noticing it in my cupboard for days, now I've had some reason to think about it. Look, what I believe happened is that, in spite of himself, Rodney half believed that about me and John Archer. He brooded over it and decided to go to the summer house; probably hating himself all the time. In fact he practically said so. When he got there he saw John with some woman who was wearing my raincoat—it is scarlet and not easily mistaken. He thought it was me and probably said something pretty nasty to John. John has a very quick temper, as you know, and may have started to attack Rodney; so, Rodney, in the heat of the moment, shot him."

Selwyn shook his head in bewilderment.

"Let's take this step by step. If there was a woman there who was wearing your raincoat, how did Rodney get hold of it? And wouldn't he have seen that the woman wasn't you? What happened to her?"

"Oh, I've thought all that out. I've been awake all night

worrying about it. The summer house would be dark inside, although there was a moon last night. Rodney might have seen the woman near the door, with John, and recognised my coat. The woman would naturally go back into the hut so that her face wouldn't be seen. Then there was a fight and she got frightened, and only thought of escaping. I suppose she threw down the coat to make it easier to run away, and slipped past the men while they were fighting."

"I see. But does Rodney usually carry a pistol, or whatever it was that killed John?"

"No, of course he doesn't. But don't you see? If he really believed that letter he might have taken the pistol with him—I told you it wasn't in his desk when the police looked—though I didn't get a chance to tell him that—and then, when John attacked him, Rodney might pull out the pistol—not really meaning to use it, but just to frighten John. And then, in the struggle, it went off; and John got shot."

"In that case, why shouldn't Rodney have told the police? If John attacked him and he shot in self-defence, or the gun went off by accident, surely he could have told the police that?"

Rosalind gave a twisted little smile. "You don't know Rodney. Although he could believe a thing like that about me, he'd never betray me. Why, he told me himself that he snatched up the raincoat so that there'd be no evidence that I'd been there. But what I don't understand is that he believes, or pretends to believe, that it was I who killed John. The only thing I've been able to think of in explanation is that Rodney doesn't want me to know that he himself did shoot John. You see, if he pretended to think I'd done it, and I believed he really thought that, then I couldn't think that he had. D'you see what I mean?"

"I do, of course; but it seems rather extraordinary to me.

I should have thought, knowing Rodney, that he'd have been far more likely to tell you the whole truth. I suppose there was no one else present when you saw him?"

Rosalind shook her head.

"Well then, that is what I should have expected him to do. And, as he didn't say he shot John, it seems to me that, for some reason, he really does think that you did. He probably tells himself that you did it in self defence. And if that's so— why then, of course he can't be guilty himself."

"Yes," said Rosalind doubtfully. "But as I didn't shoot John, then who else could have done it? And why?"

"Why not go to Rodney, now that he's had time to get over the first shock, and ask him straight out why he made such a suggestion about you?"

"He won't see me. I went first thing this morning; and that's what I was told. D'you think . . . could you possibly go and see him yourself? He'd never refuse to see you."

"Of course I will, if the police will let me."

And with that Rosalind appeared to be more happy in mind. But it was otherwise with Selwyn. That Rodney would kill a man seemed to him fantastic; but so did the idea that Rosalind could do so. Yet it looked as though one of them must have done it. Rodney's behaviour seemed consistent with the belief that his wife killed Archer. Was Rosalind's equally so with her expressed belief that her husband had committed the murder?

If she thought that, reasoned Selwyn, wouldn't she have kept it to herself? What could be her object in coming to see him and telling him of her doubts? But if, on the other hand, she were herself guilty, might it not be a good move to convince Selwyn of her innocence and enlist him on her side?

He shrugged the question away. Perhaps he was too imaginative. Maybe Rosalind just felt the necessity of sharing her troubles with someone sympathetic, since her husband refused to see her.

There was another aspect of the affair which struck him forcibly. The poison pen writer was again at work. In fact, it was possible to say that, but for the anonymous letter received by Rodney, John Archer would be still alive. And now, reflected Selwyn, through Archer's death he had lost his partner in detection. Then all the more was it up to him to unmask the vile person who had, even if indirectly, already caused two deaths. But where to begin?

Archer had hinted that he was on the trail; but had given no details. He had, however, mentioned a few days before that he had a clue as to the present owner of the typewriter which had been used for the poison letters; also that he had an appointment the same afternoon which might further his quest. More he would not say; nor had Selwyn seen him since. Here, surely, was a starting point.

His 'trouble hour' being over, Selwyn set out for John Archer's lodgings.

The landlady was effusively grief-stricken; but more, Selwyn could not help thinking, by convention than from any real sense of bereavement. She also felt the importance of her position, and told with evident relish how she had been interviewed by the police and "them newspaper chaps". Not, she added with withering scorn, "high-ups" like her late lodger; but "just ordinary reporters".

Yes, she remembered the afternoon in question. John had put on a tweed jacket and his plus-fours, and had left the house immediately after lunch. The wearing of these garments indicated a visit to the golf club, of which he was a keen if unskilful member. No, she hadn't an idea who he was playing with; nor had he said anything about it on his return. But he had seemed unusually preoccupied.

So Selwyn went on to the golf club and interviewed the secretary. From him he learned that Archer had played a round on the day in question with Sir Derrick Mathers.

Sir Derrick was at home, and engaged in painting his front door a bilious yellow-brown. He showed no pleasure at the interruption and carried on with his work while keeping Selwyn on the doorstep.

"Yes," he assented gruffly, "I played a round with John last Tuesday. I won, of course. He's a rotten player. By Gad! Of course! Shouldn't have said that. Terrible thing, his death, what? But there it is. I've often warned him there'd be trouble one day if he couldn't keep away from the mares. Fillies were his own business; but married women—well, I ask you! Just looking for trouble. However, the poor chap's found it all right so I'll say no more. But damme, I'd never have thought it of little Rosalind Ashburn."

"What d'you mean?" asked Selwyn sharply.

Sir Derrick halted the paint brush in mid air and turned on his questioner.

"What do I mean?" he repeated testily. "What d'you think I mean? What would anyone mean under the circumstances? Here's Rodney Ashburn, scouting around the summer house at Tolbay Park in the dead of night. There's a woman present and Ashburn shoots Archer. What's the answer to that, eh? *Cherchez la femme,* as the frogs say. What'd he want to kill Archer for if the woman wasn't his wife—Ashburn's wife, I mean, of course. Answer me that!"

"How do you know there was a woman present?" asked Selwyn.

"Dammit, because I use my eyes and the brains the good God's given me! Which is more than some do. Soon as I heard about the affair I went up to the park and saw the police at work, dragging the lake and searching around in the bushes by the summer house. Kept me at a distance, they did, the blighters—and that though I'm a retired J.P.! But I saw them carrying a red raincoat—

scarlet woman, what? And I saw them fish up a pistol from the lake."

"Rather slender evidence upon which to accuse a woman of infidelity and a man of murder," protested Selwyn.

Sir Derrick scowled, and set to work again upon his door. He was not one to accept criticism from anyone— least of all a ruddy parson.

"The police don't seem to think so," he growled. "Had Ashburn up before the Bench this morning and remanded him in custody. And if you're going to tell me that he'd go and shoot John Archer on account of some woman other than his wife, then I'm going to tell you to dust your brains. And, come to that"—he swung round, paint brush in hand, and a spatter of small drops decorated Selwyn's coat—"what's it got to do with you? This is a police affair; they don't need your help."

Selwyn smiled disarmingly. "I'm sure they don't. Nor should I dream of offering it. I came to see you about a totally different matter. I've been trying to investigate this poison pen letter business. It's been going on quite long enough. It has been responsible for at least one death, and it's got to stop. Naturally I shall tell the police anything I know about the matter—if they'll listen; but there seem to be difficulties about their taking action."

"A death?" echoed Sir Derrick aggressively. "What d'you mean? Oh—you're referring to old Pruin. Yes, I heard she gassed herself because of a letter she received."

"Then you can appreciate the gravity of the situation," said Selwyn simply. "The day that Archer played golf with you he told me that he was following a clue which might reveal the writer of these letters. He was trying to trace a typewriter which once belonged to him and which, he was certain, had been used to write them. He further told me that he was meeting someone that afternoon who might further him on his way. As far as I know, you are the only person he had arranged to meet. Did he mention the typewriter to you?"

Sir Derrick bent down, placed his brush in the paint kettle and straightened himself.

"Young man, he did! He did more than that. He had the damned impertinence to intimate that I had the typewriter, and that I wrote those blasted letters! I gave him a piece of my mind that he won't forget in a hurry, I can tell you! Damme, there I go again! He'll not have much chance of remembering or forgetting now."

"But why should he make such a suggestion?" asked Selwyn mildly. "John wasn't the sort of man to make wild accusations. He must have thought he had good reason—if he really did mean to accuse you."

Sir Derrick scowled. "Well, I won't go so far as to say that he accused me," he admitted slowly. "But he did say that he'd traced the damned machine to me. Isn't that the same thing?"

"And he was mistaken?" pursued Selwyn mildly persistent. "Well, in a manner of speaking I've got to admit that he was on the right track—as far as it went. I did have the thing—for a time. Look, better come in and have a glass of sherry. Can't stand talking here all day. My paint's getting too thick, anyway, and I'm sick of the job.

"Now," he said as he handed a glass of Tio Pepe to his seated guest, "I've naturally got a special interest in this. John Archer claimed that these letters have all been written on a typewriter that, as you say, he once owned. Sounds like a lot of tripe to me; but he seemed sure of it. I'd have said one darned machine writes the same as another. But there it is. He told me he'd sold the thing to a junk shop; and that's where I got it. I saw it in the window and bought it. But that was long ago; long before these letters started, anyway. You see," he became confidential and, for him, almost shy, "I've had it in mind for years to write a few of my reminiscences. Travelled a lot, you know; and seen a few things in my time. Might interest someone. You never know. But I can't face the boredom of writing by hand. Never write letters if I can possibly avoid it. Seeing that infernal machine in the window gave me an idea. I didn't suppose there was much in learning how to run the thing—after all, look at the brainless young wenches who hammer away at them in offices!

"But when I got the thing home and tried it out I couldn't get on at all. Kept writing figures instead of letters, and capitals when I wanted small ones. I kept at it for a bit—maybe on and off for a week; but I couldn't be bothered with it. So I took it to Smithers, round the corner, and sold it to him. Damned little I got for it, too. Might have got more if I'd taken it back to the shop where I bought it; but I couldn't be bothered to go all that way." Sir Derrick refilled his glass and, as an afterthought, barked: "Drop more sherry? No? Oh well, I suppose you chaps have to be careful. Well, there it is. That's the whole story. Archer said he'd go on from there; see Smithers and find out what had happened to the machine. Never heard the result. To tell you the truth I wasn't interested. I've had one of these letters myself, as I told you; but it didn't upset me!"

Selwyn thanked his host and bade him a hasty farewell. Then he hurried to the shop of Mr. Smithers. Its stock was varied and of no great value.

Smithers, a little ferret of a man, with a cast in one eye and a wispy moustache, eyed his interrogator closely.

"Now it's funny you should ask about that typewriter," he wheezed asthmatically, "for that newspaper man, John Archer, was askin' about it not more'n a few days back.

I had to look it up in me books—for 'twas some time ago as I bought it from Sir Derrick. Sold it again within the month to a woman—in the same line of business as meself—only more posh, if you get me. Took it to her shop for her; that's how I know who she was. A Mrs. Prinnett."

"Mrs. Prinnett!" echoed Selwyn with a surprise he could not quite conceal. "Dear me. That's very strange."

"Now that's more or less what Mr. Archer said," confided the ferrety one. "But what's so bloomin' strange about it?"

His curiosity went unassuaged; for Selwyn, with a brief word of thanks, left the shop.

CHAPTER XII

SELWYN SNEDDICOMBE's first, and probably natural, impulse was to call at once on Mrs. Prinnett. But there was another matter weighing on his mind; a matter which, almost subconsciously, he had pushed into the background; temporarily buried under the excuse of following the trail of the poison pen. But now it had to be faced. He must fulfil his promise and see Rodney Ashburn. This he was loath to do because, as it seemed to him, either Rodney or his wife must be guilty of the murder of John Archer. Neither supposition promised to promote an easy conversation.

At the police station he learned that Rodney had been formally charged with murder and that, as Sir Derrick had stated, he had been brought before the magistrates that morning and that they, after hearing the police evidence, had remanded him in custody for eight days. Rodney had reserved his defence.

After certain formalities Selwyn, since he was a priest, found himself face to face with Rodney.

At first the latter refused to say anything except to repeat the story he had told to the police.

Selwyn was worried. "Look," he said persuasively, "I've seen Rosalind and she is very upset because you refuse to see her. She also seems to think that you suspect her in some way. This is no time for vague suspicions. If the story you tell is the literal truth then, obviously, you had nothing to do with John's death. But why do you suspect that Rosalind is concerned in it—for she tells me that you do have some such suspicion. What evidence have you— beyond one of those vile poison letters which I hear you received yesterday?"

Rodney gave a wry smile. "You're a decent fellow, Selwyn, and I know you're trying to help; but you don't know all the facts. It's true that the starting point of my suspicions came from one of those filthy letters; but that's by no means all. It's no secret now, so I may as well tell you that I found her raincoat in the summer house. How could it have got there but through her? Of course I'm going to swear to her story—if necessary—that she lost it some time ago; but who's going to believe it? You see, I knew John Archer pretty well. He had a devil of a lot of charm when he chose to use it; and he seems to have had a knack of attracting women. I don't really blame Rosalind. I know I'm a very ordinary sort of fellow—no glamour about me or anything of that sort. And my work meant that I had to leave her alone all day; whereas Archer had a roving commission and could go, more or less, where and when he liked. Oh, I can see how it happened. Little things at first—nothing to take exception to, and then a gradual leading up to serious business. I've often wondered why Rosalind ever married me. She could have had anyone, with her looks and charm; and I've always felt I wasn't half good enough for her. What chance had she against a fellow like Archer?"

Selwyn shook his head. "Not my idea of Rosalind," he said firmly. "But, for the sake of argument, let's say that she had been meeting him and that she was there in the summer house with him. Why should she shoot him?"

Rodney shrugged despairingly. "I've asked myself that a hundred times. Jealousy, possibly; or maybe, although she'd been unable to resist his attraction up to a point, she still hadn't committed herself. Perhaps he became . . . too possessive. I don't know."

"But that's ridiculous. Would she go to an appointment of the sort you are suggesting, carrying a gun? And where on earth would she get it?"

"Well, if she were jealous of him—and you knew him well enough to know that he might give her cause—then she might have been prepared. Women in love are capable of going to extremes. As to where she got the gun, that's easy. She knew I kept a pistol in my desk. On the other hand it might have been his gun and he threatened her with it and she got it from him in a struggle. I just don't know."

"And you don't suggest to yourself that the whole thing is just a nightmare of your own invention? Invented without a scrap of real evidence?"

Rodney shook his head. "Of course I've told myself that a million times—then I remember the raincoat—the existence of which I rather foolishly denied to the police!"

"But if she lost it days before—?"

"Of course she'd have to say that. But if it were really true, why didn't she mention it to me at the time?"

Selwyn smiled. "My dear Rodney, it wasn't all that important. She tells me it was an old one. And haven't you ever lost something and then forgotten about it? Only to remember, when something brings it to mind, that you did, in fact, lose it but you just can't remember when or where? She seems to have noticed, subconsciously or nearly so, that it wasn't in her cupboard that night; and that made her recall that she hadn't seen it for days."

Rodney again shook his head. "In that case someone else must have been wearing it. Someone who had arranged to meet Archer in the summer house. No, Selwyn, it just won't do. Such a coincidence would be unbelievable. Besides, don't forget that I was warned that she would be there."

"By an anonymous letter!" There was deep scorn in Selwyn's protest.

"That's all very well. I hate the things as much as you do; but the fact remains that the things written in them do happen to be true. What about poor little Miss Pruin? And Rosalind herself had one—about me. That was true."

"All right. Now I've got a theory that might account for the whole thing. John Archer and I were trying to discover the author of these letters. I've certainly not had much success so far; but he told me that he had made some progress and was on the trail of the typewriter which was used to write them. Supposing that trail led him to the guilty party? What would the person do— faced with exposure? After Miss Pruin's death the thing became serious. Such a person might go to great lengths to prevent a showdown. So why shouldn't they arrange to have John killed, and throw suspicion on someone else?"

For an instant a gleam of hope appeared in Rodney's eyes; then he gave a harsh laugh.

"That's an ingenious theory, Selwyn; but just no good, when you come to analyse it. How the devil could such a person get Archer there? And how get hold of Rosalind's raincoat? And, even if your mad idea has any truth in it, who did shoot John? And why?"

"That's simple. The person who wrote the letters and feared disclosure, of course. Look, I'm following up the trail where John left it; and if I have any luck I shall go straight to the police and tell them. Then we'll see what will happen. In the meantime don't let yourself brood on these foolish thoughts, it'll all come right in the end."

Rodney smiled. "I admire your optimism. But I shall stick to my story all the same. If the raincoat is traced to Rosalind I shall swear that she lost it weeks ago and told me about it at the time. Whatever happens I'm not going to have her suspected. You see, foolish as it may be, I still care . . . quite a lot."

"Now that's a funny thing!" declared Superintendent Fuller to Detective-sergeant Drover as he studied a short report. "No fingerprints on the compact. Now what the devil does that mean? Girl who was using it wore gloves? Do girls make up with their gloves on? And on a hot summer's night? Damned if I know; but I shouldn't have thought so. Anyway, that's a promising line of inquiry gone to blazes. You know," he continued heavily, "it was a hell of a shock when 'Dabs' reported that the prints on the Colt were Ashburn's. We knew his pistol was missing; but someone might have pinched it; or the one in the lake might have been another one altogether—"

Drover grinned. "Not Pygmalion likely! Too much of a coincidence, that!"

"Don't you believe it. Coincidences happen a darned sight more often than most people believe. Anyway, apart from the prints, we now know that it is his pistol. The Yard rang up this morning and gave me the number. It's the same as the one in Ashburn's certificate."

"Is that so! Then, by heck, we've got a clear case!" Drover was jubilant.

"You seem to be pleased," said Fuller drily.

"I'll say I am. Do us a bit of good to cop the chap within minutes of the murder and to produce convincing evidence of his guilt."

"Yes, I suppose you're right. Mustn't have sentiment in our job, of course. Still, I've known Ashburn—Oh, let it ride."

"And what d'you make of the compact having no dabs?" persisted Drover.

"I don't. I haven't a clue. Have you?"

Drover's foxy face deepened in cunning. "Easy, I'd say. Ashburn wiped 'em off."

"And left the thing there for us to find? When he'd taken the trouble to remove the raincoat!" said Fuller caustically.

"Well, I guess he knew we'd find there'd been a woman there; so he left the compact, thinking it couldn't be identified. But he took the raincoat because he knew it was his wife's."

"That's yet to be proved," rebuked Fuller. "Well, it sounds just crazy to me; but you may be right."

"And now for Mrs. Prinnett," said Selwyn Sneddicombe to himself as he left the police station. "I must say it was a bit of a shock when I heard that she'd bought the typewriter. That worthy, if a little dull, woman couldn't possibly be the author of the letters. Now I begin to see the light. I had forgotten her son Tom. Never much of a credit to her, even as a choir boy. I greatly fear that he has deteriorated. And, when I come to think of it, the letters started just about the time when he turned up again in the town."

It was another hot summer day, such as used to be enjoyed in the good old days. The sky was cloudless and deeply blue. As Selwyn passed the ancient cathedral, its warm stone lit by the sunlight, he looked up with real affection. A gargoyle, balanced dangerously on the lip of the high roof, seemed to wink at him in friendly manner and Selwyn smiled. The time might come when he would find himself a minor canon of the cathedral. Hints had been dropped by the episcopal private chaplain. If that ever became fact. . . . He went off into a reverie. Thinking of Tom Prinnett (or Nigel Villiers) had brought Helen, never far from his thoughts, to the forefront of his mind. He was greatly tempted to tell her what had been in his heart for many a long month; and thus, in the almost inconceivable event of her feeling as he did, obtain the right to send young Tom about his business. But the original obstacle was still present: money. His stipend when compared with Helen's income—or at least the income that she might one day possess—was insignificant. On the other hand, as a Canon; even a Minor Canon. . . .

Mrs. Prinnett was in her shop. She greeted Selwyn warmly as she led him into her parlour-cum-kitchen.

"I was just about to put the kettle on for a cup of tea," she declared gaily as she installed her visitor in an overstuffed and hideous Victorian armchair. "You must join me." She waved aside his half-hearted protest. "Oh," she continued brightly, as she busied herself with the gas cooker, "I've some good news. Tom has got a job. He left yesterday to join the cast of a London production. A real leading part. I'm ever so pleased. I was afraid he was going to be content to idle away his time here and neglect his career. But now it's all right."

"I'm delighted to hear it, Mrs. Prinnett," said Selwyn, as the thought flashed through his mind that now Helen's little problem had settled itself. This was closely followed by another, more serious thought: that if his vague suspicions had any basis in fact, the poison letters might now cease.

"A West End theatre?" he asked vaguely, feeling that some further comment was expected.

"Well, not exactly West End. Somewhere in Golder's Green, I believe. But that's only for the opening, of course. As soon as people realise what a good play it is—and it must be, with Tom in a leading part—it'll soon be moved to the West End."

"No doubt. . . . Mrs. Prinnett," Selwyn was hesitant; feeling in some measure treacherous, "actually I came to see you about another matter. I believe you have a typewriter which you bought from Smithers?"

"Well now! Isn't that extraordinary? You mean Mr. Archer's machine. Poor, dear Mr. Archer. What a tragedy that was. And to think that Mr. Ashburn killed him! I'd never have believed it. Never! Why, I've always thought Mr. Ashburn one of the nicest and mildest of men. But you never know."

"My dear Mrs. Prinnett, you really must not say things like that," rebuked Selwyn with some indignation. "Until a man has been proved guilty the law presumes him innocent. Why, you might yourself be on the jury that will try him— if it comes to a trial. But I'm not at all sure that there is a real case against him. It may be that the police will have to release him after the next police court hearing." He spoke with an optimism he was far from feeling.

"Oh really?" Mrs. Prinnett was surprised. "Of course, I only know what I've read in the papers and what people have told me. But I understood that he was caught red-handed, as they say; standing over the body with a smoking revolver in his hand."

"He was the first to discover the body," said Selwyn firmly. "But there was no weapon in his hand—smoking or otherwise."

"Oh well, I'm sure I'm delighted to hear it. People do run on so, don't they! I do indeed hope he gets off. That Mr. Archer—for all his nice manners, when he chose—wasn't a good man. I can quite understand Mr. Ash—Oh, there I go again! Poor little Mrs. Ashburn; such a sweet person I always think. How she must be feeling. I do hope for her sake it's all a mistake."

"Yes. Let us hope so. Now, about the typewriter. You knew it had belonged to Mr. Archer?"

"Not when I bought it. Oh dear me no. It was not until he came in a few days ago—only a day or two before he was killed! That's why I said how extraordinary it was that you should come and ask about it. Yes, he came in and said just what you did. Then he told me that it had been his machine at one time and that he had sold it. He said he regretted it almost at once; but by that time he had bought a new one. It wasn't much of a machine—the old one—because it was getting worn; but he had got attached to it. And I can understand that, can't you? I mean, a thing that has helped to make your career becomes, well, almost a friend—if that's not silly. And now it seemed that his new machine—new comparatively speaking—was due for a general overhaul, and he didn't fancy hiring another strange one. So he wanted to buy his back or, if I didn't want to sell, to hire it." Mrs. Prinnett broke off and, with a guilty look, went to the gas cooker.

"There now!" she said apologetically, "I had a feeling something was wrong! I never lit the gas!" She proceeded to do so and returned to her chair.

"Poor man," she continued, referring to Archer, "I had to disappoint him. You see, I only bought it as a speculation. I don't know how to use the things, though I've often wished I did; thinking it would be so useful in my secretarial work. But I'm no good at mechanical gadgets. Well, as I was saying, it was just a matter of chance that I got it. I went to Smithers to see if he had a particular type of glass paperweight that a customer had asked me to get. He hadn't; but I saw a typewriter in his window marked seven pounds. That seemed very cheap to me and I thought perhaps I could make a good profit on it. You see, Smithers lives in a poky little street and doesn't get the class of customer I do." A touch of pride and complacency crept into her voice. "Typewriters and such aren't in my line, of course. I specialise in antiques, really. Though what with the tourists and visitors I'm bound to keep some cheap little things I wouldn't touch if I could afford not to. So when I saw that machine so cheap I saw no harm in trying to make a little money on it. And I was right. I hadn't had it more than two or three days—on that occasional table, it was," and Mrs. Prinnett pointed through the glass panel of the parlour door at a bogus Chippendale table resplendent with french polish.

"Yes," she resumed, "that's where it was. A man came in and bought something from the window—a Dresden shepherdess, I believe it was. And then, as I was packing it up for him, he saw the typewriter and asked how much it was. I told him ten pounds and he said he'd like to try it. I hadn't any proper typewriter paper, but I gave him one of my billheads, and he put it into the machine. I could see at once that he was used to the things. He typed something about a lazy fox and a red dog. Silly, I thought it; but he said that it used all the letters and was a good test. Well, he said it was a bit old and worn; but it would do for his purpose; and he bought it." Mrs. Prinnett paused for breath.

Selwyn had kept his patience admirably during this lengthy recital. "And this was some time ago?" he asked.

"Oh yes. Some time towards the end of last year."

"Would you know the man again? Or can you describe him?"

"Oh no. I didn't know him. I'd never seen him before. But I did describe him to Mr. Archer; and Mr. Archer said he thought he knew who he was. The man was middle aged, slim and short; and he had rather thin, brown hair. He took his hat off when he left—most gentlemanly he was—and I saw he was rather bald."

"Bald, middle aged, short and slim. Not an exhaustive description. I wonder John recognised him from that."

"Oh, I forgot. There was another thing about him. He had a slight limp. And," she added, "I think—mind, I say I think—I can do better for you than I did for poor Mr. Archer. I think I can give you the man's name! At least, the name he gave me."

"Indeed? So he gave you his name. Is that usual with a cash customer?"

Mrs. Prinnett smiled. "Oh dear me, no. But there was a reason. It was silly of me to forget when Mr. Archer asked me about him. But, you see, he took me by surprise, as it were. I just told him what I remembered. But after he'd gone—Mr. Archer, of course—that set me thinking about the matter. And then I remembered that the customer had asked for a receipt. He said something about being able to charge the typewriter to expenses, or something of the sort. So I gave him a receipt on one of my billheads that I use for people with accounts. These bill forms are bound together in a book with a blank page under each of them; and you use a carbon paper to keep a copy in the book.

So, you see, I must have a duplicate somewhere. I was going to tell Mr. Archer that, if he came again. And, if he thought it worth while, I was going to look through last year's books. I keep them in the attic. But he didn't come again and I thought no more about it. But I'll willingly go and look if you'd like me to." Mrs. Prinnett again paused for breath and looked at Selwyn diffidently. Then she rallied her courage and said:

"Do please excuse me if I'm being too curious, but why do you want to know about the typewriter? I mean, I can understand Mr. Archer wanting to get hold of it; seeing that he wanted it for himself. But why are you interested in it?"

"Well, you see, John and I were working together on a little problem and I have reason to suppose that this typewriter was a clue."

Mrs. Prinnett frowned in concentration. "A clue! That sounds very mysterious. Oooh! You don't mean those poison pen letters? They were typewritten. You remember I had one of the first? At least, I've never heard that anyone had one before me; though I understand there have been several since. Is that what you were working on with Mr. Archer?"

"Yes, it was, Mrs. Prinnett," said Selwyn simply. "You may have heard that Miss Pruin killed herself because of one of these vile things. John and I had sworn to track down the person who has been writing them. And, now that he's dead, I'm going to continue the work alone."

Mrs. Prinnett nodded gravely. "And I hope you succeed. It's awful to think someone as wicked as that is still going on doing harm, and no one can stop him." She paused and a sudden light came into her eyes. "I say! Do you think that Mr. Archer being killed had anything to do with it? I mean, if he was on the track of the person, as you say, and the person knew it—then mightn't he have . . .?"

"It's certainly a possibility, Mrs. Prinnett; and one that had already occurred to me. And in that case, of course, Mr. Ashburn couldn't possibly be guilty. No one could believe that he'd write those letters. I suppose any man *might* kill, in a moment of anger, if the provocation were sufficiently strong; but a man of his type could never write letters like those."

"Oh no! I entirely agree with you. So perhaps he didn't kill Mr. Archer after all. Oh, I do hope not. Well, I'll certainly go upstairs and look for that book."

She went to the stove and turned down the gas. "It ought not to take me long; I don't use many of those books in a year; and I'm sure it was in December that man came. If the kettle should boil would you be so kind as to turn down the gas a bit more?"

She opened a door which, as Selwyn could see, led into a tiny but scrupulously clean scullery. In the doorway she turned. "Oh, in case it takes longer than I think, there's the radio. Perhaps you'd like to turn it on." She smiled and disappeared; and a moment later Selwyn could hear her pounding up the back stairs.

From a sense of politeness he turned on the wireless, but his thoughts were not with the programme.

In due course Mrs. Prinnett returned, triumphantly waving a flimsy sheet of paper. "Here we are," she said. "I knew I'd given him a receipt. But it was November—the thirtieth; not December."

She laid before him a torn sheet which bore, in carbon, the date, the name John Hodge, an entry: "one used typewriter £10" and the signature: Emily Prinnett. Meanwhile she went to the stove and turned up the gas, talking the while.

"I do hope that will help you. It's a pity he didn't give an address; but I don't expect there are so many Hodges in Storminster."

"No, I daresay not. But, of course, we don't know that he is a native. He might have been passing through. And—if he's the type of man we suspect—that is, if he wrote those letters—then he's not likely to have given his real name. Even the limp you mentioned might have been assumed!" Selwyn was rather proud of the last suggestion. He was, after all, proving that he had the makings of a detective!

The kettle blew a shrill whistle and Mrs. Prinnett warmed the pot, swilling the water round carefully, emptied it, put in the tea and started to fill up.

"I always think it so important to warm—" She broke off suddenly with an exclamation of impatience. "Oh dear! That was a knock at the back door—and just when I'm making the tea."

"Don't worry, Mrs. Prinnett," said Selwyn pleasantly. "I'll go. You mustn't be disturbed in so important a rite."

He returned in a moment. "No one there; but I found this, pushed under the door." He handed her an envelope.

She had now made the tea and was about to pour it out, but paused as she glanced at the letter. Then she gave a gasp and looked at Selwyn with a startled expression.

"Oh dear! D'you see that? Just 'Mrs. Prinnett'; no address—and typed. That's just what that other letter was like—the one I showed to the committee. And a square envelope too! You don't think—" She broke off and held the letter before Selwyn's eyes; her hand was shaking.

"The best way to settle it," said her visitor practically, "is to open it—don't you think?"

"Oh yes; of course. But I'm upset. However—"

She tore open the envelope and scanned the few lines it contained. Then she sat down abruptly and handed it across to Selwyn. He read it aloud:

"Unless you want to share Archer's fate," it ran, "shut your mouth about the typewriter." The usual scales in red ink followed.

"I knew it! I somehow felt it was one of those terrible things," Mrs. Prinnett stammered. "Oh dear! I . . . I almost wish I hadn't told you about that receipt. What shall I do? Oh dear; I'm frightened. John Archer!"

"There there, Mrs. Prinnett," said Selwyn soothingly. "Don't let it upset you. Look, I'll pour the tea. A cup will make you feel better." He poured out two cups and handed her one. "Don't take this too much to heart," he continued. "Whoever wrote that can't possibly know that you've just given me the receipt."

"Then why should the letter come just while you're here?" demanded Mrs. Prinnett, in no wise reassured.

Selwyn considered the point as he sipped his tea.

"Yes, you've got something there," he conceded reluctantly. "Look, I expect this is what happened: the writer somehow got to know that John Archer was on his track. Whether the same person was responsible for John's death is another matter altogether. But the man may have known that John and I were working together; and he may have kept me under observation. Seeing me come to your shop he could easily have put two and two together and thought that I'd come to make inquiries about the typewriter. So he thought he'd try to frighten you by a threat. Mere bluff, Mrs. Prinnett, I'm sure."

Mrs. Prinnett shook her head despondently. "Mr. Archer's death wasn't bluff. And do you see what this means? He must live quite close! How could he have typed this letter otherwise—after seeing you come in? Why, you've only been here—say ten minutes at most! Oh no; it isn't bluff. He means it. Now I shan't know a moment's peace. Ought I to go to the police?"

"I think you're disturbing yourself needlessly," said Selwyn judicially. "He couldn't have written this since I came in—unless, as you say, he lives close at hand. In which case you'd be almost certain to have seen him about and recognised him—if it's this man Hodges. No. I think it far more likely that he found out that John had been here, making inquiries, and he wrote that note just as a safeguard—in case I, or anyone else, came to you to pursue them. That the note came while I was here is, I feel quite confident, mere coincidence. In any case, you have no need to worry. The writer can't possibly know that you've already given me his name. I shan't give it away; you may rely on my discretion. As to the police—that's another matter. I had thought, myself, of going to them about these notes; and suggesting that they might be at the bottom of John Archer's death. But I don't think the time is ripe. Superintendent Fuller seems quite convinced of Mr. Ashburn's guilt. I don't think he'd pay any attention to me, unless I could bring him concrete evidence. But go to them by all means, if you feel that it would comfort you."

Mrs. Prinnett forced a smile. "Perhaps you're right. It may be coincidence that the note came just now. And he can't know—as you say—that I've told you anything. But please don't come to see me any more; until this horrible affair is settled. That would be just asking for trouble."

"I won't," Selwyn reassured her. "And try not to worry too much. If you really do find it gets on your nerves you might join your son in London for a while."

Mrs. Prinnett brightened. "Yes! I could always do that."

CHAPTER XIII

IN anticipation of a full day, Selwyn had told his housekeeper, Mrs. Teeming, that he would be out to lunch; and on leaving Mrs. Prinnett he discovered that he was hungry. He turned in to Meakin's café and there, at a table in an alcove, he discovered Helen Battersby.

"D'you think I might join you?" he said hesitantly, "that is, if you haven't some other—"

"No one at all," Helen assured him. "But I've got to be fairly quick. I've a 'perm' at two o'clock. That's why I'm lunching here."

He sat beside her on the banquette and studied her while making a pretence of consulting the menu. She had not yet begun her lunch. No, he decided happily, she didn't look dejected or worried. In fact, she looked more desirable than ever.

"Oh, I say," he began, "I've some news for you. I really don't know whether you'll think it good or bad. Tom— that is to say Nigel—"

"Has left town for the London stage!" Helen finished for him with a smile. "He rang me up—a good thing mother was out!—and told me so yesterday afternoon. He said he didn't know when he'd be back; but as the show was a first-class one and he had a leading part—his usual modesty!—he thought it would be certain to have a long run. So I wasn't to expect him too soon!" She broke into a laugh. "D'you know, I was so relieved that I hadn't the heart to snub him. Then he said he'd write—if he could find the time. And that, I'm afraid, was a bit too much for my good resolutions. I said that he mustn't think of it; that it was most important that he spent every minute in perfecting his part. And he took me seriously! You know, Selwyn, I can't imagine why I was such a fool as to think for a moment that I liked him! Perhaps it was just that he was a change from the boyfriends mother wishes on me. Well, it's an easy way out of something that might have been very uncomfortable. Now tell me what you've been doing."

A waitress appeared and they ordered lunch. "But first," insisted Selwyn, "you must have a cocktail with me. Just to celebrate your emancipation! I'm sure you've time for that."

Two dry Martinis were ordered and produced.

Over them Helen returned to her question.

"Of course, you were working with poor John Archer on the letter business. What a shocking thing that was—his death. And I suppose it leaves you rather lost?"

Selwyn told her of the progress Archer had made and how he himself was now hot on the trail of the typewriter.

"The only thing is," he added regretfully, "that I can't think of anyone remotely answering to the description given me by Mrs. Prinnett—though she said it seemed to mean something to John." Then he said slowly, with an eye on his companion: "D'you know, when I found that Mrs. Prinnett had bought that typewriter I had a suspicion that Tom Prinnett might have been the author of the letters. But I don't see how he could have been; because she sold it before he came back to town."

To his surprise Helen nodded gravely. "It's quite within his character," she said. "You know, he's frightfully conceited. I can quite imagine him using that sort of method to get his own back on anyone who had snubbed him." She gave him a smile. "I suppose you'll think it awful of me to say that, after I became so friendly with him. But it's as if I'd woken up and can now see him clearly. He wasn't all bad—not by any means; but he had certain flaws in his character which I deliberately pretended not to see. But I'm glad, all the same, that he couldn't have done that. And now tell me about Rodney. I rang up Rosalind, poor darling, and told her how sorry I was and how stupid I thought the police had been. And she told me that you had been most helpful and were seeing Rodney.

Of course he didn't do it; but what explanation did he give you? I suppose the police wouldn't have arrested him unless they had some sort of evidence."

"He was found on the spot, within a few minutes of the murder; and no one else was anywhere near. That's about all, as far as I know—except that he had a woman's red raincoat over his arm and tried to hide it when he was chased by the police."

Helen's eyes widened. "Why, Rosalind has a scarlet raincoat! I was with her when she bought it at Stainforth's. What on earth was he doing with it in Tolbay Park? Oh, I know! That night was W.I. night. I ought to have been there myself, but I wasn't. He must have been going to meet her and took the coat in case it rained. There were some clouds across the moon that night."

"By jove!" said Selwyn artlessly, "that's a jolly good idea. I must suggest it to—" He broke off in comical dismay. "Good gracious, what am I saying? I was just going to suggest that Rodney could perjure himself!"

The following day Superintendent Fuller had a surprise. The local B.B.C. station had broadcast his appeal for the Tolbay Park witness to come forward but, until that moment, without result.

Now Sergeant Trent came in with the announcement that a Mrs. Shapley was outside and wished to see the officer in charge of the Archer case.

"Let's hope she has got something useful to say," said Fuller. "We certainly need a bit of help. We've little enough in the way of concrete evidence as you probably know."

"Haven't those C.I.D. chaps worked any wonders yet?" asked Trent with a grin. There was no jealousy in his question. He himself had had the chance of transferring to the lately formed detective branch but had preferred to remain where he was.

"Well, they've done their damnedest; but they can't manufacture clues, or evidence. Not in this country, the Lord be praised; whatever they may do behind various metallic curtains. No, barring the weapon and the prints on it, we've got little enough to go to the Crown; and we don't want to ask for another remand next week. What's this woman like?"

Trent pursed his lips and summoned a mental picture.

"She's elderly rather than middle-aged, I'd say. Wispy, grey hair—where it pokes out from a ghastly black felt hat. Face a bit wrinkled; slight moustache; small, rather frightened eyes and a hesitating manner. Clothes dowdy but respectable. Looks like a parish visitor."

Fuller laughed. "You certainly use your eyes. You ought to have joined the C.I.D., you know! Well, bring her in."

Inspector Holmslade, who was directly in charge of the new branch, had been struck down with influenza immediately after his return to Storminster from the Assizes where he had been giving evidence. Consequently Fuller found himself conducting the major part of the case. A change from his humdrum duties which would have been not unpleasant were it not for his liking for Rodney Ashburn.

The superintendent pulled some papers towards him and was making a pretence of studying them when Trent returned with their visitor. No harm in giving the appearance of intense activity; the police got enough wisecracks levelled against them by the Press as it was.

Mrs. Shapley sat nervously on one of the hard, wood chairs, pulled off her black gloves, searched in her handbag for a handkerchief with which she wiped her mouth. Then she re-donned her gloves.

Fuller, who had been covertly eyeing her, thought it time to take official notice.

"Ah, good morning Mrs. Shapley. Sergeant Trent tells

me that you wish to see me about the death of John Archer. Is that so?"

Mrs. Shapley nodded, opened her mouth, but no sound came forth.

"Good. Well, we'll just have a little talk about whatever you have to say. Don't feel nervous about it; there's no need. We police are just ordinary folk like yourself, you know. Now first of all I'd like your name and address, and occupation. D'you smoke?"

Mrs. Shapley did; and seemed to gain confidence under the soothing influence of one of Fuller's cigarettes.

"I'm Mrs. Rebecca Shapley," she said in a voice which still quavered a little. "I live at 4, Thorpe's Cottages, off Stout Street. I haven't got an occupation; not to say a paid one, that is. I used to be in the millinery; but when my husband died the shop was sold. I am Treasurer of the W.I.," she added diffidently; "and do a few odd things like that—honorary, you understand."

"Quite, Mrs. Shapley. Very praiseworthy, I'm sure. Now suppose you just tell us your story in your own words. Sergeant Trent, here, will take down your statement and you'll have a chance of reading it afterwards. Then we shall ask you to sign it."

Mrs. Shapley nodded, moistened her lips and began.

"I was walking through Tolbay Park the night of June the fifteenth. It was between half-past nine and quarter to ten. That I know because I stayed to hear the nine o'clock news on the wireless before I started out. It was hot that night; and I wanted a little air. So I thought Tolbay Park was as nice a place as any. That would take me a matter of twenty minutes from my house. So I must have got there about twenty-five minutes to ten, as near as makes no matter. There was a moon kept coming out of the clouds and it looked very nice and peaceful by the lake, so I sat down on a bench—"

"Just one moment, Mrs. Shapley. Which way did you come into the park?"

"Why, from Houlton Road, of course. That's on the way from my house."

"Of course. And you chose a seat on that side of the lake?"

"Yes. There's one just where the path first comes to the lake. Well, I sat there for a bit. Then I got up and took the path that goes round the right side of the lake. I expect you know there's a path each side and they join just by the bridge that leads to the summer house on the island?"

Fuller nodded.

"So I walked along the path," continued Mrs. Shapley, "until I got to near where the two paths join." She paused and looked embarrassed. Fuller, with quick intuition, helped her out.

"That would be somewhere near the ladies' convenience," he said in a matter-of-fact tone.

Mrs. Shapley nodded gratefully. "That's it. Well, I went in there for a minute. As I came out—you know there's a lot of bushes just there, on one side of the path?" she broke off.

"Planted to conceal the building," assented Fuller.

"Yes. Well, they sort of hide you from anyone coming up the path from the Portman Road end of the park. You can see them, but they wouldn't see you. Not unless they were looking for you in a manner of speaking. Just as I was going to step back along the path to go home, I saw a man coming up from the Portman Road direction and making towards the summer house. Well, I'm a bit nervous; and you never know what sort of person you may meet there at night. One reads such dreadful things in the papers! So I thought I'd just wait in the shadows; hoping he'd take the path that goes round the other side of the lake—or even go into the summer house. When he got to the bridge he started to cross it. Then I saw he'd got something sort of shiny in his right hand. Not shiny like a knife, you know; but a sort of dark shine—" Mrs. Shapley halted at the difficulty of rendering her impression in speech.

"Like the reflection from a black car?" suggested Fuller helpfully, carefully avoiding the obvious leading question.

"That's it!" said Mrs. Shapley gratefully, "except that it was duller. Then the moon went behind a cloud. I could still see him—as a figure, you know; but that was all. He went across the bridge to the summer house—"

"Was he carrying anything else?" interrupted Fuller. "A raincoat, perhaps?"

"No. I don't think so. But he was wearing one."

"Did you see his face at all?"

"Well, I caught a glimpse of it. It wasn't anyone I know."

"Would you be able to recognise it again?"

"Oh, I think so. He had a hat on, but it wasn't pulled down over his eyes or anything. Yes, I think I'd know him again."

"Good, And what happened then?"

"I was just going to slip out of the bushes and go home when I heard a man's voice say: 'What the—' I'm afraid he used a swear word there," said Mrs. Shapley nervously.

"Never mind. We understand that you aren't saying it of yourself, Mrs. Shapley. So he said 'What the—'?"

"Yes. He said 'What the hell does this mean?' And then another man's voice said something but it was quiet like, and I couldn't hear the words. Well, after that there was a lot of shouting but all mixed up. Both speaking at once and a woman joining in. I didn't make out any words. But the men got angrier and angrier and I got frightened. I thought I'd better get away while I could, and perhaps get a policeman to stop them. Then I remembered the phone box at the beginning of Portman Road. So I hurried that way instead of going straight home. I hadn't got far along the path when the woman screamed. So I ran. And then—just as I got near the park end—a clock struck ten and immediately after that I heard a shot, coming, I'm sure, from the summer house. So I went into the telephone box and asked for the police. That's all."

"And what did you do after that?" asked Fuller. "Did you wait for the police to come?"

Mrs. Shapley shook her head. "No. I didn't. I'm afraid I'm a dreadful coward about publicity. I was afraid I'd be asked to give evidence, if there was anything bad going on in the summer house; and I couldn't face the thought of going to a police court. So I started for home as quick as I could; but going round the outside of the park instead of through it. When I got back to Houlton Road I saw a police car standing by the side of the road, close to the edge of the park. There didn't seem to be anyone in it, but I kept away from it all the same."

"And why didn't you give your name over the telephone?" asked Fuller, knowing the answer but wishing it to appear in the statement.

"Why, because I didn't want it to be printed in the papers—or to have to give evidence; like I said."

"And what made you come forward now?"

"It was that radio message. That made me keep thinking. That and the papers. I'd thought the girl would be able to tell the police all they wanted to know—if there'd been an accident. But when I read a man had been arrested and there wasn't any talk of the girl being seen, I thought it was my duty to come and tell you what I knew. If the man who's been taken up isn't the man I saw, then perhaps I could help to get him off, you see. So I came along."

"Very public spirited of you, Mrs. Shapley, seeing how nervous you are of publicity. All the same, you know, the man we've got might be the man who was already in the summer house; and the one you saw may have been the victim."

Mrs. Shapley nodded. "Yes, I thought of that. But I thought I ought to come. Just in case, as it were."

And with that Mrs. Shapley concluded her evidence.

Later that day she attended an identification parade under the auspices of the station sergeant, and had no hesitation in pointing out Rodney Ashburn as the man she had seen.

CHAPTER XIV

For a while things hung fire in Storminster and the good people thereof returned to their peaceful ways, while the old cathedral, basking in the sun, brooded in motherly fashion over her sons and daughters.

Rodney had been committed for trial at the next assizes, which were to be held in the neighbouring, manufacturing town of Littleborough. The Crown, having considered the evidence, decided that there was a case to answer.

Rosalind had given up attempting to see her husband; while he, for his part, stuck to his original story and stubbornly refused, in spite of the counsel of his legal advisers, to alter or amplify it—save for one detail. As for the story told by Mrs. Shapley, he could, or would, offer no explanation of the object she declared she had seen in his hand.

The detail which he now admitted, referred to the raincoat. As his solicitor pointed out, it was mere stupidity to deny all knowledge of it, since Trent had seen him with it and it had been later recovered from bushes which, as his footprints showed, he had passed in his flight. His explanation was that he had seen the raincoat lying on the floor of the hut and had picked it up purely mechanically, hardly realising that he was doing so. Far from 'hiding' it in the bushes, he asserted, it must have slipped from his arm in his flight.

"But, my dear Mr. Ashburn," urged his solicitor, George Grant, "your wife has already told me that the raincoat is hers, and that she lost it some time before this incident. Seeing it there, and recognising it as your wife's, it was a perfectly natural thing to do to pick it up. Why make a mystery of it? Of course it's a pity that you denied it in your original statement to the police; but we could have pleaded shock, and you could have amended it later."

"You say Rosalind admitted that the coat was hers?" asked Rodney dully.

"She had to. The police got hold of your daily woman and showed her the coat and asked her if she recognised it. She didn't realise what it was all about and said at once that it belonged to Mrs. Ashburn. Later she felt a bit uneasy and told your wife what had happened. Lucky she did, because the police saw Mrs. Ashburn about it the same evening; and, of course, she said at once that it was hers but she had lost it some time before."

"I see. And did my wife offer any explanation of my being on the scene of the crime?—isn't that what you legal chaps and the police call it?"

"She said that the whole thing was a ridiculous mistake. That you often took walks at night, and that Tolbay Park was one of your favourite spots for the purpose. She said, further, that you and John Archer had always been good friends and that there could be no possible motive for you to kill him."

"And what of the police? What do they suggest as motive?" Grant gave a dry little cough; presumably to cover embarrassment—or maybe merely from force of habit.

"The police," he began didactically, "work on certain definite lines. When two men quarrel and there is evidence that a woman has been present, they assume that the quarrel was on her account."

"And do they go so far as to name the woman?" pursued Rodney sarcastically.

"They have not been precise on the point as yet. But their questioning of your wife rather suggests that they think she might have been present. And that brings me to what I think should be your line of defence. If you chanced to meet Archer in the summer house and there was a woman present who, let us say, escaped without your seeing her face, and then you saw, and recognised, your wife's raincoat—well, not knowing, or forgetting, that she had lost it some time before, you jumped to the very natural conclusion that the woman was her. You and Archer had a furious quarrel and he threatened you. So much so that, in self-defence you shot him."

Rodney smiled coldly. "I see. I'm to plead guilty to manslaughter. Is that it?"

"Well, I'm bound to point out to you that it is better than being charged with murder—if, indeed, the prosecution would accept such a plea."

"And just suppose, for the sake of argument, if you like, that I am guilty of neither?"

"But look at the evidence! You were seen with the weapon in your hand—"

"Wait a minute," interrupted Rodney sharply. "Has it now become a weapon? When I was told about it it was a 'dull, shiny object' or some such vague stupidity."

"Quite . . . quite," agreed Grant hastily. "I should not have said 'weapon'. I fear I put upon the testimony the construction that I also fear the jury will. But, as your solicitor, if you persist in assuring me of your innocence, and your entire ignorance of the circumstances that brought about the death of John Archer, then, of course, I am bound to accept that and to plan a defence in accordance with it. But we really must have a little more detail to your statement. Why, for instance, were you in Tolbay Park at the time?"

"My wife has already explained that."

"As far as the police are concerned, yes. But she asked me, somewhat anxiously, I thought, if she would have to swear to that in court. She confessed that she said the first thing that came into her head as an explanation; but she is afraid that if the statement is challenged it may be proved to be false. No one else, it appears, could corroborate it. And that suggests, does it not, that it is not strictly true?"

Rodney laughed harshly. "My dear sir, there's not a shred

of truth in it. As an architect I loathe Tolbay Park and all its works; and the summer house is an abomination."

"Then why, in fact, did you go there?"

"Now listen, and I'll tell you what I've told no one else but Rosalind. But you are clearly to understand that in no case whatsoever is it to be used in my defence. Nor is my wife to be called as a witness."

"I quite agree with the latter stipulation. I had no thought of calling her. She has, I gather, no material evidence in your favour; and one never knows what cross-examination may bring to light. As to what you are about to tell me, that will not, of course, be used in evidence unless you so wish it. But I reserve the right to advise you upon the point when I know what it is."

"All right. But I tell you frankly that no advice you can give will make me change my mind. The fact is that I went to the summer house that night as the result of receiving one of those damned poison letters that have been going the rounds. It said I should find my wife there, with John Archer. And I was fool enough to go there—if only to prove to myself that it was a lie."

"I see!" Grant pursed his lips and nodded solemnly. "And when you got there you saw, if not your wife, at least her raincoat. Yes, yes. Very natural to assume that she had been there. But of course you realise that it would never do to bring this up in your defence? It gives motive and to spare. Besides, the police would maintain that as you went there with that thought in mind, it would be most natural for you to take your automatic. Premeditation. Oh no. We couldn't use it."

"That's as may be. I told you I wouldn't allow you to use it, anyway; but not for that reason. I am not going to have my wife's name brought into this business for any reason whatever. Understand that. It's bad enough for her to have a husband charged with murder, without having mud flung at her for other things in addition."

Grant shook his head dolefully. "I really do not see, for the moment, what line of defence we can take. The circumstances are so very much against you. This woman, Shapley, has sworn that she saw you going into the summer house before the shot was fired. She then heard voices raised in anger—not to mention the scream of a woman— and, later, the fatal shot. What have you to say to that?"

"That she's either a damned liar or she has made a genuine mistake in identification. She may have seen my photograph in the papers at some time and recognised me on the parade as someone she had seen before. An easy enough thing to do. In any case, she says she only saw the man by moonlight, and then only for a moment."

"Then if, as you suggest, there was another man there, and you only came up after the shot was fired, why didn't you see either the man or the woman escaping? I take it that you saw no one after you had entered the park?"

"I didn't. But if I were guilty, as you obviously believe, how easy for me to say that I did!"

Grant coughed. "In that regard I must point out that when you made your first statement to the police—the moment when you would, surely, have mentioned seeing others—you had not heard Mrs. Shapley's evidence. You neither knew that you—or, let us say, a man—had been seen by her or that she had heard a woman's scream. No, I'm afraid that is what the prosecution would undoubtedly point out."

"All right. Let's get back to where we were. I didn't see anyone; but what was to prevent them from running off in the opposite direction? Escaping by the north entrance?"

"Nothing at all. But even so, unless they waded through the lake—as you did—they would have to cross the bridge. I have made some study of the park since you called me in and it seems to me that if you were half-way along the

146

path leading to the summer house when you heard the shot fired, then the bridge would be well within your sight—for there was a moon that night."

"There was. But it kept going behind clouds. Anyway, all I can say is that I didn't see anyone; and I certainly could see the bridge. But this Shapley woman has got her times all wrong. I say the shot was fired at about seven or eight minutes before ten, and that I was then half-way between the southern park entrance and the island. She says it was fired just after ten, and that at that time she was herself at the park entrance, having come straight from the summer house—or close to it. If that's true, why didn't I see her? She says she ran down the path; and that must have been just at the time when I was walking along it. That is," he added, "timing it by the shot."

"Exactly! And she called the police from the telephone kiosk at ten five. So she cannot be far out in her actual timing."

"Not if the call really came from that box."

"Oh, that has been verified. There's no doubt about it."

"Then why didn't we meet somewhere on the path?" persisted Ashburn.

"It would certainly seem that you must have done so—unless you are mistaken in the time of the shot. If, however, it was fired just after ten, then, by that time you, according to your own evidence, must have reached the summer house. In that case she could easily, as she claims, have slipped from the bushes and run down the path."

"So one of us is a liar," declared Rodney flatly.

"Have you any reason to suppose this woman is lying?" asked Grant. "Could she possibly have a grudge against you?"

"Of course she's lying—or making several genuine mistakes.

As for a grudge, why I'd never even heard of her until

147

she came into the case; much less seen her."

"Then we must assume she is genuinely mistaken. But it is difficult to do that when her time of telephoning corroborates her evidence."

"Yes," said Rodney thoughtfully. "But she was, admittedly, in a bit of a flap. Suppose she was hiding in the bushes when the shot was fired. That is to say, at about seven minutes to ten. That would be enough to paralyse her. She may even have fainted. Women do, you know—even in these days. All right. When she comes to she hares like mad for the park exit and hears the clock strike ten as she gets there. At the same moment she may have heard a car back-firing; or she may simply have got mixed up between the times she heard the shot and the clock. In that case, as you say, I might well have been in the summer house when she crept out of the bushes and did her dash to the telephone booth."

Grant nodded dubiously. "Well, we must see if we can do better than that. It doesn't sound the sort of story a jury is going to appreciate."

"In other words, as I said before, you're quite convinced of my guilt but, nevertheless, will do your best to get me off! Well, thanks for that much."

Superintendent Fuller regarded the paper before him with acute distaste and rang a bell. To the constable who came in response he said:

"This thing"—pointing to the missive and its envelope—"how did it get here? Do you happen to know?"

"Yessir. Found it in the box this morning with your other letters."

Fuller grunted. Extracting a pair of tweezers from a drawer he placed the letter and its cover in a wire correspondence basket and handed the latter to the man.

"Take this to Sergeant Blake and get him to test it

for prints, though—as far as the envelope's concerned anyway, there'll be plenty—P.O. Staff and yours as well. But the letter may prove more helpful. And tell 'em to make it quick!"

The constable departed on his errand. Fuller sat back in his chair and filled a much burned briar with loving care.

"'Mrs. Ashburn was having an affair with Archer. She was with him in the summer house that night. That's why Ashburn killed him. It was his gun'", he repeated slowly, from memory. "That, and a drawing in red ink of a pair of scales were the contents of the note."

"Tell us something we don't know, damn you!" he said savagely. 'Know it, and don't want to believe it', said an inner voice quietly.

"But," continued Fuller, addressing his blotter with a scowl, "how the hell do *you* know—about the pistol, for instance?"

But no inner voice offered a solution to this problem.

And a later report from the fingerprints department proved equally unhelpful: there were no fingerprints on the letter. The envelope, on the other hand, was plastered with them—all defacing each other with the exception of a large finger and thumb which proved to have been made by the constable who had placed the missive on Fuller's desk.

"Nevertheless," said Fuller despondently, "we've got plenty on him already. I'll wager my pension the case comes to trial."

And so it did.

CHAPTER XV

THE CLERK OF ASSIZE: Rodney Warner Ashburn, you stand charged that you, on the fifteenth day of June of this year in this county, murdered Arthur John Archer. How say you upon this indictment, are you guilty or not guilty?

The Clerk of Assize, fully conscious of his momentary importance yet unable to slough the veneer of over familiarity with his task, sounded merely bored.

"Not guilty," replied Rodney Ashburn firmly but with a note of despondency.

Sir Gregory Cummings, Counsel for the Crown, rose slowly to his feet and surveyed the Court. He was an imposing figure. His face, long and pale, was deeply scored with lines running from nostril to mouth. A roman nose, bushy eyebrows and strongly jutting chin betokened a force of character not to be lightly thrust aside. He affected a monocle, which he could drop with devastating effect at the right moment; for the rest, he was without mannerisms—excepting, perhaps, those of speech.

SIR GREGORY CUMMINGS: May it please your lordship, ladies and gentlemen of the jury, I will begin my address with a word upon circumstantial evidence. Direct evidence, in a case of murder, is seldom come by—since murderers are prone to commit their crimes in secrecy and without an audience. Circumstantial evidence, however, in its cumulative effect, may be far more damning, far more convincing, than the testimony of a human being; liable, as are we all, to errors of judgment and observation, coupled with lapses of memory. Circumstantial evidence is, as I may say, a rope woven of many strands. Each strand, in itself, may be a frail, an unconvincing thing. Yet such strands when twisted together and integrated to form a rope, may well become proof positive. And it is such a case that occupies our attention today. Briefly the facts are these: (Sir Gregory, letting his eyeglass fall to the length of its cord, fixed the jury with his steel grey eyes while he paused for a tense moment).

SIR GREGORY: On the fifteenth day of June at five minutes past ten at night, the police received a telephone call from a woman, who gave no name, reporting that she had heard two men quarrelling and a woman shrieking in the summer house on the island of Tolbay Park; and that a shot had just been fired. Now I want you to remember the times I shall give you. They are of the utmost importance. This, then, was at ten five.

A patrol car was at once directed by wireless to the spot and reached the north end of the park at about ten or twelve minutes past ten. The occupants, under Sergeant Trent—whom you will hear in evidence—proceeded towards the summer house but taking different routes. Sergeant Trent himself crossed the bridge, which leads to the island and summer house, alone.

Just as he was about to step off at the island end of this bridge a man, who later proved to be the prisoner, collided with him, gave a startled exclamation and switched on an electric torch, by the light of which he must have seen that the other was a police officer. (Again the pause with the eyeglass dropped.)

Now what did the prisoner do at this juncture? You may consider that a man who has nothing to hide would have apologised for the collision and had a friendly word with Sergeant Trent. You may think that. But what, in fact, did the prisoner do? He made a bolt for freedom; even going to the length of plunging into the lake in his effort to escape. Unfortunately for him, Sergeant Trent at once dispatched his men to the other side of the lake and was able to direct them so that they arrested the fugitive as he reached the far bank. The sergeant then made his way to the summer house and there, by the light of the moon—which had hitherto been behind a cloud—he saw a man, lying face downwards across the threshold, arms outstretched. A brief examination showed that the man was dead, and had been killed, presumably, by a bullet which had entered his forehead. At the same time Sergeant Trent recognised the dead man as John Archer, a critic and journalist of this town, and on the staff of *The Clarion.*

And now, members of the jury, the other police officers had arrived at the summer house, bringing the prisoner with them. He was at once cautioned by Sergeant Trent and told that he need make no statement. Nevertheless he insisted on saying: "I know nothing whatever about this. I don't even know who the dead man is." He added that he would reserve his statement until arrival at the police station where, as he himself agreed, the sergeant had no option but to take him. On arrival there he was again cautioned but elected to make a statement.

You will hear the statement in detail from Superintendent Fuller, to whom it was made. I need not, therefore, give it to you in its entirety. But I would call your attention to one or two significant points in it. Briefly, then, the prisoner— Rodney Ashburn—stated that he was having a stroll, with no particular object in view and taking little notice of his surroundings, when his attention was aroused by a clock striking the quarter before ten. He then realised that he was at the south entrance of Tolbay Park. He thereupon decided to continue his stroll through the park, and had reached a point about half-way between the entrance and the island summer house when he heard what he imagined to be a revolver shot. The time at the moment was, according to the prisoner's statement, just about nine forty-seven. You will remember that the telephone report gave the time of the shot as close upon five minutes past ten; for the woman who made that report said that she had "just heard the shot". One may suppose that it was the fact that a shot had been fired which inspired her to telephone. But you will hear her evidence from her own lips; for she has now come forward to perform an unpleasant duty which she would have done much to avoid. Now there, members of the jury, is the first discrepancy in the prisoner's statement as compared with the evidence of this witness. It is not suggested that two shots were fired. Yet the prisoner gives the time as close upon nine forty-seven—and instances the chiming of the clock in support—whereas the woman witness declares that she telephoned within at most two minutes of hearing the shot. And it is upon record that her call came through to the police, from that kiosk, at ten five. At least a quarter of an hour's difference, you will observe. Unfortunately, exhaustive inquiries made by the police have failed to reveal any other person who heard the shot.

Now why should the prisoner insist upon the earlier time? You may think that he did so in the hope that someone had seen him entering the park at nine forty-five; in which case he could not have shot a man in the summer house two minutes later—let alone prefacing the shooting with a quarrel. You may think so, I say. This suggestion may occur to you. It is for that reason that I mention it—as a warning. For, as his Lordship will tell you at the proper time, you must come to your verdict solely upon the evidence which you shall hear. It is not for you to suggest motives which have not been proved to your complete satisfaction.

Now, members of the jury, having dealt with the vital matter of the times let us return to the point where the prisoner claims to have heard the shot. What was his reaction? You may think that it was a perfectly normal one.

He hastened to the spot whence came the shot and there—so he tells us—he found the body of a man face downwards across the threshold of the summer house. Face downwards, you will note.

Later, when apprehended by the police, he stated that he had no idea who the victim was. And again, in his statement at the police station, he maintained that he merely felt the man's pulse and heart, and thus satisfied himself that death had supervened. He did not, he insisted, move or otherwise touch the corpse. (The monocle dropped and the jury, already conditioned to this manifestation, craned forward eagerly.)

And yet, ladies and gentlemen of the jury, he told the police that it appeared to him that the man had been shot by a small calibre weapon. Now—I want your close attention—the bullet which killed John Archer, as you will hear from the medical testimony, entered his forehead and lodged in the skull. There was no hole of exit. How, then, did the prisoner know what sized bullet had killed the man—unless he turned him over? And if he did this, then he must inevitably have recognised the dead man as John Archer. And yet he said that he had no idea who the dead man was. Why did he say that? When you have heard all the evidence you may think that he had reason—or believed that he had reason—to bear John Archer some ill-will. But if the police believed his statement that he had no idea of the identity of the victim—what possible motive could he have for killing him? You may think on these lines. It is for you to decide, according to the evidence you shall hear.

And now let me continue with an outline of the evidence which you will hear from this woman witness, Mrs. Shapley. She will tell you that she was near the summer house that night at about five minutes to ten. She saw a man coming up the path from the south entrance to the park; that is, from Portman Road. She waited, screened by bushes, as she did not wish to confront a strange man in the park at that time of night. This man, she will tell you, crossed the bridge leading to the summer house and, by the light of the moon, she could see that he was carrying in his right hand an object which she describes as having a 'dark shine'. A moment later she heard an altercation in which she could distinguish two men's voices and the voice of a woman. The voices rose in anger and excitement and Mrs. Shapley, fearing that the men might become violent, slipped out of the bushes and hastened towards Portman Road; having it in mind, as she will tell you, to summon the police by means of the telephone kiosk at the park entrance. While traversing this path she heard a woman scream and then, when she had nearly reached the kiosk, the sound of a shot which followed closely upon a clock striking the hour of ten. It was this shot which crystallised her former—perhaps vague—intention of telephoning the police. She has since identified the prisoner as the man she saw. But, members of the jury, I must again administer a warning. Even if you accept this witness's testimony, you have no right to assume, on that account alone, that the prisoner, even though he was present in the summer house, fired the fatal shot. But we shall hear more on that subject later, from a firearms expert.

Now what of the weapon? A Colt automatic of .32 calibre was retrieved the next morning from the waters of the lake in Tolbay Park at a spot close to the line taken by the prisoner when he waded across the lake. This weapon will be proved to have belonged to the prisoner and, as you will hear, bore his fingerprints—and his alone. You will also hear, from the firearms expert, that this weapon undoubtedly fired the shot that killed John Archer. You may consider it significant that an attempt had been made to erase the registered number of the pistol.

And what of motive? Ladies and gentlemen of the jury, it is a popular fallacy that in a case of murder it is necessary to prove motive. It is no more necessary than it is to have a body before proceedings for murder can be instituted. Naturally it is more satisfactory if motive can be proved. But the human mind works in such unpredictable ways that what might seem to one man to be an adequate motive for murder might be nothing of the sort to another. Hate, jealousy, greed, revenge—these and many others have been motives for murder time and again. And who can say that he knows any of his fellow men well enough to say whether or no that man harbours any or all of these feelings?

In this case there is a peculiar feature which you may think suggests a motive but, again, you will be guided by evidence alone. And the evidence you will hear in this connection will show that the prisoner, when he started to run away from Sergeant Trent, was carrying a lady's scarlet raincoat. When questioned about this he denied all knowledge of such a garment. Yet it was later found in a bush where footprints showed that the prisoner had passed on his way to the lake. It has also been identified as the property of his wife. If the prisoner was carrying such a coat, why should he deny it? It is not against the law for a man to carry a woman's raincoat with him when he goes for a walk—however eccentric it might appear to the casual observer. You may think that it has something to do with the unknown woman who, as the evidence will show, was in the summer house at the time of the tragedy; and with the prisoner's reluctance to admit to knowing the identity of the dead man. But I stress yet again that motive is not of primary importance.

(Sir Gregory laid down his notes, let his eyeglass fall, and fixed the jury with his piercing gaze before continuing solemnly):

That, members of the jury, is, in brief, the case for the Crown. Everything I have said has been said in order to give you a picture of this case as a whole. You will not, of

course, take from me any of the details I have recounted.
They must all be proved in undeniable evidence and to
your complete satisfaction. For, as you must all know, it is
for the Crown to prove the prisoner's guilt; not for him
to prove his innocence. But (a long pause)—if the facts I
have outlined are so proved you will, I am assured, have
no hesitation in bringing in a verdict of guilty. Putting
aside all sentiment you must do that duty which you have
sworn to perform and a true verdict give in accordance
with the evidence. No one has the right to kill, no matter
what his motive. Society must be protected from those
who presume to take the law into their own hands.

I shall now call the evidence to which I have referred.
Sergeant Trent! (Sir Gregory sat down with the air of one
who has well and truly performed his duty.)

"Not a word about the compact," whispered Archibald
Mainstay, Counsel for the defence, to his junior.

"No. They evidently don't like the absence of prints.
But we can bring it in in cross-examination."

"We can—if we think it will do any good."

Mr. Mainstay, Counsel for the defence, was a man of
full habit, red of face. He had a deceptively lazy manner
of interrogating witnesses which often led them into
relaxing their vigilance. Then he would pounce. Voice
raised to a fierce bark, eyes flashing beneath thick, black
brows bent in a fierce frown, he would lead them into
contradictions from which their own counsel had the
greatest difficulty in extricating them.

Sergeant Trent then recounted the story of events
on the night in question and in cross-examination was
forced to admit that a metal compact had been found
and that there were no fingerprints upon it. The medical
testimony followed. Evidence was given as to the recovery
of the Colt automatic and its identification with the
weapon for which the prisoner held a certificate. It was

also demonstrated that the prisoner's fingerprints were on the pistol; and that it bore no others.

Some excitement was shown in Court when an officer from Scotland Yard explained how he had been able to decipher the registration number in spite of an attempt to erase it.

A ballistics expert next proved, with enlarged photographs taken by means of the comparison microscope, that the pistol in question had undoubtedly fired the bullet which had been recovered from the skull of the murdered man.

The Ashburns' daily woman then identified the scarlet raincoat as being the property of Rosalind Ashburn but admitted, in cross-examination, that she did not remember when she had last seen it.

Mrs. Ashburn herself did not appear. Despite her urgent request Rodney had steadfastly refused to allow her to be called, saying that he feared she might be trapped into some incriminating admission which would throw suspicion on her. Counsel for the defence was the more ready to agree with this decision since he felt that nothing which Rosalind might say could be of help to her husband.

The star witness then took the stand:

Mrs. Rebecca Shapley, sworn.

Examined by Sir Gregory Cummings—I am a widow residing at 4, Thorpe's Cottages, Stout Street, Storminster. I am of independent means. On the fifteenth day of June this year I was in Tolbay Park in the neighbourhood of the summer house at about . . .

Her story was as she had given it to the police. When asked if she could recognise the man whom she had seen on that fatal night she pointed nervously at the prisoner.

In cross-examination by Archibald Mainstay her testimony remained unshaken. There was a moment of excitement when he produced from beneath his gown an electric torch and directed its beam on the face of the witness.

MR. MAINSTAY: I suggest, Mrs. Shapley, that this is the 'shining object' which you say you saw in the prisoner's hand?—Oh no. That's a plated thing. What I saw was dark; like a pistol.

You did not suggest a pistol in your statement to Superintendent Fuller?—No. I didn't want to suggest a thing like that in case I was mistaken.

But you don't mind suggesting it now—when a man is on trial for his life?—Well . . . I'm on my oath. I have to tell everything. Besides, we know now that Mr. Ashburn did have a pistol.

MR. JUSTICE SWALE: That is a most improper observation. The jury will expunge from their minds the witness's suggestion. For the purpose of evidence the object stated to have been seen in the prisoner's hand will remain 'a dull, shining object' and no more.

CROSS-EXAMINATION CONTINUED

Mrs. Shapley, you have told the Court why you did not give your name when you telephoned to the police. It would not be because, at that time, you had not perfected the details of your story?—I don't understand.

SIR GREGORY (rising in all his might): My lord, I object. My learned friend is, to all intents and purposes, accusing the witness of committing perjury; and that without a shred of evidence to support such an accusation.

MR. JUSTICE SWALE: Mr. Mainstay, I do not think that you must attack the witness unless you have some sort of evidence with which to confront her.

MR. MAINSTAY: As your lordship pleases.

CROSS-EXAMINATION CONTINUED

You tell us that you paid a visit to the ladies' convenience in Tolbay Park on the night of the murder at a few minutes before ten o'clock?—That's right.

Are you aware that that convenience is locked up by the park attendant at nine every night?—I didn't say I went in. (Witness paused noticeably before replying.) I don't think I need go into details. It's not a subject a lady can discuss in public.

I see. The jury will, no doubt, form their own conclusions. The night of the fifteenth of June, we have learned from the police testimony, was overcast; the moon appearing only fitfully and for short intervals?—I daresay.

Was it not a most fortunate coincidence that the moon came out just in time for you to get so good a view of the prisoner that you were able to identify him later?—Not for the prisoner, I should think. (Laughter in court; instantly suppressed.)

Mrs. Shapley, I am going to ask you a very simple question.

In answering it I want to remind you that you are upon your oath. Did you know the prisoner by sight before that night in Tolbay Park?—No, I never. (Answer came immediately.)

He is not an unknown figure in Storminster?—I wouldn't care to say.

But you had never seen him?—No.

Mrs. Shapley, I understand that you were born in China?—I don't know who told you that. (Witness visibly startled.)

And that your parents were missionaries there?—Yes, they were.

And that you, when you became of age, were yourself a missionary?—Well, I worked with them.

As treasurer?——

By Mr. Justice Swale: Mr. Mainstay, anxious as I am to give the defence every latitude, I don't quite follow your line of questioning. What has the witness's former occupation to do with the present proceedings?

MR. MAINSTAY: I hope to show very shortly, my lord, that it is germane to the creditableness of the witness; upon which I attempted to throw doubt when your lordship restrained me.

CROSS-EXAMINATION CONTINUED

You were treasurer of the local branch of the society for which your parents worked?—For a time.

For a time. Yes. And did you resign your post of your own free will?—Yes. (Witness paused before replying.)

And shortly after that you left China?—I came home to get married.

Do you mean to tell the court that you came home in order to get married?—Well, not exactly. It was some years later.

Mrs. Shapley, I suggest that you were asked to resign from your post of treasurer and that you were also asked to leave China?—It wasn't true. I never touched a penny!

(Mr. Mainstay partially concealed a smile.) I was not aware that I had made an accusation. Then you were, in fact, asked to resign your post?—It wasn't fair. I——

Please answer my question!—Well, yes.

And you were also asked to leave China?—Yes.

And when you returned to this country you no longer carried on missionary work?—No. I had been unfairly treated and I didn't want to have anything more to do with them.

What did you do?—I went into the millinery. Then I got married; but my husband died and I sold the shop.

And you are now treasurer of the local branch of the

Women's Institute?—Yes.

Have you held the post for a long time?—Not very.

For a year, perhaps?—Not a year. Some months.

And you hope to continue in the post?—Why shouldn't I?

No reason at all—I hope. Thank you, Mrs. Shapley.

There was no re-examination of this witness.

SIR GREGORY: That, my lord, completes the case for the Crown.

CHAPTER XVI

M R. MAINSTAY rose and surveyed the Court with a smile on his red and cherubic face. In particular he smiled at the jury.

MR. MAINSTAY: May it please your lordship, members of the jury. I propose to call only one witness: Mr. Rodney Ashburn.

(There was a gasp of suppressed excitement as the prisoner left the dock, took the stand and was duly sworn.)

MR. MAINSTAY: Now, Mr. Ashburn, I want you to tell the jury quite simply, in your own words, what really happened on the night of June the fifteenth.

RODNEY ASHBURN (facing the jury; pale but composed): On the night of June the fifteenth I was working at my home on some architectural plans. My wife was at her usual meeting of the W.I. In the course of my work I came upon a rather difficult problem and, as has always been my habit, I decided to go for a walk while I thought it over.

I don't know if everyone is the same; but I know that with me, when I'm concentrating on a problem of this sort, it seems to occupy that part of my brain which chooses where I go. I find the same thing while driving a car. I observe all the traffic lights, other traffic, pedestrians and so forth, and do the correct things; but I lose all sense of direction. Often I have found myself miles from where I intended to go. (A nervous laugh which the jury observed in stony silence.)

And that's how it was that night. The chiming of a nearby clock brought me back to the present and I found that I was at the entrance of Tolbay Park. My wrist-watch confirmed that it was a quarter to ten. Since my wife never gets home before half-past ten on her W.I. nights I decided to walk through the park and home to my house in the Cathedral Close by the longer route.

I had hardly left the entrance when I heard the sound of what appeared to be a shot. For a moment I took it to be a car back-firing; but the sound seemed to come from the direction of the summer house on the island in the park lake; and there could be no cars there. So I hurried towards it. When I reached it I saw, by the light of the moon, a man lying face downwards across the doorway. There was a pool of blood under his head. I felt his pulse and put my hand underneath him to see if his heart was still beating; but there was no movement. He was obviously dead; and, as obviously, had been killed by the shot I heard. I wondered if he had killed himself, or been murdered. So I flashed my torch round the hut but could see no weapon. Nor was anyone else there. The first thing that came to my mind was that I must not touch anything. I suppose it was a subconscious realisation of that which prevented my turning the body over. Had I done so, of course, I should have recognised John Archer. As it was I had no idea of his identity.

Counsel for the prosecution has made the suggestion that I must have turned the body over because I said in my statement to the police that I thought the man had been shot by a small calibre weapon and, since I owned a pistol of this description, became afraid of being accused of killing the man if I were found on the spot. I can only explain my supposition of a small calibre weapon by saying that my mind must have registered the sound of the shot and judged from that. And besides that, there was very little blood. A large bullet would have made more. But all this was subconscious. I wasn't aware at the time that I had formed that opinion.

The next thought I had in mind was that I ought to get the police. But what about leaving the body? Wouldn't it be better to stop with it until someone came along who would call the police for me? And then I realised what a terrible position I was in. Here was a man who had just been shot. Suppose a policeman had heard the shot and came to investigate! I should be found there—alone. I decided to get away at once. I got as far as——

MR. MAINSTAY: Were you carrying anything?—Oh, yes; of course. I had noticed a raincoat lying on the floor just inside the hut and I picked it up and put it over my arm.

Had you any particular reason for doing that?—Well, yes. I thought I recognised it as a coat that my wife had lost some time before. It was an unusual colour for a raincoat—scarlet. And I satisfied myself that it was hers by a tear on one of the pockets. Naturally I didn't want to leave it there.

Very natural. Pray continue?—Just as I got to the bridge I bumped into someone. My torch was still in my hand and I switched it on. Then I saw that the other man was a policeman. Well, I suppose it was silly, but I got into a panic and tried to get away. The rest the Court knows.

Thank you. Sir Gregory—your witness.

SIR GREGORY CUMMINGS: You have referred to a torch. Do you usually carry a torch when out upon these, shall I say irresponsible, rambles?—Always. Some of the lesser streets of Storminster are not too well lit; besides, being an architect, I often stop to look at a piece of stone carving or the like.

Even though, as you have just explained to us, you are not fully conscious of your surroundings?—(Hesitation.) Oh, well, I'm not like that all the time. Only when I'm worrying over some problem.

I see. This raincoat, now. My learned friend considers it quite natural that you—on finding what you took to be your wife's raincoat in close proximity to a murdered man—he finds it quite natural that you should throw it over your arm and carry it away. I suggest that you did so because you feared that your wife was in the vicinity. That she might even have been implicated——

MR. MAINSTAY: My lord, I object. There is not one particle of evidence before the court to support this outrageous theory.

MR. JUSTICE SWALE: As I understood counsel's question he was not suggesting that the prisoner's wife was in the vicinity; only that the prisoner might have thought so. Nevertheless, Sir Gregory, I think I should refrain from making an unfounded suggestion which might prejudice the jury. The jury will erase that suggestion from their minds.

SIR GREGORY: As your lordship pleases.

CROSS-EXAMINATION CONTINUED

You have heard the evidence proving that the automatic pistol which was used to kill John Archer is your property?—I have. I told you that my wife had lost her raincoat days before——

MR. JUSTICE SWALE: You will confine your replies to the question under consideration. You must not make statements on your own account when answering counsel.

THE PRISONER: I beg your pardon, my lord. I was only anxious to have that fact on record.

CROSS-EXAMINATION CONTINUED

You agree then, that the pistol is yours?—Yes.

Can you give the Court any explanation of how it came to be found in the lake at a spot where you are known to have been?—Of course; the murderer threw it there.

I fully agree. That is what I had supposed. Did you, then,

throw it there?—No.

Then how did it leave your possession?—I kept it, and some ammunition, in a drawer in my study at home. I thought it was still there when the police asked me about it. Then I heard that it had been found in the lake and that it had been used for the murder. But anyone could have got in and taken it. My study windows are open all day in the summer and they face the public roadway in the Close.

What can you tell us about the attempt to erase the identification number of the pistol?—Nothing. All I know is that I didn't do it.

Yet your fingerprints are on the weapon?—Naturally, since I handled the thing when I put it into the drawer. But the prints were not, you will remember, on any places where one would have to hold the pistol in order to fire it. (No rebuke from the judge on this occasion.)

Would it be correct to say that you went out that night with the deliberate intention of going to the summer house in Tolbay Park?—It would not. No.

And that you were acting upon information contained in an anonymous letter?

MR. JUSTICE SWALE: One moment, Sir Gregory. Is any such letter amongst the exhibits? I fail to notice it in the list I have before me.

SIR GREGORY: No, my lord. I appreciate your lordship's point and will not press the matter. (But Sir Gregory, had produced upon the jury the impression he desired to make.)

RE-EXAMINATION by Mr. Mainstay.

When did you last see the pistol which you kept in your desk?—(Prisoner paused to consider his reply.) I really couldn't say. I put it there when we first went to the house and, at first, I used to clean it now and again. But I haven't done so for some time—months, I suppose. It was at the back of the drawer and I had no occasion to look at it.

Are people frequently shown into your study to wait for you when you are out?—Well, I suppose they may have been, on occasion. I wouldn't say it was a general practice.

MR. MAINSTAY: That, my lord, is all the evidence I intend to call.

CLOSING SPEECH FOR THE PROSECUTION

SIR GREGORY CUMMINGS: May it please your lordship, members of the jury. I think you will agree with me that we have before us a plain and simple case of murder; and that the Crown has proved its case. But I will refresh your minds.

In undisputed evidence we have the following facts:

The prisoner was found on the scene of the crime within a few minutes of its commission. The weapon used to kill John Archer has been shown to belong to the prisoner, and his fingerprints—and no others—were found upon it. (Pause and dropping of eyeglass while the point sinks in.) Moreover it was found in the lake at a spot which the prisoner is known to have passed in his flight from the police.

You will bear in mind the fact that an attempt had been made to erase the identification number of the pistol. An attempt which, but for the resources of modern science, would have been wholly successful; and you may ask yourselves who but the prisoner had an interest in removing the number? If the weapon were—as the prisoner suggests—stolen, then surely the thief would have been only too glad for the weapon to be identified as the property of another party.

Then, ladies and gentlemen of the jury, you will recall the incident of the torch; and you may ask yourselves if a torch would be a normal thing for a man to take with him during an evening walk in the streets of Storminster—unless he had reason to suppose that he might need it for a specific purpose. You have heard the prisoner's attempt at an explanation; but why should he choose, for a walk where movement was all he required, dimly lit back streets? And would not daylight be a more reasonable time to examine sculpture, than night—assisted by a torch?

We also have the discrepancy in time. The witness Shapley has stated that the shot was fired at a moment after ten o'clock.

A statement in some measure supported by her voluntary call to the police which is recorded as having been made at ten five. But the prisoner alleges that it was at a minute or two after quarter to ten. In my opening address I gave you a possible explanation of this.

But all these details pale into insignificance in comparison with the main evidence of Mrs. Shapley. Here, if not an actual witness to the crime, is an independent person who observes the prisoner entering the summer house, hears an altercation and, after she has left the spot, a gunshot. She heard only two men's voices—and the voice of a woman. Must we not, then, take it that there were only two men, and that one killed the other? It may cross your minds that the woman might have fired the fatal shot. But, in that case, what of the second man? What was he doing? Why did he not apprehend the woman or, if that were not possible, tell the police as soon as they arrived that it was a woman who had done the shooting and that she had escaped? Only one person was found on the scene when the police arrived; and that person is the prisoner; picked out, as the man she saw, by Mrs. Shapley from a group of ten men at the police station. Men, I may add, chosen for their general resemblance to the prisoner as far as is humanly possible.

To my mind Mrs. Shapley's evidence is sufficient to prove the case without the many added details which have been proved in this Court. But it is for you to decide.

Now let us consider the answers made by the prisoner to what may seem to you to have been extremely awkward questions:

'How did your pistol come to be in the lake?' An answer that I can only characterise as flippant—or unwittingly revealing: 'The murderer must have thrown it there!' And again, when asked how anyone but himself could have gained possession of the pistol: 'I kept it in a drawer in my study ... the windows are always open in summer. Anyone could have stolen it.' Possibly so—if we believe that a man in the prisoner's position could be so criminally careless as to keep a pistol and ammunition in such a place. But no complaint has been made of other articles stolen at the time. What sort of burglar is it who breaks into a house in broad daylight and steals only a pistol? (Again the eyeglass dropped.)

And now to the raincoat which, you will remember, has been identified as the property of the prisoner's wife. Here I tread upon delicate ground. It is alleged by the prisoner that this coat had been lost 'some days before' the murder. But has any evidence been called to prove this extremely important point?

It is probably common knowledge to you, members of the jury, that a wife cannot give evidence against her husband—except in a few specific cases with which we are not concerned. Nor can she be compelled to give evidence for him. But there is nothing to prevent her being called by the defence—except her own unwillingness or that of her husband. You may perhaps consider that the evidence she could have given would not have helped her husband's case. I think it is fair to make this comment because the raincoat presents a vital piece of evidence in that it suggests a possible motive for the crime. But I will say no more upon that matter, save to remind you that the prisoner in his first statement to the police denied the existence of this raincoat. What could be his motive for such a denial?

Then we must consider the prisoner's explanation—if we can call it that—as to why he imagined that a small calibre weapon had been used to kill John Archer. You may think this explanation reasonable—or you may not. You may think that he could only know such a fact from observation of the bullet wound; and if you think that, then you may also think that he must have recognised John Archer.

But here, ladies and gentlemen of the jury, we must avoid confusion. (A long pause.) The case for the Crown is that the prisoner did in fact shoot and kill John Archer. If this is true—and it is for you to decide upon the evidence you have heard—then of course he knew the identity of the dead man, and knew that he had a reason for shooting him—whatever that reason may have been. But if he could make it appear that he had no idea who the dead man was—then all motive disappears. But he betrayed himself by stating that the man had been killed by a small calibre weapon. I suggest that he could only know this in one of two ways: he himself used such a weapon; or he did, in fact, examine the face of the murdered man. And this, ladies and gentlemen of the jury, you have heard him strenuously deny.

I will labour the point no further; but you will agree that it is a vital one.

To sum up. The prisoner was on the scene of the crime both before and shortly after the time of the shooting. His was the weapon that fired the fatal shot, and his fingerprints were on it. He attempted to escape from the police and, in his first statement to them, denied all knowledge of the raincoat.

That, members of the jury, is the case for the Crown. And on this evidence I call upon you to do your duty and, if you believe the evidence, to bring in a verdict of guilty.

I sympathise with you in what must prove an extremely unpleasant task; but the law must be upheld and the sanctity of human life preserved. Nevertheless, as his lordship will shortly tell you, if the Crown has failed to prove its case beyond all reasonable doubt—the reasonable doubt of plain, honest persons like ourselves—then you will acquit the prisoner.

CHAPTER XVII

CLOSING SPEECH FOR THE DEFENCE

M R. MAINSTAY: My lord, ladies and gentlemen of the jury; it will be my purpose to show that there is no case against my client and that you, the jury, are bound to return a verdict of not guilty.

You, members of the jury, may be wondering why I am addressing you last—after the closing speech for the Crown.

This is because, in our law, if an accused person brings no witness in his defence but himself, the defence is allowed the last word. There is an exception—to do with the presence of the Attorney General or the Solicitor General; but that need not concern us.

This provision is a good and a just one. It is made especially for such a case as we are considering today. Here is a man against whom the evidence is entirely circumstantial. That being so, he is in the unfortunate position of having no witnesses to speak on his behalf. The witnesses for the prosecution, you will have remarked, are witnesses only to this circumstantial evidence; not one of them is a direct witness as to the commission of the crime.

My learned friend, in his opening speech, has given you a very apt if—unintentionally, I am sure—somewhat macabre simile with regard to circumstantial evidence. He compared it with a rope, woven of many strands, each of which, by itself, is a frail and unreliable thing. But, members of the jury, he failed to bring to your notice the phenomenon known as the multiplication of errors. Let me give a simple illustration:

You start with a basic fact which is given a wrong

interpretation. In this case, a man found on the spot where a murder has been committed, is at once assumed to have done that murder. To this wrong interpretation you add another fact; but—and this, ladies and gentlemen of the jury, is the crux of the whole matter—you interpret the meaning of the second fact in the light of the first. The initial error has now become magnified. And so it goes on. With each additional error of interpretation the initial error becomes larger and larger until an apparently solid edifice stands before you—but, members of the jury, it rests upon an unsound foundation.

Let us return to my learned friend's simile of the rope.

The rope in this case is constructed of frail and weak strands; not one of them capable of standing on its own merit. Twisted together they appear to form a reliable whole. But once let the strain of unbiased examination be put upon this rope, and one strand after another will fail—until your seemingly sound rope cannot support even its own weight.

It is my duty to unravel this faulty rope; to pick it to pieces and show the weakness of the separate strands.

My learned friend also has duties to perform. The duty of proving his case—if he can; but also the far greater duty, as he himself would be the first to admit, of seeing that justice is done. Yet, from the very fact that he is conducting the prosecution, he must inevitably view the evidence available to him from the standpoint of the prisoner's guilt. And this he has done in very able fashion.

But I approach the case from the opposite angle; and it is my conviction that I shall be able to prove to you, from these selfsame facts, the innocence of my client.

You have heard the simple and direct story that he has told, Let us assume—using my viewpoint—that it is true in every detail. He takes a walk, as any of us might, and finds himself—through no fault of his own—involved in a case of murder. His natural inclination—as, surely, would be yours—is to get away from the scene of the crime as quickly as possible. How right he was to feel that if found there he would be suspected! For that, members of the jury, is exactly what has happened.

Now let us take the incident of the raincoat. He recognises a coat which he sees on the floor near the body of the murdered man; a raincoat which has been mislaid or—mark my words, for I shall return to this subject later—stolen from his wife. He has a very natural reluctance to having his wife's name dragged into this grave and unpleasant case; and he realises that, although the coat had left her possession some days before the murder, it will no doubt be traced to her—as it has been, members of the jury; as it has been. So he does what you or I would have done. He removes it. Then comes the unfortunate incident with the police and the prisoner's momentary panic. Surely understandable in the circumstances, and in view of the shock which anyone must feel when coming suddenly upon the corpse of a murdered man. He does not realise that the raincoat has already been seen by the sharp eye of Sergeant Trent; and he feels that he may not make good his escape. So he thrusts the coat into a bush—where it is later discovered.

Touching the matter of the raincoat it has been remarked that my client's wife has not been before the court to testify. Members of the jury, I ask you frankly, what purpose would this have served? There is no suggestion that she was present at the time of the crime—or, if there was such a veiled suggestion it has, very properly, been ruled out of evidence. And neither she, nor her husband, remembers the exact date or circumstances under which the coat was lost—or stolen! And remember this, ladies and gentlemen of the jury, had she appeared as a witness I should have forfeited the right to be the last—saving, of course, his lordship—to address you. A right which is all important if you are to view the evidence from what I maintain to be the correct standpoint.

And so we come to the pistol. My client has told you that he kept the weapon in a drawer in his study. You may think this was very careless of him—and I think he will now agree with you. But many of us do careless things without finding ourselves charged with murder. He suggests that someone stole the pistol. Again I ask you to mark that word 'stole'. When I asked him if persons were often left alone in his study what was his answer? Instead of leaping at the explanation, as a less honest man would have done, he said that it might happen, but that it was not a normal practice.

What of the fingerprints? Who could doubt that a weapon owned, and handled, by a man would bear his fingerprints—unless they had been deliberately wiped off. But you will remember that, according to the testimony of the police themselves, no prints were found on such parts of the pistol as would have to be handled in the act of firing. What does this suggest? Surely that such prints of his as were found by the police upon the weapon were left—deliberately; while those which were bound to be erased when the pistol was fired by another person, were so erased—by the gloved hand of the murderer.

And now we come to another matter of erasure. I think it probable that a man of the education and standing of the diocesan architect would be sufficiently acquainted with modern methods of scientific detection to know that a number merely filed off a metal can, by using certain rays and reflections, be read with ease. I say I think it probable, but I do not stress this; nor do I rely upon it. Supposing that the pistol was stolen with the deliberate intention of throwing suspicion on my client. You might think that in such a case the thief, knowing for what purpose the pistol was to be used, would leave an identification number that would lead inevitably to the rightful owner of the pistol. But there is a second degree of cunning.

If it were already known that that owner would be present at the scene of the crime, and that the weapon would be recovered from the lake—a more obvious place to throw it one can hardly imagine—then it might well be assumed that the police, having a description of the weapon in their registration records, would be satisfied that it was the property of that owner—my client; and that the filing away of the number would, in that case, tell against him. I may even go so far as to say that the fact that the filed off number could be resurrected may have been known to this hypothetical robber and murderer.

And now, members of the jury, we come to what I can only style a negative piece of evidence. I refer to the compact. You cannot have failed to remark that no mention of this compact was made in the original statements by the police; and that I had to drag it out in cross-examination. Why (you must have asked yourselves) was this? The raincoat was mentioned; and much play made in its regard; but not the compact.

I will tell you why. The compact—as you heard in the evidence I extracted—bore no fingerprints. It has a bright, plated surface, ideal for retaining such prints— yet there were none. You, ladies of the jury, will be in a better position than we mere men, to say whether it is reasonable to imagine that a woman would, whenever she uses her compact—and I venture to suggest that a frequent, rather than an infrequent use would be made of such an article—whether it is reasonable, I ask, to imagine that she would carefully put on gloves every time she powdered her nose? Indoors and out; by night and by day? And yet, members of the jury, that is exactly what must have happened, since there were no fingerprints on the compact—unless—I say unless—*the compact was deliberately wiped clean of prints before being left on the floor of the hut!*

Let us consider this implication. If there had been a woman present at the shooting, can anyone conceive of such a woman carefully wiping her fingerprints from her compact and then deliberately leaving it on the floor? Why leave it at all? Had it been covered with prints one might have assumed that it had been dropped unnoticed in a moment of panic. But the picture of a panicking woman wiping off her prints and then throwing the compact on the floor is so ludicrous that it insults your intelligence.

You will understand, members of the jury, why the prosecution, while using the raincoat, wisely omitted to use the compact. And the raincoat? Isn't it stretching credulity just a little too far to believe that it was left behind by accident? You may or may not think so; it is for you to decide, and I am content to leave it to you.

By now I think you will have seen the purpose of my remarks—and will understand my asking you to mark my references to stolen goods. It is the submission of the defence that the whole affair has been a plot to implicate my client. Viewed in this light, surely the evidence—as I suggested at the beginning of my address—takes on a very different complexion?

But why, you may ask, should anyone go to such fantastic lengths to incriminate an innocent man?

Let us suppose that there is in this city someone who had good reason for killing John Archer. Not a wild supposition—for someone did kill him. No one wishes to speak evil of the dead; nor may I refer to things which have not been proved in evidence; nevertheless, members of the jury, one can readily imagine why a man—men, for that matter—might want to kill him.

But I must not ask you to pay too much attention to what is, after all, merely a theory unsupported by proven facts. (Counsel, while keeping just within his rights, was well aware that the reputation of John Archer with regard to married women was a matter of common talk in Storminster). But my learned friend himself has already told you that it is not necessary to prove motive—nor, indeed, has he attempted to do so in the case for the prosecution. We may, then, leave it at that in my hypothetical case.

But to continue the supposition. Let us call the unknown 'X'.

X desires to kill John Archer; but does not want to suffer the penalty for murder. He must, then, have a suspect; one who will bear the punishment for the crime X intends to commit. He lays his plan carefully. First he steals the suspect's pistol. Not a difficult feat, as we have heard, provided that X had the knowledge that the weapon was habitually kept in the drawer of the study desk. I do not suppose that my client made any great secret of this fact. Next comes the raincoat. Motive must be suggested—or, rather, in view of my learned friend's remarks—motive is desirable. Jealousy! The wronged husband! If it could be suggested that the suspect's wife was present at the time of the murder, the minds of the police and public alike would find no difficulty in suggesting a motive. So X steals a raincoat—an unusual raincoat—belonging to the suspect's wife. But this, perhaps, is not sufficient. So our murderer—Mr. X—proceeds to do what so many murderers before him have done: to gild refined gold; to paint the lily. Not satisfied with what might have proved a very convincing picture he must needs over-reach himself and be just a little too clever. Women use compacts, he reasons, therefore, in case the raincoat fails in its object—it might even have been anticipated that the suspect himself might remove it—let there be a compact. And there Mr. X must have had a difficult problem before him. Had he been able to obtain on the compact the fingerprints of the suspect's wife, all would have been ideal. But this is impossible. Ah! thinks he, people often wipe off fingerprints in cases of murder; then let the compact be printless. It may even be thought by the police that the suspect himself erased them. We do not know what was in the mind of Mr. X; but we do know the actual fact: that the compact was found and that—most remarkably—it bore no prints. I ask you to consider this with the most earnest attention.

And now, members of the jury, I come to what you must be thinking is the most damning part of the case against my client. I refer, of course, to the evidence of Mrs. Shapley.

Two possibilities occur to me in this regard. One: that Mr. X is not unlike my client in general appearance—a likeness which could be emphasised by copying his clothes, his hat and so forth—and what Mrs. Shapley has related in evidence refers to such a man; and that she was genuinely mistaken in her identification at the parade. I ask you to remember that she only caught the barest glimpse of the man in question; and that by moonlight. And moonlight, as one of our most successful dramatists has pointed out, 'can be cruelly deceptive!'

And now for the second possibility. You may have thought me a little cruel in my questioning of Mrs. Shapley. Why dig up what may have been a painful episode in her past? I did so, members of the jury, with the greatest reluctance. But I had to remember that the life of a man was at stake; and in such a case we cannot afford to spare feelings. Moreover, in attacking the character of a witness for the prosecution, I was exposing my own client to a like attack. An attack, you will have remarked, which was not made.

Why?—Because my client bears a blameless character. A fact which you must bear in mind when considering all the aspects of the case.

My intention, then, was to show that Mrs. Shapley is a person who is not worthy of credence. You heard her admit that she was asked to relinquish her post as treasurer of a missionary fund and, further, was asked to leave China. You may think that one is not treated in such a manner without very good reason—particularly not by persons so earnest in their beliefs as to become Christian missionaries. And you will recall that Mrs. Shapley herself stated—whilst denying the implication—that missing money was at the root of her misfortune. A fact, members of the jury, which I could not have been the first to mention; since I have no proof to place before the court. So you may decide to discount the evidence of this witness as being that of an unreliable person. It is for you to decide.

One last word, and I have done. As my learned friend, with his scrupulous attention to justice, has already told you, it is for the Crown to prove its case; not for the accused to prove his innocence. Therefore, members of the jury, I claim from you, unless you are convinced beyond all reasonable doubt of the guilt of my client, a verdict of not guilty.

In his summing up, which was scrupulously fair, Mr. Justice Swale made reference to the 'highly ingenious' theory of counsel for the defence, but felt bound to point out that counsel had offered no real explanation as to why the prisoner was at the scene of the murder at the vital hour. If this theory were to be accepted by the jury as a possibility, then they must ask themselves how the person referred to as 'Mr. X' could have arranged to have his suspect and his victim both on the spot at the crucial moment. And in this regard it was noteworthy that the prisoner himself, when giving evidence, made no mention of any reason for his presence, other than pure chance—a chance which no plotting villain could possibly have foreseen, let alone have embodied as a part of his plot.

In the event it was hardly a surprise to anyone in Court when the jury, after a long absence, brought in a verdict of guilty.

CHAPTER XVIII

Selwyn Sneddicombe gazed through the window of his study at the sun-drenched Close. 'Plane trees,' said one part of his mind, 'why do people like plane trees so much?' They always reminded him of the time when he had scarlet fever and had reached the peeling stage. Another part of his mind was more seriously occupied. Throughout Ashburn's trial Selwyn had sat in Court, an absorbed and anxious spectator. He had a genuine affection for both Rodney and Rosalind, and his heart went out to them in their dire trouble.

And the thought of that word drove his mind in yet another direction. It was behaving, he reflected, rather like that out-of-time hover fly which was helicoptering over his autumnal flower beds—darting now here, now there; and getting nowhere. This was supposed to be his 'trouble hour'—and no one had come. Unusual. He glanced at his watch. Barely a quarter of an hour to go. For once he'd take a chance. Not likely that anyone would turn up now.

He sought his hat, threw a word to Mrs. Teeming to the effect that he would be out for lunch, and set forth purposefully for the police station.

"Well, Superintendent," he said when face to face with Fuller, "are you satisfied with yesterday's verdict?"

Fuller gave his visitor a keen look.

"Sounds from your tone, Padre, as if you weren't. But it's not for me to be satisfied or otherwise. That's a matter for judge and jury—and they seemed to be in no doubt. To tell you the truth, Mr. Sneddicombe, I don't rightly see how they could have found otherwise." Fuller pulled at his moustache and frowned down upon his scribbling pad, richly embellished with doodlings.

"Oh, logically," replied Selwyn absently, "yes, I daresay. Yet there's something beyond logic and legal proof. . . .

But of course," he added more briskly, "you have to deal with facts, not fancies. So let us consider them. I don't see any harm—now—in telling you something you may not know. Rodney Ashburn went to the summer house that night because of an anonymous letter he received the same morning. It told him that his wife would be there—with John Archer."

"You don't say!" Fuller showed a lively interest.

"Yes. But he wouldn't allow his counsel to bring it up in Court. He was afraid it might reflect on his wife."

The superintendent gave a short laugh. "He needn't have worried. No sane counsel for the defence would dream of bringing that out; and Mainstay is no fool. Why, my dear Padre, there's the motive—sticking out like a barber's pole." Fuller tweaked the ends of his moustache and added triumphantly: "So that's why he took his pistol!"

Selwyn looked worried. "Now wait a minute, Superintendent. You've got it all wrong. That's not what I meant at all. Look! To my mind the whole thing is tied up with these vile anonymous letters that have been going about. You must have heard of them—even if unofficially?" Fuller nodded. "Very well. Now just listen to this: John Archer and I were working on those letters; trying to trace the writer. He told me that he was hot on the trail—and what happened? He got shot!" Selwyn paused dramatically.

Fuller smiled, but nodded encouragement.

"Now suppose," continued the padre earnestly, "that the writer knew that John was on his trail and wanted him out of the way. He sends a letter to Ashburn that will make certain that Rodney goes to the summer house—he'd have been more than human if he hadn't!—at a time when the real villain has just killed John Archer. There's a scapegoat, right on the spot."

Again Fuller smiled. "And what of the lady?"

"Oh ..." Selwyn dismissed the question with a shrug. "Of

course there never was one. The raincoat was planted—
isn't that what you call it in police circles?"

"Then why was John Archer there?"

"Well, I haven't thought that out—yet. But I shall!
Rosalind Ashburn told me herself that she had lost that
raincoat several days before the murder; and I believe her.
Then," Selwyn continued with mounting excitement,
"there's the compact! Why, my dear man, that was
obviously planted! Even the prosecution realised that—
for they deliberately left out all reference to it at the
trial; knowing that it would tell against their case. No
fingerprints, you remember!"

Fuller shook his head. "That's not the way we work—
in this country. If the Crown had thought that, then they'd
have mentioned it in Court. That's our idea of fair play.
But you've got nothing there, I'm afraid. How's this for
an explanation: the girl pulls out her compact to powder
her nose. It's in one of those soft, suède cases—you know,
just a loose cover. You'll remember the compact was
described as plated—highly polished. What more natural
than it should have a sort of glove, to keep it bright—like
a smoker has for his best-loved pipe? Just then Ashburn
arrives and the row starts. The girl gets frightened. The
compact slips out of the glove and falls on the floor,
leaving the suede cover in her hand. No time to feel
about for the thing. It's dark, remember——"

"Wait a minute!" interrupted Selwyn in triumph.
"Dark—and yet this girl is able to powder her nose!"

Fuller burst into a roar of laughter. "Good for you,
Padre! You've got me there. Oh well, maybe she had a
little flashlight. Even so, she wouldn't stop to look for the
thing if she was really scared. She shoves the cover into
her bag and gets cracking. Well, if the compact had just
slipped out of its cover you couldn't expect it to have

fingerprints. No, I'm afraid there's no more to it than that."

"All right," persisted Selwyn stubbornly. "We'll leave it for the moment. But what about the raincoat? Obviously planted! Even if there was a woman there, it wasn't Rosalind Ashburn."

Fuller smiled tolerantly. "Don't much matter who she was—as long as Ashburn *thought* it was his wife. But leave that aside, like the compact, Padre. What about Shapley's testimony? You can't get by that—although Mainstay tried his damnedest."

Selwyn nodded gloomily. "It's going to be hard to do so. But she may have been genuinely mistaken. She may have seen the real murderer and then Rodney came on the scene immediately afterwards. According to him the shot was fired several minutes earlier than Mrs. Shapley said it was. Oh, I know you don't believe him; but I do. Anyway, I'm going to work on that theory."

"Well, I wish you luck," said Fuller warmly. "I like the Ashburns; always have. No one will be more pleased than I if you can prove his innocence. But there it is. Any man might kill in a moment of anger; and jealousy's a powerful motive. Mind you," he finished, judicially, "I'm not saying you mayn't be right; that this letter-writer may have been behind the whole affair and planned for Mr. Ashburn to kill John Archer; but that doesn't affect his guilt."

"Now this," said Selwyn to himself, "must be just about where Mrs. Shapley stood. She'd tried to get into that building and found it locked. Funny that had to be brought out by questions. She spoke at first as if she'd been in there. But perhaps that was only maidenly modesty. Yes," he nodded soberly, "she's that sort."

Dusk was falling; but it never occurred to Selwyn that there might be something a little equivocal in a parson hanging around such a spot at such an hour. In some ways he was singularly guileless.

There was no moon, so he had chosen dusk, as reproducing as nearly as possible the conditions of that fateful summer night with its fitful moon.

'Yes,' he mused, 'this must be the spot. I can see the path leading to the south entrance for quite a distance. Bless my soul!' he exclaimed aloud in his excitement, 'now that's extraordinary! You can't see the bridge from here. Those bushes on the corner of the island screen it. Of course, they may have grown since that night; but would they have grown that much? And yet she was quite positive. It was as the man stepped on to the bridge that she saw the thing in his hand, and then his face. Well then, she couldn't have stood here.' He glanced round; but his choice of *locale* had not been at fault. If he advanced further towards the main path he would be compelled to leave the shelter of the bushes which so modestly hid the building; and Mrs. Shapley had specifically stated that she was lurking in the shadows of the bushes. There was nothing but open ground between him and the whole stretch of path leading to the south entrance. And yet, as he had remarked, from the most advanced position amongst the bushes it was quite impossible to see the bridge. Funny that the police had not spotted that.

At that moment a distant footfall on the asphalt path aroused him from his preoccupation. Someone was approaching from the south entrance. Soon, in the fast deepening twilight, he was able to make out a dim figure. Almost instinctively he drew back into the bushes. Now he could discern the form of a man, wearing a raincoat and carrying a large, square parcel; but the light was insufficient to reveal the man's face. Then the figure was lost to view behind the island bushes and a second or two later Selwyn heard the sound of his footsteps on the planks of the bridge.

He nodded to himself with satisfaction. It was as he had thought: it was not possible, from where he stood, to see anyone on the bridge.

'Now what a queer coincidence!' he remarked. 'And what can the chap be doing?'

The question was reasonable. Guileless though Selwyn might be he yet knew that couples were wont to frequent Tolbay Park after dark; but not, he thought, on a distinctly chilly autumn night. Besides, this wasn't a question of a couple. It was one man, alone; and carrying a parcel.

A loud splash made him jump. The next instant he rushed from the bushes and raced towards the bridge. Thoughts of suicide darted through his mind. But as he neared the approach a figure came swiftly across the bridge, brushed him roughly aside and made off towards the park entrance.

Without pausing to reason Selwyn called out: "I say! Just a minute."

For answer he heard the footsteps break into a run and he gave chase. But it was now almost dark and the other had a start. Selwyn arrived, panting, at the entrance only to find that his quarry had eluded him. For a moment he stood irresolute. Was it any of his business? But there is no zeal like the zeal of the self-appointed sleuth; and Selwyn had come to the park in just that capacity. 'Visit the scene of the crime,' he had told himself. 'That's the first and most important step.' The police wouldn't move—then he must.

And surely, he reasoned, as he regained his breath, it was more than coincidence that a man had come up the path at that moment and had thrown something into the lake?

He remembered with relief that evidence in Court had shown that nowhere was the lake deep. Nor, he reflected, could one throw a large parcel very far. His next step was obvious—if unpleasant. Switching on a torch which he had brought with him in readiness for his return, he went back to the bridge, crossed it and examined the terrain. He found himself at the junction of three paths. One led direct to the summer house, the others branched right and left of it. On the outer sides of the latter two paths grew bushes.

Since no one had been pursuing the man with the parcel it was reasonable to suppose that he would have followed one of these paths on his way to the lake, rather than plunge through the undergrowth. Selwyn chose one and shortly found himself on the farther side of the summer house, where the bushes ceased and there was a small plot of grass sloping down to the lake.

This, he decided, must be the spot from which the unknown had thrown his parcel. He paused for a long moment. Then, fired by his detective fever, he removed his shoes, socks and trousers, and rolled up the ends of his long, woollen pants. The good Lord be thanked, he thought fervently, that it was dark. He made slow and shivering progress into the turgid waters of the lake, sliding more than walking down the slimy cement slope. To his relief he came upon the bottom at no worse than knee deep. Then began a tedious minesweeping operation: back and forth, a pace forward and the manoeuvre repeated. Patience is sometimes rewarded; and it was so in this case. Before long he stubbed a toe on something which, surely, had no place on the bottom of a lake.

He regained the shore, chilly but triumphant, and then, with commendable restraint, wiped legs and feet on his handkerchief, re-donned his clothes and set out for home without so much as a peep at the contents of the parcel, which was bulky and moderately heavy in its sodden wrappings. A thin trickle of water marked his trail—had any been there to follow it.

CHAPTER XIX

SELWYN, when in reminiscent mood, could never decide whether he was surprised at the contents of his parcel or whether the rush of excitement which assailed him at its unveiling was merely due to fulfilment of his expectations.

Without waiting to dry the typewriter he seized a sheet of paper and wound it into the machine. From memory he typed the wording of the anonymous letter which he had himself received, tore the paper from the platen and rushed to his desk. It was but the work of a moment to pluck the original from its hiding place and lay the two specimens side by side. There was no doubt that both had come from the same machine. It could hardly have been otherwise.

'Who,' demanded Selwyn, 'but the villain of the piece would want to get rid of the typewriter?' Then the mysterious stranger was—must be—the author of the poison pen letters and, *ipso facto,* the murderer. At the thought Selwyn gnashed his teeth. If only he had managed to run a little faster—or to have started earlier. Then a disquieting thought struck him. What of the limp? Mrs. Prinnett had certainly said that the purchaser of the machine had a limp. But the man in the park was far too fleet of foot to be so handicapped. Had the machine, then, changed hands yet again? Not necessarily! A ray of hope crept into Selwyn's mind. If the chap bought the thing with the very intention of writing poison pen letters, then he would hardly want to be identified as the purchaser if ever such letters were traced to a certain machine. His appearance, it had already been established, was not such as to remain in the memory. Safe enough there. But a *limp,* now; that would be remembered. So why not adopt a limp? Then, if ever there were a hue and cry, the pursuers would be nicely led up the garden path. Selwyn liked this conclusion.

But what should be his next step? Take the typewriter to the police? With what object? Fuller might be persuaded that there was the machine that had written the anonymous letters; but even so—*cui bono?* The superintendent had not suggested that Rodney Ashburn had never received such a letter. To the contrary. He had immediately decided that there, then, was the motive for killing John Archer. Nor had he taken kindly to Selwyn's suggestion that the author of the letters had done the killing. No; he would get little help from the police.

Mulling over the affair after the cold supper which had been left for him he was again struck by the two discrepancies in the story related by Mrs. Shapley. She had let it be assumed that she had entered a building which was known to have been locked at that hour; and she had claimed to have seen a bridge from a spot where—under present conditions at least—it was not visible. Allowing for the unobservant habit of the average human being, there was still room for questioning the ultimate veracity of her statement. This, Selwyn decided, he would do on the morrow.

But morning found him going first to Mrs. Prinnett. Hoping against hope, he intended to probe into her memories in order to get a better description of the man who had bought the typewriter. Since the trial was over he felt released from his promise not to visit her.

But Mrs. Prinnett was far too excited to think of that—or to let her visitor do more than open his mouth.

"Oh dear!" she exclaimed breathlessly, as she motioned Selwyn into her kitchen-parlour. "I don't know whether to be glad to have him home again or sorry he's lost the part!"

"I suppose you are referring to Tom?" suggested Selwyn.

Mrs. Prinnett nodded and dabbed at her eyes with a

wisp of tissue. "Yes. I'd such high hopes this time—and so had he. But you never can tell!" With which profound reflection she subsided into a chair and searched her bag feverishly for a cigarette.

"It's the fickleness of the public," she continued resentfully. "That's what it is. Tom's show didn't run above three nights. All that rehearsing—and then where are you? He turned up yesterday afternoon. Quite downhearted he was."

"Dear me; I'm sorry to hear that. And where is he now?"

Mrs. Prinnett shrugged. "I don't know. He went out before I came down this morning. Gone after that Helen, I shouldn't wonder. Didn't think twice about leaving her when there was a chance of a job; but now the job's off, he's off too—after her. Serve him right, I told him, if she turned him down flat. But she won't! You'll see. Tom has a way with him."

A wild and grim thought came unbidden to Selwyn's mind. Tom Prinnett was said to have left Storminster before John Archer's death—but had he? He had also, it now appeared, returned to the city on the very day that an unidentified man had thrown the typewriter into the lake.

With a cunning foreign to his nature Selwyn suggested; "I suppose he needed a lot of comforting last night?"

Mrs. Prinnett bridled. "If he did, he didn't come to his mother for it. He went to his room after an early supper and I haven't seen him since. I suppose he took his failure in London very much to heart."

Selwyn then stated the object of his visit; but, in the light of his new theory, was not unduly disappointed when he failed to elicit a more exact description of the elusive typewriter purchaser.

"This Mrs. Shapley," he pursued, "what do you know of her?"

"What should I know?" Mrs. Prinnett sounded affronted.

"It was she who got poor Mr. Ashburn into trouble."

"Yes, I know. No doubt the poor woman thought she was doing her duty. But—seeing that you're secretary of the Women's Institute and she's treasurer—I thought you might be able to tell me something about her."

Mrs. Prinnett shook her head. "We meet when we have to," she said stiffly. Then, with a burst of feeling she could not conceal; "We don't meet socially. Like me and several round here that I could name. 'Oh, get Mrs. Prinnett to do it—she's always willing to oblige. But ask her to come to our houses?' " A snort concluded the words.

Selwyn felt an unworthy urge to tell the good lady that she was talking nonsense—was over-sensitive; but his natural honesty restrained him. It was, as well he knew, nothing but the truth.

There was no more to be gained by further questioning; and the thought of Tom, in his role of Nigel Villiers, making the running with Helen in his quest for comfort was one which gave him no pleasure. Why not drop in on Helen—quite casually. That is, if she were at home, and not already out with Tom Prinnett.

The fresh air (it had been stuffily hot in the Prinnett parlour) restored to him his sense of proportion. If Helen really preferred Tom, then there was no more to be said. In any case, he was a detective on the job; not for him to be side-tracked by personal considerations.

Never in his blameless life had he bullied anyone; least of all a woman. But a man's life was at stake and there was no room for squeamishness. 'Dear me', he reflected ruefully, 'here have I been using guile with Mrs. Prinnett, and now I am about to browbeat Mrs. Shapley! *Facile est.* . . .'

Mrs. Shapley was at home. With pince-nez on her bony nose she pored over some sheets of accounts.

"Mrs. Shapley, I don't think you know me," began

Selwyn, assuming with great difficulty an air which he hoped was menacing. "I am——"

"Oh, I know who you are, Mr. Sneddicombe," interrupted Mrs. Shapley, removing her glasses and pushing aside the accounts. "I've often seen you about in the town. You must be feeling it about poor Mr. Ashburn; he was such a friend of yours."

A little spark of excitement thrilled through Selwyn.

"Oh? Now what makes you think that, Mrs. Shapley?"

"Well, I've seen you about with him, you know—from time to time."

Selwyn pounced.

"What made you tell those lies in court?" he demanded fiercely. "Who was behind it?"

Mrs. Shapley turned an unpleasing greenish white.

"I'm sure I don't know what you mean. . . . I. . . ."

"One," said Selwyn with cold and terrible emphasis, ticking off the score upon an accusing finger, "you lied about going to that . . . building in Tolbay Park. Two, you could not have seen the bridge from any position amongst the bushes near the building. Three, you said that you didn't know Mr. Ashburn by sight; and had never seen him before the identification parade."

Mrs. Shapley burst into tears. "I'm sure I never meant it to go so far. I didn't see any harm in telling what happened as if I'd seen it myself. And once I said it to the police it was too late. I'd have got myself into terrible trouble if I'd gone back on it—on top of what else would have happened to me. And I was told to say I'd never seen Mr. Ashburn—to make it more convincing like."

"You'll certainly get into terrible trouble now, Mrs. Shapley," pronounced Selwyn remorselessly. "And the best thing you can do is to make a clean breast of the whole thing. They may let you off more lightly if you do that."

"Hullo, lovely! Back again, you see!"

Helen turned in surprise not unmixed with indignation.

"How nice for Storminster," she said coldly. "To what do we owe the pleasure?"

"Can't talk here. Let's go to that café place and knock back a 'cuppa'. You see before you someone in dire need of comfort and mental recuperation."

Moved, perhaps, by curiosity rather than any urge to administer spiritual comfort, Helen allowed herself to be led into Meakin's café.

"Well, what's been going on in this dead-alive hole since I robbed it of my sparkling presence?" began Nigel (for as such he would wish to be known). "Any more poison pen manifestations?"

There was a levity in his tone which angered Helen.

"No—they seem to have stopped when you left. Let's hope they won't start again—now that you're back!"

Nigel gave her a peculiar look. "You're not insinuating that I wrote them, I hope?" His tone was only half jocular.

"I shouldn't think so—considering what the one I had received said about you."

"I say! What do you mean? What did it say? Of all the damned cheek!"

A waitress with coffee forced an interlude.

"Well?" persisted Nigel when she had gone.

"Oh, nothing that mattered. Just that you were a fortune hunter, and that sort of thing."

"My God!" Nigel spoke with a depth of feeling which caused Helen to look at him in surprise.

"Then you didn't write it yourself? I thought——" She broke off abruptly. She had thought that perhaps it had been his way of getting out of a situation which no longer appealed to him; but she could hardly tell him that. "It would have been a clever thing to do—wouldn't it?" she substituted. "To write one against yourself—if you had been responsible for the others."

"I say! You can't mean that!" Nigel scowled moodily at his plate. "If you think I wrote them," he went on defiantly, "I can tell you I damned well didn't. But I know who did—and I can also tell you that there won't be any more of them."

But in this he was wrong.

As soon as Helen could free herself she hurried to Selwyn's house in the Close. He had just returned from interviewing Mrs. Shapley.

"I say!" she said when Mrs. Teeming had shown her into Selwyn's study, "Nigel Villiers has come back; and he knows who wrote the anonymous letters! He's just told me so."

"And well he might," said Selwyn drily. "Hardly a case of the right hand not knowing what the left is doing."

"Oh no," Helen shook her head. "He didn't do it himself. I asked him that."

"You would hardly expect him to admit it! But let that pass. Who does he say wrote them?"

"He didn't. But he did say that there wouldn't be any more."

"Well, it's nice to have his assurance," said Selwyn.

Helen looked at him with a little frown. "You sound awfully sort of . . . sarcastic this morning, Selwyn. And that's not a bit like you. What's wrong? You don't care for Nigel—do you?"

"I could manage without him," agreed Selwyn, smiling for the first time. "And you? Have you still a . . . leaning towards him?"

Helen laughed gaily. "Good Lord, no! That was midsummer madness. I think I have more of a leaning . . . towards the church."

"You . . . you don't mean you're thinking of entering a convent?" asked Selwyn anxiously.

"Not exactly. Oh, Selwyn, you are a silly idiot sometimes!"

Then, as though she had said too much, even for one of Selwyn's lack of perception—or lack of conceit—she hurried on lightly: "No convent to hide a broken heart for me. I'm far too modern. But let's stick to work. I came along as fast as I could to tell you about the letters; because I know you've been working on them for ages. Aren't you pleased?"

Selwyn nodded. "I am indeed; for it bears out what I already have in mind. Look, Helen, this matter is far more serious than you can possibly realise. You know, of course, that poor little Miss Pruin killed herself because of one of these letters. But what you don't know is that it was because of one of them that Rodney went to the summer house that night. The person who wrote them has a lot to answer for; maybe even more than indirect murder!"

"My dear!" Helen was startled into seriousness. "But it's impossible! Things like that don't happen in places like Storminster. I can hardly believe it."

Selwyn then told her that he had every reason to believe that the whole of Mrs. Shapley's evidence was a tissue of lies.

"But why? What on earth had she to gain by lying?" asked Helen in bewilderment.

"It wasn't what she had to gain by lying; it was what she had to lose . . . if she didn't bear false witness."

CHAPTER XX

S ELWYN next called on Rosalind Ashburn. He found her
listless and resigned.

"I haven't come to you before," he began, "because I had
nothing definite. Nothing but my own personal belief in
Rodney. But now I've a lot more to go on. I think we're
nearly out of the wood, Rosalind."

The girl smiled wanly. "It's awfully nice of you to try
to help, Selwyn; but what's the use? I know it was silly of
Rodney to believe what that beastly note said; but he did
believe it. And that explains why he killed John. I suppose
they quarrelled and Rodney lost his temper. John could
be awfully cynical at times. I can quite imagine him being
delighted to go on fooling Rodney when he saw how
much he cared."

"But, my dear Rosalind, you don't really believe that
Rodney did kill him?"

"What else can I believe? Why, he never even attempted
to defend himself at the trial. Not properly."

"And don't you know why? Because he believes that you
killed John! He thinks that you were there that night—oh,
he doesn't think it was anything really serious; he wouldn't
believe that of you—but he thinks that you may have gone
there out of . . . well, just for excitement. And then John
became offensive—and you shot him."

Rosalind gasped. "You can't mean that! Why, he behaved
as if he believed that when I saw him in prison; but
I thought it was just an act to make me believe he was
innocent. If he could make me think he believed I'd done
it, then of course he couldn't have done it himself. Oh,
why didn't you tell me before!"

Selwyn smiled a little sadly. "My dear, you wouldn't have
believed me. I had to have some sort of proof. And now I
think I've got it. Now you can understand why Rodney

put up no real defence. He thought you were guilty and he was afraid that anything he said might implicate you. I assured him that you weren't—to the best of my ability; but it was no use. You see "Selwyn broke off and gave Rosalind an appealing look. "I wasn't quite sure myself!"

But Rosalind seemed not to hear him. Her whole face was transfigured as the understanding of Rodney's sacrifice found its way into her mind. The fact that he had been capable of believing her guilty of an intrigue with John Archer paled into insignificance before this proof of his abiding love. And mingled with the joy was a deep shame that she herself had doubted him. But Selwyn had mentioned proof. Thrusting aside emotion she became calm and forceful.

"You spoke of proof, Selwyn. What proof? Who did kill John?"

"I think he was killed by Tom Prinnett—the man who calls himself Nigel Villiers. The man who has been behind all the poison letters. For him I can have little sympathy; but I fear very much for the effect this may have on his mother."

Selwyn then recounted the steps in his investigation. How he had been led to Mrs. Prinnett's shop in search of the typewriter, and how she had described the man who had bought it.

"Poor woman!" he said. "When John Archer first asked her about the machine she must have realised that it had to do with the poison letters. So she invented the story of a lame man who had bought the typewriter; knowing all the time that her own son had taken it. She even went so far as to leave me while she faked an invoice to prove her story. But I don't think for a minute that—at that time, at any rate—she suspected Tom of killing Archer. She was only concerned with the letters, and with shielding him from the consequences of writing them."

"But you said that one of these letters was delivered to Mrs. Prinnett while you were there," objected Rosalind.

"Yes, I've thought about that. I believe Tom had no idea his mother suspected him. He must have known that I was making an investigation, and thought that a letter delivered to her house would put me right off the scent—as it did."

"But Tom was away at the time!"

"He was supposed to be away. But what proof have we of that? Or that he was away on the night of the murder? His mother may have believed it was so; but what was to prevent his returning—or even remaining hidden in the town? Then we must remember that the letters more or less stopped when Tom was in London. Also that on the very night of his return someone tried to get rid of the typewriter. His mother must have tackled him on his return and told him of her suspicions—for they could have been no more. I suppose she was afraid to try to get rid of the thing herself—alone and unaided. But when he came home from London she told him all that John and I had been doing and advised him to get rid of it at once. She told me that he went to his room immediately after supper and stayed there sulking. Either she said that to give him an alibi—because he told her that he had been seen at the lake—or she really believed it. In which case he must have got out of his window.

"I imagine he chose the lake so that, if the police found the machine by any ill chance, they would immediately connect it with John Archer's murder and, probably, think that it meant that Rodney not only killed John Archer but was also guilty of writing the anonymous letters."

Rosalind nodded. "Yes, I can see that. And you think that Tom Prinnett killed John Archer because he had discovered that Tom was the author of the letters?"

"Yes. It hardly seems an adequate motive. But when you come to remember that Miss Pruin killed herself because of one of those letters, you can imagine what sort of outcry there would be in Storminster if it became known that he was responsible. And Tom, in his character of Nigel Villiers, would be branded for life. He couldn't change his name and his identity without also sacrificing any reputation he has already gained on the stage."

"I see. But what about Mrs. Shapley's evidence?"

"I looked at it in this way: we learned at the trial that Mrs. Shapley had been driven out of China because of the embezzlement of missionary funds of which she had charge as treasurer.

"And now we find her as treasurer of the W.I. One doesn't want to give a dog a bad name and hang him for it; but what, I asked myself, if Mrs. Prinnett, as secretary of the W.I., discovered that Mrs. Shapley was appropriating funds to her own use? By now I am assuming that Mrs. Prinnett must have suspected or known that her son killed John Archer.

"Very well. There was a broadcast appeal for the woman who had reported the quarrel to the police to come forward. Mrs. Prinnett herself couldn't appear to tell the tale she had invented; that would be to lead the inquiry straight to her own home. So she blackmailed Mrs. Shapley into taking the part and coached her into it word by word. What happened to the real woman I don't know. Probably afraid to go to the police when she realised there had been a murder. But she must have been very astonished when she read of Mrs. Shapley's evidence in Court. Mrs. Prinnett, no doubt, made a hasty reconnaissance of the summer house and concocted what she thought was a plausible story that would prove Rodney's guilt—and thus shield her son. A most wicked thing to do; but we must remember that she is his mother.

"Well, that's how I reasoned the thing out. So I went and tackled Mrs. Shapley. She confessed to me that my supposition was correct. It happened exactly as I had imagined; except that Mrs. Prinnett told her that she, herself, had actually seen all that she described; but for certain reasons which she did not explain—understandably enough!—she couldn't give evidence. All she asked Mrs. Shapley to do was to give the evidence that Mrs. Prinnett would have given if she had been free to do so. A weak story; but I imagine that Mrs. Shapley—under the threat of blackmail—was only too glad to have that much to salve her conscience."

"But what a vile woman Mrs. Prinnett must be!" exclaimed Rosalind indignantly. "To save her own worthless son she was going to let Rodney die!"

"I can quite understand your indignation; and I make no excuses for her. I think the law will take care of her. But, although I told you that I have proof, it's not yet such that I can go to the police and hand over a complete case. I've got to prove, somehow, that it was Tom Prinnett who threw the typewriter into the lake. I must also explain how he got hold of your raincoat. That was one of the most damning pieces of evidence against Rodney. If only you could remember when and where you lost it!"

"Oh, but I have! I didn't tell you about it because it didn't seem to matter any longer. It wouldn't prove Rodney's innocence. The fact that he saw it in the summer house, and thought I'd dropped it, was sufficient to give him a motive. Yes, I remembered the other day, when I was at a W.I. meeting. It suddenly came to me that I wore it to one of those very meetings not long before that awful night. It was raining. But when I came out I was busy talking to someone or other; and the rain had stopped. So I just forgot it."

The simple explanation seemed to stun Selwyn. He just gaped at Rosalind. When he did recover the power of speech his words meant nothing to her. He said:

"Gosh! What a fool I've been! I've missed the wood for the trees. What's the time?" He looked at his watch. "A few minutes after eleven. Good! I can just make it."

Relations between Mrs. Prinnett and her son Tom had been severely strained from the previous afternoon when he, returning unexpectedly and unannounced from a London that wanted him not, discovered his mother in the little attic room at the top of her house in process of concocting one of the pleasant little letters that had wrought such havoc in Storminster.

The first surprise that Tom experienced was to see his mother typing; for it had never crossed his mind that she could do such a thing, let alone that she possessed a typewriter. The next surprise was her patent attitude of guilt, as she tried to cover up what she had written.

Roughly pushing her hand aside he wrenched the paper from the machine and read it:

How does it feel to have a husband who's going to the gallows? You won't have so much to be proud about in three weeks' time.

He looked at his mother in horror.

"Good God! So it has been you all the time, writing these beastly things!"

Mrs. Prinnett attempted to maintain her dignity.

"I don't think that's the way to speak to your mother," she said tartly, "particularly when it's mostly because of you that I've thought it necessary to put some of these stuck up fools in their places. I don't mind so much for myself. I've got used to 'Oh, Prinnett'll do it. She's so good at donkey work; and she loves being asked to slave for others!' And the same creatures would never dream of asking me to their homes—except to do work for them. But when you came back to live here I just wasn't going to stand for it. Treating you as they did me! Not good enough for their beastly homes!"

"Look, Mother, it's no use trying that on. You were writing these stinking things before I came back. Oh, I've heard all about them. But I never dreamed it was my own mother who was responsible. What in hell made you start it?"

Mrs. Prinnett told him with a queer sort of pride how she had read a book in which a woman who thought herself slighted had got her revenge by writing anonymous letters; and the idea had appealed to her as very well suited to her own case. She prepared the plan of campaign most carefully. She explained how she had acquired the typewriter and had at once hidden it in the upstairs room. Then she had sent herself, as secretary of the Organ Fund Committee, one of the first notes. She had thought that reading it before a number of influential people would make it quite impossible for anyone to suspect her. It would always be remembered that she had been the first to receive such a note.

"But how on earth did you get hold of the details you put in these things?" asked Tom, curious in spite of his loathing.

"Oh, that was easy enough," said his mother with contempt. "In a deadly place like Storminster there are always heaps of people who just live on scandal—they've nothing better to do. But I had a bit of luck with that stuck-up Battersby woman! You remember you went to her party, and I asked you to leave a note for me? That was one of my best efforts. My sister Alice—your aunt, of course—used to live in the same Cotswold village as Jane Stunning—as she was then. She was the postman's daughter. Then some rich uncle died in Australia and left her a lot of money. Her parents had her educated above her station and got some person who needed cash to launch

her in society in London. That was where she met Harold
Battersby; and married him! She was one of the worst, as
far as I was concerned. They always are, these jumped-up
nouveau riche. 'Dear Mrs. Prinnett, it would be so *sweet* of
you if you would copy out this list of subscribers for me. I
know my handwriting's *too, too* poor; but you're so clever
at reading bad writing.' Ugh! the posing fool. I often had
it on the tip of my tongue to tell her I knew who she was.
But then I thought of the better way. She wouldn't have
an idea who it was who knew about her; and she'd always
be in fear of it coming out. She's just the sort to dread a
disclosure like that worse than death itself.

"Then there was that conceited Rosalind Ashburn. No
girl has any right to be as pretty as that! I put a flea in
her ear all right; and I had you to thank for it! D'you
remember telling me what you heard about Ashburn
when you were up at Cambridge? About that girl Anita
Pedler?"

"Mother! You didn't tell her about that! Why, I told
you it wasn't to go any further."

"I know, dear. But don't worry. I merely told her to ask
her husband about the girl. That's all."

Tom's face had darkened during this recital. He now
said menacingly: "And I suppose it was you who wrote to
Helen Battersby to tell her I was a fortune hunter!"

Mrs. Prinnett winced at his tone.

"It was for your own good, my dear boy. I knew you'd
never stick to the stage and all its hard work if you could
marry money and live idly. And I believe in you as an
actor. It was for your own good."

Tom gave a contemptuous snort. "And I suppose it was
for her own good that you drove poor little Miss Pruin to
her death. Helen told me about that. How did you find
out the poor thing's secret?"

His mother explained how she had come across a

place in the receipt book where a counterfoil had been removed: and how she had matched the amount, showing as an indentation on the following counterfoil, with the hundred pounds given by Miss Carson; and how she had used this knowledge in her note and, later, allowed Selwyn to be the one to make the discovery.

"But what the hell!" said her son wrathfully. "Why on earth did you want to hound the poor old thing to her death. What harm had she ever done you?"

"I wasn't to know that she'd kill herself. I thought she deserved punishment for stealing like that—and her pretending to be so pious. Besides, she'd slighted me on several occasions when I'd tried to be friendly. The cheek of it! A woman like that without two pennies to rub together. But," she added plaintively, "I didn't think she'd kill herself. That put me in a most awkward position. If ever it came out that it was my letter that caused her to gas herself, my life wouldn't have been worth living. You know what people are like! They'd all have blamed me—when I was only doing my duty in trying to frighten her into returning the money——"

"Look, Mother," interrupted Tom who was getting restive, "the fact of the matter is you've been a damned fool, if nothing worse. Well, that can't be altered. The only thing to do is to try to hush it up. And the first step, obviously, is to get rid of that blasted machine. Surely you knew that typing can be traced, to the machine that did it, just as easily—and more certainly—than handwriting to an individual? I can't think why you didn't get rid of it long ago."

"I didn't know typing could be traced—until John Archer came here asking awkward questions. Then I did realise, in spite of the silly story he told me. I kept wondering why he wanted to get hold of the machine, and suddenly I thought it might be that. So I typed a few lines and examined the letters carefully. Then I saw that some weren't perfect.

"But as for getting rid of it—well, for one thing, I didn't know how. Besides, I didn't want to give up ruling people's lives. Once you've done that it's not easy to give up. But perhaps it ought to go now. Will you see to it?"

"I suppose I've got to. I don't want this sort of scandal to come out when I'm just on the high road to success on the stage. But what the hell shall I do with it? It's not the sort of thing you can just dump in someone else's dust-bin."

"I know!" said his mother brightly. "You know all that business in Tolbay Park—Ashburn shooting John Archer? Well, there was a lot of gossip at the time that it was about the letters. That one of them had written them and the other had found out. So why not drop the machine into the lake? The police have already dragged it once, so they're not likely to do it again. But if by any chance they do, they'll think it was there all the time—as well as the pistol. You see they stopped dragging as soon as they found the weapon. So they'd be bound to connect it with those two."

"All right," agreed Tom reluctantly. "Seems silly reasoning to me; but I've nowhere better to suggest. I'll see to it tonight." He flung himself into a chair and stared sulkily at his shoes. "You've properly queered my pitch with Helen! I saw her this morning, as soon as I got back to this plague spot. She was as frosty as an English May morning. And that's all your doing. She wouldn't even lunch with me; I had to have it by myself. Still," he brightened a little, "I guess I can turn on the charm and have her feeding out of my hand again—given time. I must think up some way of getting her alone."

That night under cover of dusk, Tom fulfilled his mission; quite unaware until too late that his actions had been observed. Even then he had no idea of the identity of the watcher.

But, as has been stated, relations between his mother and himself were strained the next morning. A worse shock was in store for him.

His mother, opening her midday post, took up a letter and looked at it curiously. It was unstamped and the envelope was square. Her face paled as she tore it open hurriedly. After one glance she gave a cry of alarm. The paper dropped from her fingers and Tom picked it up.

" 'Be sure your sin will find you out,' " he read. " 'The mills of God grind slowly; but they grind exceeding small'." At the foot was a red ink representation of a pair of scales.

"I suppose," he said with a sneer, "that this is a copy of your style? This is the sort of tripe you've been sending out?"

His mother was too upset to resent his tone. She nodded mutely, and picking up the paper, looked at it intently.

"Oh dear!" she exclaimed, "I was afraid so. It's been done on that same machine!"

"What?" Tom was startled. "Are you certain?"

"Quite. When John Archer, and later Selwyn Sneddicombe, came making inquiries about it I realised— as I told you last night—what they were after; and I typed out every letter on the machine and took note of all the ones that had any defects. This comes from the machine you threw into the lake last night."

"Damnation! I didn't want to add to your troubles. That's why I went out this morning without seeing you. I wanted to think things over. Someone saw me get rid of the thing last night, and chased me; called out to me to stop. But I got away all right and I don't think the blighter could have recognised me. Anyway, to play safe, if that snooping Sneddicombe, or anyone else, comes asking about me, say I was in all the evening."

"I will, dear. In fact, I did. He was here this morning; but I said that very thing; and he was quite put off the scent. But how did whoever it was watching you get hold of the typewriter?"

"Obviously he must have gone back to the lake after he lost me and fished the damned thing up. But d'you see what this letter means? That he—whoever he may be—knows that you are the author of those others."

Mrs. Prinnett took up the envelope and examined it with shaking hands. "I'm not so sure. Look, there's no name on it at all. It was just amongst the others in the letter box."

"You mean it might have been meant for me! Thanks very much."

"Well, you've just said that you were seen when you threw the machine into the lake. Whoever saw you can hardly have thought it was me! But no," she continued thoughtfully, "that's no good. Not, at least, if John Archer had an opportunity of telling Mr. Sneddicombe what he knew."

"What's all this? What d'you mean? Did Archer know that you——"

"Yes. I'll tell you about it. One night, when I was out late delivering one of my letters, I found that I was being followed. The streets were empty; but I could hear footsteps behind me. I looked round and there was a man—too far away for me to see by the street lights who it was. I tried to shake him off; but he just kept the same distance away. So I turned down a side street with houses that had little gardens in front. The one on the corner had some bushes; and there was a street lamp close by. So I hid behind one of the bushes and waited.

"And who should come round the corner but John Archer! He looked up and down the pavement with a puzzled air, then walked slowly along the road, peering into each garden as if he expected to find me at the front door. I suppose he thought he'd catch me in the act of delivering a note. The silly fool!

"Well then, of course, I knew what I had guessed before: that he suspected that I had written the notes. So that *was* why he'd come round with that silly story of the typewriter having been his and wanting to trace it.

"As for Sneddicombe—it was you first told me he was on the trail; after you saw him at the Battersbys'—I sent him a note to keep his nose out of the business. He didn't really count—simple little man that he is; Archer was the real danger. So, of course, he had to go. You see, it wasn't only that I couldn't face people knowing about me; it was the sense of power the notes gave me. I could revenge any insults, and even control people's lives—like Miss Pruin's. I just couldn't give that up. You don't know what it's like to have that sense of power over people when you've been treated like dirt by them for so long."

"So," said Tom slowly, with fresh horror dawning on his face, "you arranged things so that Rodney Ashburn shot Archer. That's as bad as murder. How did you manage it?"

"I sent Ashburn a note saying that his wife would be in the summer house of Tolbay Park at ten o'clock that night, with John Archer. And I rang up Archer, disguising my voice, and told him that if he wanted a scoop for his paper he'd better be there at nine forty-five sharp. I told him to hide in the summer house and warned him to keep quiet. I knew he'd have to go, even if he half believed it was a hoax. Luckily he doesn't seem to have told anyone else. Afraid of looking a fool if there was nothing in it, I suppose.

"But of course there had to be some sort of evidence to convince Rodney Ashburn; and that's where the raincoat came in. You see, I planned the thing days before it happened. Rosalind Ashburn used to come to W.I. meetings wearing a scarlet raincoat—when it was wet. A thing no one could mistake. So, a week before the summer house meeting was planned to take place, I took her coat from the cloakroom at the W.I. meeting. I guessed she wouldn't make a fuss about it—it was getting old, anyway. Besides, I got talking to her after the meeting and kept it up until we got outside the building. The rain had stopped and, thanks to my talk, she never even went to the cloakroom to look for the coat.

"The following week, being secretary, you know, I managed things so that the meeting ended early and I reached the park by half-past nine. I'd got the raincoat, wrapped up in paper. So I planted it on the floor of the summer house. Oh," she added with a bright smile, "I forgot to tell you that I'd bought a brand new compact in the town; and I left that too in the summer house—just to make it more obvious that a woman had been there. It would have been better if I could have got Rosalind's fingerprints on it; but I didn't see how to do that; so I just wiped it clean before dropping it on the floor. I thought the police would be mystified by that and think the criminal had wiped it for some reason. I also had an idea that Ashburn might recognise the coat and take it away with him if he managed to escape before the police came. So there had to be something else for the police to find. I didn't suppose Ashburn would notice the compact if I put it in a corner. The coat was different, because I threw it down just inside the door, to intrigue Archer when he came.

"Then I hid in the bushes, to be certain that Archer came along. Well, he did; at quarter to ten exactly. He went into the summer house and I saw him flash a torch. He must have seen the raincoat, because, when he came to the door, he was holding it. Then I heard steps on the path leading from the south entrance, and knew that Rodney Ashburn had swallowed the bait and was coming. So I waited in the bushes until Ashburn got to the summer house and started to quarrel with Archer—seeing him with the coat, I expect. Then I slipped out and went to the telephone box by the park entrance. I waited there until I heard the shot and then rang the police. After that I went round the park to the north entrance to see if they came. The police station is that side; and anyway I didn't dare to hang around the telephone box after making the call. They came all right, for there was their car, left at the entrance."

Tom had become more and more bewildered as the long story unfolded itself. When his mother stopped he waved a hand and said: "Give me time to think. There's something wrong here."

For a while he sat in silence, anxiously watched by his mother, as he ran over in his mind the essential details of her explanation.

"You say you rang the police," he said at length. "But it wasn't you at all. It was that woman Shapley!"

His mother laughed. "I wasn't silly enough to give evidence myself; so I got her to do it. I told her what to say. You see, I had a hold over her. She was no trouble. Naturally, I couldn't afford to be mixed up in the affair, in case Archer had told someone what he suspected about the letters. To go back to that night. The timing was difficult, but I knew the police wouldn't believe Ashburn when he said he heard the shot just after quarter to ten——"

"You knew what?" demanded her son. "How could you possibly know that he would say that?" The horror deepened on his face. "No! You don't need to tell me. I can see it all now. You shot Archer yourself! And you arranged matters so that Ashburn would arrive immediately afterwards. Then you went to the telephone kiosk and said that you'd just heard the shot—at ten o'clock."

His mother slumped in her chair. "All right. You may

as well know. It's a relief to be able to tell someone—particularly someone safe. Yes, I did shoot him. It was the only thing to do. But I had to have someone there to take the blame; and I chose Ashburn. Not that I'd anything much against him; but I can't stand that stuck-up little fool of a wife of his. And, considering Archer's reputation, if the police thought she'd been with him in the summer house—why, there was Ashbarn's motive as clear as anything. Besides, it was so easy to get hold of her raincoat; and that would make splendid evidence."

Mrs. Prinnett broke off and gave a harsh laugh. "I thought it would serve her right to be involved in a murder case. Why, when I went to his house to get the pistol she just showed me into his study to wait. That's because I was only 'Mrs. Prinnett—not on her social list'. Anyone else would have been asked to have a cup of tea with her. Mind you, I was counting on her behaving like that—knowing her; but I resented it just the same."

"Look, I can't take all this in," protested Tom. "You'll have to explain it gradually. I can't really believe you did this awful thing. What's this about getting the pistol?"

"Oh that! That was easy. In fact it was because of the pistol that I first thought of Ashburn as a scapegoat. At one of the meetings where he was present and I, as usual, was secretary—it was an architectural matter—the men were talking while waiting for the chairman. They got on to the war and from that to the subject of their revolvers and pistols. Sir Derrick—you know him—said he'd still got his, locked up in a safe. Ashburn said he supposed he ought to keep his under lock and key; but he'd never bothered. He'd just chucked it into a drawer of his desk and hadn't thought about it since. So that gave me the idea of shooting Archer. I'd been wondering how to kill him and, if I decided to shoot him, where I'd get the weapon.

"Mind you, at that time I wasn't certain that he'd spotted me as the letter writer; but I was preparing things in case he had. I thought he'd probably try to blackmail me. Then, as I told you, he followed me one night and that settled it.

"So I worked out the whole plan from that beginning—getting hold of the pistol. It was quite fascinating, really. I'd never have thought I'd got it in me. I rang up Ashburn's office and asked if he'd still be there if I called to see him at six o'clock. His secretary said no, he left at five-thirty, unless he had to work late for some special reason. So I went to his house just before five-thirty and, as I've explained, was shown into his study to wait. I got the pistol and some ammunition out of the drawer—wearing gloves, of course—and had a bit of luck. There were fingerprints all over it, and of course they must be Ashburn's. So I took care that those on the barrel weren't rubbed off. The others, naturally, were bound to be destroyed when I fired the pistol. When Ashburn did come I just asked him to explain a technical detail for the minutes, which I said I didn't understand.

"Next came the W.I. meeting when I got Rosalind's raincoat. Then I had a week to finish my plans.

"I had read an article in a newspaper which said that anything stamped into metal could always be deciphered—even if filed off so that no sign was visible to the naked eye. Ashburn's pistol had a number, which I knew the police would have in their records, so I filed it off to make them think he must have done it to avoid identification.

"But to come back to that night. As soon as I heard Ashburn's footsteps on the path I called to John Archer from where I was hiding in the bushes close to the summer house—on the island, of course. He came to the door, holding the raincoat, and I shot him, and threw the pistol into the lake. That was when Ashburn heard the shot—just as he said. Then I slipped back into the bushes until

Ashburn came up and bent over Archer's body. When he went into the summer house I crept out and went to the telephone box. I rang up, disguising my voice like I did with John Archer, and said I'd just heard the shot. That was in case anyone had seen Rodney Ashburn going into the park. It wouldn't have done for the shot to be timed several minutes before he could have got to the summer house.

"I meant to leave it at that. But then Sneddicombe told me that he didn't think the police had a real case against Ashburn; and the wireless asked the woman who had telephoned to get into touch with them. So I thought of Mrs. Shapley. I worked out a story that would be certain to hang Ashburn and made her learn it by heart and then go to the police. Of course she knew him well by sight, so the identification parade was a complete farce; but I told her to say that she had never seen him before.

"Well," Mrs. Prinnett sighed with relief, "that's all there is to it. But you can imagine how worried I was when that little Sneddicombe came round after Archer's death, asking questions. I'd heard Archer and he were working together on the letters; but I didn't know how much Archer had passed on before he died. However, my mind worked wonderfully quickly. I not only made up a story about a lame man buying the typewriter but, on the excuse of finding a copy of the receipt, I went upstairs, wrote a false receipt in one of the old books and actually typed myself an anonymous letter—all while Sneddicombe was below waiting for a cup of tea—with the wireless on to drown the noise of the typewriter! I slipped the note half under the back door as I passed it on my way from upstairs and then, when I was busy with the kettle, pretended that I'd heard a knock at the door. I made him go and find the note; so that he'd be quite certain it had been left by someone from outside.

"It was a pity I had to kill John Archer; such a risk for me; but there was nothing else I could do. And, as that was the case, you must admit I managed things very well. And now Rodney Ashburn will be hanged and the case will be closed. I'm sorry about him; but it serves his stuck-up wife right!"

"He won't be hanged!" said Tom tersely. "D'you really think I'd stand for a thing like that! Besides, suppose the truth came out later—and that note you've had shows that someone knows a good deal about it! Suppose it all came out—and that I had known about it and done nothing! I'd be had as an accessory after the fact with regard to Archer; and maybe before and after with regard to Ashburn. I suppose that deliberately letting an innocent man hang would amount to murder. No bloody fear! Filial affection's all very well; but it doesn't go that far; not with Tom Prinnett. And don't try that yarn on again that you did it for my sake. You did it out of sheer spite because you thought people didn't take enough notice of you. I'm going to the police."

"You can't do a thing like that!" gasped his mother. "You that I've looked after all these years! To your own mother!"

"Precious little looking after! I've seen to that. Why, I've earned my own living ever since I left school—and sent you money when I've been flush. And you tried to queer my pitch with Helen. No, I'm not taking a risk like that. All I'll do is give you a chance to get away. I've got my own life to live—and I'll be famous before I'm done; whereas you're old, and there's nothing much left for you in any case.

"Maybe, if they do catch you, they'll bring you in as insane. You must have been, I should think, to do such a crazy and damnable thing. I'll give you until five o'clock this afternoon and then I'm going to the police. I'm taking a chance, even then; for the chap who wrote that note may get in before me."

The outer door slamming had an ominous air of finality.

So it came about that while Selwyn Sneddicombe was recounting his discoveries to a dubious superintendent, Tom Prinnett (alias Nigel Villiers) was announced and bidden to wait.

"And you've actually got this Shapley woman to confess?" said Fuller incredulously. "She admits she made up the whole thing?"

"No. Mrs. Prinnett did that part of it; but Mrs. Shapley admits that the story she told in court was taught to her, word by word, by Mrs. Prinnett. I should think that that alone would be enough to incriminate Mrs. Prinnett. I thought at first that Tom—her son—had killed Archer; and that his mother was trying to shield him. But when Rosalind Ashburn told me that she'd lost her raincoat at the W.I.—*before* the murder—and I remembered that Mrs. Prinnett was the secretary, why then it was obvious that she was at the bottom of the whole affair.

"This was the way I worked things out: The raincoat was the key to the mystery. It was deliberately planted in the summer house to provide a motive for Rodney killing Archer. That meant that the whole affair was planned. But how could Tom Prinnett have got hold of the coat? I didn't see how. But his mother could! So I thought I'd give her a dose of her own medicine. A little cruel, perhaps; but just think what she'd done to others! And I thought if I got her really frightened she'd be more likely to confess. So I dropped her a note this morning, typed on her own machine, telling her that her sin had found her out. I put it in her letter-box just before the midday delivery, so she can't have missed it. After a spot of brooding over that I think you'll find it easy enough to get her to confess."

"All right if she does," agreed Fuller doubtfully; "but if she doesn't, I don't see that you've got much real evidence. It'll be a question of Shapley's word against hers. Why, you can't even prove that the typewriter is hers. She may have sold it as she said."

"Then what motive would she have had for killing Archer? Oh, no; it was hers all right; and it must have been Tom Prinnett I saw last night when he threw it into the lake."

"Maybe. Well, Tom Prinnett's outside. I'll see him. Perhaps he's got something that will help us. You can stay, unless he objects."

Tom Prinnett had a deal to say. And when he had done, Fuller himself, accompanied by a sergeant, went at once to the antique dealer's shop. The smell of gas as they opened the door to the parlour-kitchen told them that they were too late. Miss Pruin had been avenged.

"Well," finished Selwyn when he had told the whole story to a devoutly thankful Rosalind, "I'd just as soon it ended that way. Poetic justice! It's my first attempt at being a detective—and it's going to be my last! I shouldn't have liked to have been responsible for having that woman hanged. Poor soul, she must have been quite insane to have acted that way. A sort of persecution mania, I suppose. She let her imagined slights obsess her—and that was the result. And, to be honest, they weren't all imagined. There were far too many people who were quite ready to make use of her but wouldn't admit her into their own homes.

"Now Rosalind," he went on with sudden diffidence, "it's my turn to ask your advice! Helen Battersby happened to tell me that she had 'a leaning towards the church'; and when I asked her if she meant she wanted to enter a convent, she laughed as if I had said something funny and said I was a silly idiot! You don't think she could have meant——" But the sentence trailed away into silence. It was not in Selwyn to make so immodest a claim.

Rosalind laughed in turn. "My dear Selwyn, I entirely agree with Helen! Anyone with half an eye can see that you two have been in love for ages past. Why, it's the talk of the town. Why on earth haven't you told her that you love her?"

"You don't think so, really?" Selwyn blushed all over his eager, smiling face. "Oh, I say! D'you really think it's possible? I mean, I'm such an ordinary chap—and she. . . . Well, she's Helen! As to why I haven't asked her," and his face clouded, "that difficulty still remains. Her parents have such pots of money and I've only my stipend. But," his face brightened, "I've been almost promised a more paying post. We would at least have enough to live on. I wonder——"

"My dear Selwyn, you're terribly old-fashioned—and rather sweet. In these days men don't refrain from asking their lady loves to marry them because the girl's parents are rich! On the contrary, it's usually considered a most fortunate coincidence. Anyway, I know Helen pretty well; and I know she'd rather marry you without a penny than——" an impish light came into her eyes as she altered what she was about to say and concluded: "become an old maid!"

Other Golden Age Detective books published by Galileo (for full listings please go to https://galileopublishing. co.uk/category/golden-age-detective-fiction/).

Curiosity Killed the Cat   Joan Cockin   9781915530141 | £10.99

Villainy at Vespers   Joan Cockin   9781912916900 | £10.99

Dancing with Death   Joan Coggin   9781912916603 | £9.99

Who Killed the Curate?   Joan Coggin   9781915530134 | £10.99

The King and the Corpse Max Murray   9781915530158 | £10.99

Catt Out of the Bag   Clifford Witting 9781912916375 | £8.99

Dead on Time   Clifford Witting 9781912916634 | £9.99

Let X be the Murderer   Clifford Witting 9781915530004 | £10.99

Measure for Murder   Clifford Witting 9781912916528 | £8.99

Midsummer Murder   Clifford Witting 9781912916733 | £9.99

Murder in Blue   Clifford Witting 9781912916504 | £8.99

Subject Murder   Clifford Witting 9781912916993 | £10.99

The Case of the Michaelmas Goose Clifford Witting

9781915530127 | £10.99